Chasing North Star

Chasing North Star

A Novel

Heidi McCrary

She Writes Press

Published 2020
Printed in the United States of America
ISBN: 978-1-63152-757-9
ISBN: 978-1-63152-758-6
Library of Congress Control Number: [LOCCN]

For information, address:
She Writes Press
1569 Solano Ave #546
Berkeley, CA 94707

She Writes Press is a division of SparkPoint Studio, LLC.

That which does not kill us makes for a great story.

—Heidi McCrary

Author's Note

The majority of this story takes place in the year 1970, a time when mental illness was still thought of as something to shove into the shadows. Misunderstood by those around them, people dealing with mental illness were often overwhelmed, and overmedicated by professionals eager to *fix the problem*. This tale is not meant to make light of mental illness, but rather, inspire those who experienced similar challenges during this era and persevered.

Today, use of the word, *crazy* is insensitive and inappropriate. After much contemplation, I have left the word in the dialogue of the characters in this book to reflect the times and essence of the story.

— 1 —

August 4, 2005
New York City

Sunlight slaps me with jarring rhythm, jumping out from behind the abandoned buildings lining the street. "This is how epilepsy gets started," I say, tapping the top of my head in search of my sunglasses, and sliding them down over my eyes. As the train gathers speed, I lean in against the window to get a better view of the buildings in the distance as they pop up out of the morning fog, one after the other like that old Whac-A-Mole game. At least I hope it's fog and not the dull-white film covering the windowpane, formed from the sticky fingers of countless travelers.

"See over there?" my husband says, standing up and leaning over the seat in front of us. Our boys both look out their window as he continues. "That's Yankee Stadium. What do you say we check it out if we have time? It's a long way from where we're staying but we can take the subway to the Bronx . . ."

As Jon continues pointing out other New York landmarks, I gaze out my window, drinking in the energy of the emerging city. Jon knows we're not just here to stand at the top of the Empire State Building or to catch *The Lion King* on Broadway. Across the aisle, an older woman in a worn housecoat lets out a hacking cough, reminding me just how my window acquired the lovely white filter. I lean back from the glass and look over to the young man who has been sitting next to the woman for at least as long as we have been on the train. He was sleeping but his eyes are open now. He shifts his position away from her just as she lets out another dry cough that comes from deep inside her chest.

"This is our stop," Jon says, grabbing his luggage. He turns to me and smiles. "We're going to find it, honey. If it's out there, we're damn well going to find it for you."

"We'll see," I say, throwing back a half-cocked smile.

As we step off the train, rolling our suitcases behind us, we're blocked momentarily by the woman fishing around in her large mesh bag. She pulls out a cigarette and lights it, taking a long drag so that the bright ash on the tip grows before our eyes. She exhales, and I'm hit with a familiar scent: Virginia Slims, the preferred choice for my mother who only smoked using her black cigarette holder even though the cigarettes had filters—all while striking the pose of Audrey Hepburn on a movie set.

Only it wasn't a movie . . .

— 2 —

1940

Eschbach, Baden-Württemberg, Germany

"*Ich bin* home!" Didi called out, kicking the door shut behind her. She tossed her mittens across the floor, watching them land just short of the heater. For the third day in a row, snow had fallen hard outside, making her half-mile walk from school seem longer. It felt good to be inside again. She slipped her boots off and set them on the braided rug, careful to keep the melting snow from landing on the hardwood floor. Thawed ice crystals dripped from her hair as she pulled her coat off. Picking up her satchel, she started for the kitchen, dreading the afternoon chores that she had to complete before getting started on her homework.

Suddenly she stopped and looked towards the kitchen. Someone was crying.

"*Mutter*?" she called out, setting her bag down. Just past the kitchen table, she found her mother crumpled on the floor in the corner of the room, crying so hard that she gasped for breath between each sob.

"Oh, *mein gott*," Didi cried out, covering her mouth with her hands before running to her mother. "*Was ist* wrong?" she asked, kneeling down to help her up. Her mother raised her hand, and Didi reached out only to be met with a violent slap across her face causing Didi to lose her balance. As her feet flew out from under her, her head slammed against the linoleum floor.

"Wha-what did I do?!" Didi stammered, climbing back onto her feet while cupping her ear in an attempt to stop the painful ringing.

"What did you do? The better question is, what did *we* do?" Didi's mother whispered, looking down toward the floor, making no attempt to brush back her long bangs hanging over her eyes. "What didn't we do?" She gasped for breath and let out another sob. "That is the problem, isn't it? No one is doing anything to stop it."

Still holding her ear, Didi stared at her mother who made no attempt to get up and remained sprawled on the floor. Slowly, her mother sat up, and, with her back to Didi, she looked down the hall toward the front door and pointed in the general direction of the street. She let out a long shuddering sigh. "This wasn't supposed to turn into madness. He boasted about giving power back to the people—back to us. But this . . . this is a nightmare."

Didi stood still and waited for her mother to continue, but her mother only let out another sob. Afraid that her mother might strike her again, Didi backed up and kept a safe distance. In a soft voice, she asked, "What are you talking about?"

"Don't act so innocent. You know what I'm talking about, or at least you should. The Shusters are gone. They took them." She spun around and gazed at her daughter as if she had just noticed her. She brushed her bangs away from her eyes, but they immediately fell back. "I knew something was wrong when I saw that damn swastika on the truck in front of their house." She let out an uncontrollable sob. "God damn him and his ideals. God damn him! We should never have listened to his promises! 'I'm going to bring pride back to the German people!' he said. He sucked on our fears, and now he's spitting on us." She looked back toward the street and whispered, "Dear Lord, what did we do?"

Her mother began sobbing again as Didi walked back into the

front room to look out the window. Snow was gently falling and it was starting to get dark out, but she could still see across the street. A car drove by, and everything looked just how it should. She peered down the road over to the Shusters' house and noticed the snow-covered front stoop. Mr. Shuster was meticulous about keeping the front walk free of snow and ice. The front curtains were open, showing a lighted living room, but no one was moving about inside the house. Everything looked normal, but in recent months it was difficult to call any day normal, where it was common for Jewish children and their entire families to disappear without notice. "They're being relocated," was the official answer provided by nervous teachers questioned by students as to the whereabouts of their friends. Thinking back on the day, Didi realized that Elke didn't show up for school, and as she looked out the window again toward the Shusters' house, she knew that her friend wouldn't be opening the front door.

Didi stepped away from the window but before she could walk back into the kitchen, a thunderous explosion shook the house, making her stumble. She steadied herself on the arm of the sofa, and the sharp pain in her ear returned as she looked to her mother for guidance as to what to do.

Meanwhile, her mother stopped crying and her face hardened. Without emotion, she picked herself up from the floor and started rubbing her dress, trying to smooth out the creases. She laughed as sirens blared in the distance. "Of course, there it is—it never stops. They never hurt anyone!" she screamed while raising her shaking fist. "Frieda never hurt a flea, so what in the hell did she ever do to him? What the hell did she ever do to anyone? Tell me what she did to deserve this!"

"Mother, the sirens. Should we go down to the—"

"I don't care what the hell you do, just get away from me! What do I need with you anyway? You only care about yourself, sassing back, ignoring your chores. Just go." When Didi didn't move, she repeated sharply, "Go!"

Didi ran out of the kitchen and pulled the cellar door open, shutting it behind her. At the top of the stairs, she reached for the string, turning on the light as it swayed in the darkness, casting a dancing shadow while Didi made her way down the narrow staircase. She stopped at a small table that held three cardboard boxes containing Christmas decorations, reminding her that her mother had told her to put them away days ago. She moved one of the boxes over and looked around the room, regretting not bringing her satchel down with her. Sometimes the sirens would go off for hours, and with no radio for information on where the bombing was taking place, she had no idea as to how long this one would last. She looked up the staircase, wondering if her mother would soon follow her, but the door remained shut. Didi cocked her head and put her hand to her ear, which was still hot from the slap. She remembered a time when her mother didn't hit her, but in the past two years, her mother's anger grew, and Didi seemed to be the closest and easiest target more often than not.

Didi sighed, picked up one of the Christmas boxes, and started toward the back room, but as she spun around, another blast exploded, shaking the house and causing her to trip. As she fell onto the cold cement floor, the box landed with a crash, and a light-blue Christmas bulb rolled out and stopped beside Didi. Heat rose from her ear as a thin stream of blood formed a small puddle on the cement floor beside her. She tried to get up, but her muscles stiffened, and her body shook uncontrollably. As the sirens screamed, her vision faded to black.

— 3 —

January 17, 1970
Kalamazoo, Michigan

I scrunched my nose at the funky but familiar smell—a mixture of cough syrup, ammonia, and body odor. Few children ever set foot in this place, and probably no more than a handful knew of its existence, but you would find me there as regularly as kids go for dental cleanings. Only there wasn't a *Highlights* magazine to be found anywhere in this lobby—sparsely furnished with four mismatched vinyl chairs and two art deco end tables. It was not exactly inviting but not surprising considering the inhabitants. I slid down further into the worn seat cushion of my chair until my feet touched the floor.

"I'm not supposed to tell you this," Silvia whispered, glancing around like she was searching for someone, but there was no one in the lobby but the two of us. My sister then bent down so we were face-to-face, with our noses almost touching. "Don't let your guard down for one second while you're down here all by yourself." She paused as if afraid to continue. "They keep the craziest patients locked up in the very top of the tower here, and every once in a while, one of them escapes and comes bursting through . . . that door!" With great exaggeration, she threw her finger out toward something I couldn't see. I pushed the hood of my parka down and turned to see what she was pointing at—a closed door on the far side of the lobby. Hanging above the door, a faded yellow sign warned visitors with one lone word—Private. "The escapees have been known to sneak up on small children hanging out here all by themselves. They snatch them up and run off with them into the woods."

"Oh, shut up," I said, swatting Silvia's arm away from me. I was finally warming up, so I took my parka off and threw it over the back of my chair.

"Silvia," Hanna, called out from the top of the staircase. "Come on!"

A sour-looking woman dressed in a thick white cotton dress, even thicker white nylons, and white orthopedic shoes stood at the top of the stairs next to Hanna, my oldest sister. Her black hair was pulled back into a bun with such force that she looked pained. Standing beside this ray of sunshine, Hanna looked even more miserable. I couldn't say I blamed her.

"Brat. You're so lucky that you're not old enough," Silvia said.

"Being the smallest doesn't work to my advantage very often. You have to give me this one."

"I hate you," Silvia groaned, slapping down on the bill of my baseball cap before climbing the stairs to join the others. As she reached the top, the nurse unlocked a door, and the three of them walked through the doorway. The door shut behind them with a thunderous *clank*, and with that, the Kalamazoo Insane Asylum swallowed up my sisters.

Good riddance, I thought, pushing my cap back. Looking around, it occurred to me that the next hour would be incredibly boring. Since there was two feet of snow on the ground and it was continuing to fall, I wasn't going to be venturing outside. I looked back over toward the door marked Private. Of course, Silvia was just pulling my leg. *Right?*

A Sunday edition of the *Kalamazoo Gazette* from the previous month and a *Health Matters* magazine sat on the end table next to me. Even if I did want to read about prostate cancer, the lighting would have made it a challenge. As the low insistent hum from the fluorescent bulbs drilled through my ears, I sighed and slouched further into my seat.

For the first time since we had arrived, I noticed a man sitting behind the reception desk. His stringy uncombed hair and dull white uniform contrasted sharply with the nurse who was holding my sisters captive. He was watching several TV screens displaying a variety of community patient areas. Or rather, he was supposed to be watching the screens. Instead, his eyelids drooped, and his head bobbed—like that drinking-bird toy that slowly rocks back and forth until his head finally dips into the glass of water. I kept watching, mesmerized. Just when the man was about to hit the top of his desk with his forehead, he jerked awake. Quickly scanning the room, his eyes landed on me staring back at him. Embarrassed, he let out a cough and glanced down at his watch as I just as quickly looked away, only to find myself staring at that damn door again. *Crazy people do not sometimes come screaming through that door, snatching up innocent children.*

Stupid door.

Still, I had to admit I was relieved to be down in the lobby instead of upstairs in the pulsing heart of the mental hospital where our mother had been spending the last week. With good intentions, our father believed it would be nice for her to see her children. Again, I was thankful that visitors under the age of twelve were not allowed beyond the lobby—my win.

"Son of a—!" I yelled as two hands came down heavily on my shoulders from behind. Jumping in my seat, I turned to find Silvia standing over me, with Hanna walking up. "Don't you know that you don't sneak up on someone in an insane asylum?"

"Sorry, kiddo," Silvia said, snatching my baseball cap.

Hanna took a seat next to me, with a serious look on her face. "Popi asked us to check on you since it looks like we're going to be here for a while. The doctor is talking about moving Mutti to a hospital in Detroit."

"Why would they move Mutti to a different hospital?" This was a new development, and as I tried to weigh the importance of Hanna's announcement, a weird smile appeared on Silvia's face. She pulled a brochure out from under her coat and handed it to me. On the cover was a photo of a three-story brick hospital along with a photo of a woman lying in a hospital bed. A doctor stood next to her bed, and they were both smiling, because who wouldn't be smiling while staying in a mental institution? Just another spa vacation. The woman's hair was styled, and she looked like she had just finished writing out her postcards. *Having a great time. The doctors are so nice. Wish you were here!*

I read the caption below the photos. *Eloise Sanitarium—Part of Wayne County Hospital. Serving Detroit and beyond. Offering the latest treatments in insulin and electroshock therapy.*

"Shock what?" I asked, looking up at Hanna. "Are they really going to shock Mutti?"

"Oh man, Mutti is getting electrocuted!" Silvia said, yanking the brochure away from me. "That should finally fix her or kill her. Either way—"

"Knock it off," Hanna snapped, grabbing the brochure out of Silvia's hands.

"Um, Hanna?" I asked, putting my feet up onto the wooden frame of the chair. "Are they really going to electrocute Mutti?" I was suddenly acutely aware of my wet socks inside my sneakers. Hanna had told me to put on my snow boots, but I didn't listen, and I was paying the price with cold feet.

Hanna reached over and tucked my hair back behind my ear so she could see my face. I let her do it only because she was old—seventeen, and years smarter than me. She took her glasses off and started rubbing the lenses clean with her shirt. They were cool aqua-colored cat-eyes, making me wish that I had bad eyesight and had to wear glasses. "Don't worry," she said in a soothing voice. "No one is electrocuting Mutti. They're talking about moving her to the Detroit hospital for a new treatment called electroshock therapy. The doctor here thinks that Mutti might be a good candidate for it. She'll go through a series of electric zaps. It's like jump-starting the brain."

Silvia leaned over and whispered into my ear, "They're electrocuting her." A vision appeared in my mind of our mother lying on a bed with jumper-cables clamped onto her ears, with flames shooting from her hair. "Hopefully they'll shock the cuckoo out of her!"

"Shut up," I said, giving her a shove.

"Stop it," Hanna scolded, shooting Silvia a look, but Silvia responded with another "cuckoo" while rolling her eyes in circles. Hanna turned back to me. "All you need to know is that she's not getting electrocuted. Electroshock therapy is supposed to help people with epilepsy and other mental problems. Come on," she said softly, handing me my hat and throwing her coat on the back of the seat over my own coat. "Let's walk around. I need to find a bathroom."

I stayed seated, running my finger along the raised English D on the front of my baseball cap. Without looking back up at Hanna, I whispered, "How long will Mutti be in the hospital this time?"

"I don't know," Hanna sighed, looking out the front lobby windows, where the snow was coming down harder. "I wish I knew."

— 4 —

April 26, 1970
Alamo, Michigan

No one can possibly think of black licorice as a real candy flavor. I can only imagine that this bitter treat was invented back in the covered wagon days when sugar was scarce and folks had to find other ways to satisfy their sweet tooth. I put black licorice in the same category as those butterscotch hard candies our father and every other old person used to keep in their cupboards. I'm convinced that he bought those horrible candies only because he knew they would be safe from his children.

I handed the man behind the counter my quarter, and, reaching over the licorice in the box that held a wonderful assortment of candy bars and gum, I grabbed the last $100,000 Bar. Chocolate, puffed rice, and caramel—nothing fancy on their own but put them together, and *bam*, sweet music in my mouth. With the candy bar safely tucked away in my pocket, I hopped back on my bike and pedaled down the road to the school, where I was hoping to find a friend or two on the playground. But it was quiet there, which wasn't surprising since it was still early on a Sunday morning, and frankly, I was OK with not having to share my candy bar.

While most kids were cruising the streets on glistening new Stingray bicycles, I was still pedaling around on a bike with handlebars that didn't reach for the sky and a seat that wasn't named for a long yellow fruit devoured by monkeys.

Looking down at my faded blue bike, I touched the cold rusty bell and hit the lever, emitting a scratchy ring that sounded more like an ill Canada goose than a singing bell. Another reminder of being the fourth born.

Fourth.

Nothing is new about the fourth child. They do nothing the previous three hadn't already done or at least attempted. They do little that requires new clothes, toys, beds, or bicycles, nor do they inspire parents to pick up the camera. My baby photo album contained four photographs, and I'm suspiciously absent from one of them. Fourth-borns also enjoy being the last one in the bathtub on Sunday nights, and yes, sitting in cloudy lukewarm bathwater that three teenagers already bathed in is as uncivilized as it sounds. In short, the last-born is lucky to get new socks and underpants.

Zipping my previously owned Barracuda tightly against my neck, I stepped into the shade, thankful that as I ran out the door earlier, Hanna yelled at me to grab my jacket. Aside from it being chilly in the shade, this was my favorite time of day—with brilliant white morning glories, still wet from the morning dew, blanketing the playground.

"What are you doing?"

"Huh?" I asked, surprised that I wasn't alone. "Oh, hi Jenny. You want to seesaw?"

"Do I want to . . . no, why would I do that, dressed in this?" She grabbed the sides of her frilly pink and white skirt and twirled around so I could get the full effect of the taffeta material, making her look like she just stepped off the set of *The Brady Bunch*.

"So," I said, trying to look past the ribbons and bows, "I imagine that hanging from the monkey bars is out of the question."

"Do I look like . . . never mind. How about the swing sets? I can swing with you for a while. But then I have to get back home. Mummy wants to give me a permanent wave." She paused, and I suspected she was looking for an, "Ooh that's so fabulous!"

"Cool," I said, keeping my hands in my jacket pockets.

On the swings, the sun warmed our backs, and I closed my eyes while pushing hard into the air with my outstretched legs. Meanwhile Jenny casually pumped with her long legs and had no problem finding heights I could never attain. She was a year ahead of me at school, and it would seem like we should be friends, but I actually had more in common with her brother who was two years younger than me. Lee had a quirky way about him, and while most kids in school kept their distance from him, I found him . . . interesting.

"And after I get my permanent wave, we're all going into town for ice cream. The new High Wheeler has a chocolate sundae that is five scoops of . . ."

As she carried on about gourmet ice cream, I stopped listening and focused on a daddy longlegs crawling up the metal pole. Funny how spiders freak me out when I find them in the corners of my bedroom, but watching them do their thing in the beauty of the outdoors is calming.

And then there was Jenny, who was anything but calming. Her family was the closest thing we had to celebrities in this town. Her father owned Paulson AMC Car Dealership in the next town over, and his wife operated Alamo's only beauty parlor out of their home. Our mother claimed that Mr. Paulson had the beauty salon built off to the side of their house for his wife, not so they could generate extra income by having her do hair, but rather as an attempt to keep her out of his.

"And get this, my daddy had the nerve this morning to ask me to help him get the swimming pool ready for the season!" She laughed as if the idea of her partaking in menial labor was absurd. "Even Daddy had to laugh when I gave him the look."

I glanced down at my wrist, wishing I owned a watch so I could see how long it took for Jenny to bring up the pool. About three minutes? Because they had an image to maintain, the Paulsons were the only family in town to have an in-ground swimming pool. Never mind that we were never invited to swim in it. As she swung higher into the air, I decided I couldn't wait for her to get her hair done so I could yank out the permanent wave with my hands. Dragging my feet in the dirt with each swing, I put my hands back into my pockets.

"Is that yours?" Jenny asked, pointing down to my candy bar which was laying on the ground.

"Oh, yeah." Skidding to a stop, I stooped over to pick it up. "Um, Jenny, would you like part of my—"

"Oh my, I need to get going. Can't keep Mummy waiting!" She scurried off, leaving me alone and relieved that I hadn't finished my sentence.

Bored, I walked over to the monkey bars, where I climbed to the top, moving my hands quickly to avoid gripping the ice-cold metal. It was quiet here, the silence broken only by a barking dog and the honking geese overhead. As I watched my breath float away, I hung upside down, imagining myself flying away.

— 5 —

May 23, 1970
Alamo, Michigan

"Come on, guys. Can you slow down a little?"

"Shh!" Mickey said, looking back to find that I was no longer in lockstep behind him, but instead slowly disappearing into the shadows of the night. In my defense, Mickey was at the age when all of his body parts were growing at different speeds. At fourteen, he was as thin as me but already as tall as our father. Each long stride of his lanky legs required three leaps by me just to keep up with him, and at four foot nothing, I was losing the race.

Taking pity on me, Hanna slowed, allowing me to catch up with her. I normally would have been running circles around all of them, but we had been wandering around Alamo for hours, and I was no longer sure if it was still tonight or tomorrow morning. Our parents thought we were asleep in the pup tent in the woods on our property, so it was only logical that we were now roaming the streets of Alamo like a band of G-rated hooligans—me, Silvia, Hanna, Mickey, and two of Mickey's friends, Jeff and Robbie.

We kept conversation to a minimum as we walked down the middle of the street. It's funny how the volume of the smallest sound ramps up at night so even a whisper travels across town. I forced myself to jog, rubbing my eyes, and telling myself that sleep was for sissies. But with each successive slap of my sneakers against the pavement, I was hit with that same lightheaded feeling I had earlier taking a couple of puffs from the Virginia Slims Silvia had swiped from our mother's cigarette box. With the first drag, I just blew the smoke back in Silvia's face. I was instructed that if I was going to smoke, I had to do it right, which meant breathing the smoke into my lungs. After I finally stopped coughing, I decided I might have to rethink following in every footstep of my glamorous sisters.

As we made our way to the four-corners, I kept quiet, honored to be tagging along with this ragtag team of teenagers, and I was relieved that Mickey's pals were too busy vying for Hanna's attention to notice my presence.

No one would blame Hanna for doing her best to ignore Jeff, a boy who proudly sported a dark smudge above his upper lip masquerading as a mustache and who wore more hairspray than any woman walking out of the Alamo Beauty Parlor. "Hey beautiful," was his favorite saying, and it was usually spoken while looking into the mirror. But I had to wonder how she resisted the quiet charms of Robbie, a boy with sun-drenched blonde hair and feathered bangs that couldn't hide his shy grin that could light up all of Alamo.

"Hey Squirt," Robbie said, turning around. His hands were cupped as he walked back towards me. "I think this guy is yours." He relaxed his grip to reveal a warm blinking glow.

"A firefly!" I marveled, not because fireflies were unique on any summer night in Michigan, but because Robbie could have handed me a rock and received the same level of appreciation from me. But as I reached for his open hand, the lightning bug flew away, happy to be free again.

"That's all right, Squirt. We'll get you another one before the night's over."

"Keep up," Silvia said, pushing me in the back, obviously jealous of the special attention I was receiving. "Hey guys," she suggested to the group as we walked through the school playground, "what if we

TP-ed the school?" She tried blowing a smoke ring, but the smoke simply floated away.

"TP-ing's for amateurs," Mickey scoffed, climbing up the monkey bars and perching himself on the top bar. He ran his hand through his hair, pushing his long bangs back. Looking at him under the parking lot lights, I noticed how he resembled our mother, with his dark eyes and straight, almost-black hair framing his face. But because he was more likely channeling Mick Jagger, I'm sure he wouldn't have appreciated my comparisons of him and our mother at that moment.

"No, we need to do something better, something this town will never forget," Mickey said, leaping from the top of the monkey bars. "Well, at least not for a while." Inspired, he grabbed one of the legs of the structure and started shaking the monkey bars. "Come here, everyone. Grab a bar and lift!"

"Seriously," Hanna said, not doing as instructed. "We're stealing the monkey bars? And we're going to take it where?"

"Don't think of it as stealing. We're just borrowing it," Mickey replied with a wink.

And before I could figure out what was happening, the five teenagers all tugged in unison and lifted the monkey bars off the ground. I joined them, pretending to carry my weight as the equipment glided off the schoolyard and floated down the middle of the street. Anyone looking out their front window that night might have thought they were witnessing an alien spaceship passing by their house.

Slowly and quietly, we walked, with the spacecraft finally coming to a landing in the middle of the intersection, complete with a streetlight shining on it like an FBI helicopter flashing a spotlight on that alien spaceship.

"OK, this is good," Mickey announced. "Set it down."

"Good," Hanna said. "This damn thing is heavy."

With that, she and everyone else let go of the monkey bars, making it land on the asphalt with an echoing *clank*. Stepping back, we marveled at our handiwork for a moment before scurrying off to the front steps of the church across the street. Congratulatory cigarettes were lit, and everyone took a seat on the steps. A sliver of the sun was showing itself, and I closed my eyes, thinking how nice sleep would be at that moment. Slowly, I pried my eyelids back open, and, trying to shake the sleep, I stood up and started jumping around. Rays from the predawn sun were bouncing off the cross that sat at the top of the steeple, like God was giving us a thumbs-up for a prank well done.

"Ha!" Mickey boasted, admiring our handiwork sitting in the intersection. "Can you imagine the first guy who drives up to this? He's going to scratch his head, go home to his wife, and say, 'Honey, you will never believe what's sitting in the middle of Alamo Center.' I wish I could—"

"Shit!" Silvia said, dropping her cigarette. "Ditch it!"

A car drove up to the intersection, and as it coasted to a stop in front of the monkey bars, Hanna grabbed my jacket sleeve and yanked me into the hedges where Silvia was already hiding. Meanwhile, Mickey and his friends moved into the shadows behind the church.

"Shh," Hanna whispered, placing her hand on my shoulder, while I squirmed, trying to move away from a twig that was sticking into my back.

Silvia carefully bent a branch back and peered through the opening. "The driver's door is opening," she whispered. "OK, I think it's closing again."

"Thank God," Hanna said.

"Wait—it's opening again. He's getting out, he's looking around. I think he's looking at us!" She let the branch spring back and leaned back against the wall of the church.

From behind the hedges, I could see Mickey and his friends standing in the shadows, and they were not exactly invisible in the early morning light.

"Oh, shit," Robbie said, suddenly aware that the man was coming after them. "Run!"

I started to stand up, but Hanna yanked me back down and turned my head so that our faces were two inches apart. She put her finger up to her lips, and together, we stayed crouched behind the hedges, not daring to move.

The sound of the boys running off was followed by the slower footsteps of the man.

"Get back here!" he shouted after the boys. "I know who you are! I know your parents, and I'm going to tell them what you did! You little shits are going to regret running from me!"

The boys laughed at the man's threats as they quickly outdistanced him. Unfortunately for us, the man gave up on the chase directly in front of the hedges. He stood, breathing hard as the three of us remained crouched where we were, frozen. As he stood just feet from us, trying to catch his breath, I feared he would spot us through the branches, but the crinkle of paper and the snap of a lighter told us he believed he was alone. Not long after, we heard footsteps walking away, followed by the opening and slamming of a car door. With the sound of the car engine, Hanna relaxed her grip on me, making me realize how scared she must have been.

Silvia peeked through the hedge. "He's driving around the monkey bars. We're good."

"Oh my god, that was close," Hanna said, plucking a twig from her sweater as we crawled out of hiding. "What if the man actually did recognize Mickey or one of the other boys, and tells Popi? Oh man, Popi will take a *gürtel* to every one of us."

"A girdle?"

We turned to see that the boys had returned. Between snorts of laughter, Jeff added, "And who the hell is Boppy? Will they really hit you with a girdle?"

This got Jeff laughing all over again, which triggered an outburst of laughter from Robbie, who looked embarrassed to be laughing but couldn't help himself. With arms crossed, Hanna let out a long sigh.

"Popi is our father, smart-asses. And don't you get spanked with a *gürtel*?" Strangely, Hanna's question got the boys laughing all over again, and I laughed with them even though I had no idea what was so funny.

"Popi" is what we called our father. It's like Papa, which is German for father. As a result of our mother's German heritage, we kids grew up speaking Germlish, which is basically English with an occasional German word thrown in because the folks in town didn't think we were weird enough already. Growing up speaking Germlish, we had no idea we were slaughtering both languages until it was kindly brought to our attention by understanding friends like Robbie and Jeff.

"Can't say my dad has ever taken a girdle to me," Jeff said with a wide grin and tears of laughter rolling down his cheeks. "A belt sometimes, but never a girdle!"

And that's when we learned that while *gürtel* is German for belt, it had an entirely different meaning in English, which gave Mickey's friends a visual of all of the Phillips kids being spanked with a women's undergarment. And so went our life in Alamo.

As the laughter died down, the sun quietly rose, creating long shadows and heavy eyelids. Hanna yawned and started walking in the direction of our woods, and we all fell in line behind her. *Finally*, I thought, following Mickey and his friends. The only thing I wanted at that moment was sleep. Mickey looked back toward the intersection and reached for my hand. "Car coming our way!" We raced down the road, laughing, drunk on a mixture of hijinks and a lack of sleep.

When you live in a small town, it's only a matter of time before the news of the day (or night) becomes the topic of conversation where grownups converge, like the town church or beauty salon. Or if you're a real man-about-town, the Marathon Station.

As Ernie Harwell broke down the day's baseball game over the radio, Dale and Kevin discussed the day's business over a Chevy engine. *"They've had a lot of groundballs so far today. Here's a pitch on the way. Swings and fouls it off. It'll reach the seats over back by the Tiger dugout—caught by a young lad from Taylor, Michigan."*

"You know he just makes that shit up," Dale said from under the hood. "Harwell doesn't know who the hell is sitting in those seats. I love that guy. The Tigers wouldn't be the same without him." With a strong yank, he pulled the battery out from under the hood of the Chevy and grabbed a brush to scrub the battery acid caked onto the cables while Kevin rummaged through an industrial-sized toolbox.

Our father leaned against the open garage door, taking it all in. He never did talk much. With an exceptionally high IQ, he never felt the need to show off his superior intellect, preferring instead, to have the people of Alamo think that he was simply a quiet man—an identity that put few demands on him from a social aspect and allowed him to soak up tidbits of information that the guys at the Marathon were only more than happy to share with anyone within spitting distance.

"So, Rob and Beth's son was called up for duty a couple of days ago," Kevin said, pulling out a wrench, and buffing grease off of it with a dirty towel. "Apparently, Beth went crazy when Robbie's draft number came up on the television set. Rob had to hold her down to keep her from throwing the television across the room."

"You served, didn't you, Larry?" Dale asked, looking out from under the hood.

"Yes, sir."

The guys at the Marathon Station called our father "Larry," his first name. At Fuller Transmission, where he worked nights, he went by the nickname "Smokey," but he referred to himself as "Merle," his middle name, which was also the name our mother used for him.

And with all of us calling him "Popi," it was amazing he responded to anything at all.

"Overseas, right?"

Larry nodded.

"See any action?"

"Little bit."

Sensing that Larry wasn't going to share any war stories with them, Dale went back to installing the new battery. "Well, I heard that Beth said that she'll be damned if she lets the government haul her son overseas. I wouldn't be surprised if she takes that sissy kid and heads to Canada. She should be damn proud to have a son fighting for our country."

"Does Rob know he married a Commie?" Kevin asked.

"He does now," Dale answered, wiping his brow as he stepped back from the car. He put his hands on his hips and stretched, making his back crack. "Kids today don't have the same sense of duty we had growing up. Isn't that right, Larry?"

"No, they sure don't."

"And the pitch. He swings, hits the ball. A hard bounce toward third base—caught by Jones who throws it to first. He's out! And that finishes the second inning. A great play by Dalton Jones."

"Let's hope Lolich doesn't throw the game away today like he did on Wednesday against the Blue Jays," Dale said.

As the game went to a commercial break, the owner of the Chevy, sitting quietly on a rusty metal chair, waited for a pause in the conversation. "You guys will never believe what happened to me this morning," he said, slapping his knee. "So, I was driving home after third shift when I come up to the intersection here. And what do you think I saw? A set of playground monkey bars sitting smack-dab in the middle of the damn intersection!"

Dale popped his head out from under the hood.

"If I had been going any faster, I might have crashed into it!"

"No shit? You saw that, too?" Dale asked. "I had to enlist three guys to help me carry the damn thing back to the schoolyard. Did you happen to see who did it?"

"Hell, yes, I did," the man nodded, waving his hands around. "There were half a dozen of them! Older boys." He spit on the floor and wiped spittle from his chin with the back of his hand, relishing everyone's attention. "Well, I wasn't going to let them get away with that, so I jumped out of my car and chased after them. I think there were six of them, maybe eight. Almost caught one of them—nearly tore his tennis shoe right off his foot!"

As the tale grew taller, Larry dropped a couple of coins into the pop machine and pulled out a Coke. Miss December 1968 smiled down at him from the greasy calendar. She was dressed in tight denim overalls with one of the straps hanging down over her chest and discreetly over her tight T-shirt that seemed to be missing a bra. Larry smiled at the photo and shook his head ever so slightly before taking a long drink from the aqua-colored bottle. Setting the Coke down, he took a packet of tobacco out of his pocket and packed his pipe, inhaling as he kept the lighter lit over the pipe's bowl. As the man finished his tale, Larry scrunched up his face and thought about his children who supposedly spent the night asleep in the woods. He had a feeling that the children of his free-spirited wife had something to do with the Landing of the Monkey Bars. Putting two and two together, he came up with four—four Phillips children.

"Gentlemen, I think I hear the missus calling." With a nod to his friends, he walked out, debating whether he needed to reprimand his children, admitting to himself that their prank wasn't destructive, and he smiled, thinking back to the anger their prank drew out of the weaselly man in the garage. But still, he knew what he had to do. As he walked across the yard, he found his youngest playing in front of the barn, kneeling in the dirt with a bag of marbles, practicing boulder shots.

—

"Hi Popi," I said, looking up.

He nodded as he continued across the yard and into the house. Not more than five minutes later, the back door opened again, and surprisingly, he walked directly toward me, stopping a few feet away.

"Come here, please," he said with no indication that I was in trouble, yet I had a feeling. I got up and wiped the dirt from my knees as he continued. "Tell me where you all went last night, when you should have been sleeping in the tent."

Darn, I thought as I looked up into his eyes and saw that he meant business. I didn't know how to answer his question without getting the whole lot of us in trouble, but I knew telling a lie wouldn't wash since he obviously knew we were out gallivanting around the night before or we wouldn't have been having this conversation. Our father never wasted energy with chitchat.

"We were walking around," I mumbled, unable to look him in the eye. "Just walking."

"Did your brother and sisters move the monkey bars?"

And with that direct question, I knew to stop dancing around. Looking at the marbles in my hand, I took a deep breath and in an even quieter voice, I whispered, "Yes, sir."

Germlish wasn't the only hint of our heritage. Looking like extras from *The Sound of Music*, we ran around regularly in lederhosen, which are leather shorts with suspenders and a leather strap across the chest that holds the suspenders in place. And it wasn't just me decked out in shorts that could stand up by themselves, but all of us Phillips kids. Our mother was damn proud of her heritage, never mind that we all looked like Hummel figurines. Like everything else in my life, my lederhosen were handed down, with the leather so worn it was shiny, which allowed me to clean it by simply scraping off any offending grime.

Along with being easy-care, there was a secret we kids shared with one another—and one that Mickey remembered as he looked out his bedroom window and saw our father talking to me on that afternoon after the Monkey Bars Landing. Having no idea what our father had learned down at the garage, Mickey had insisted that we never left the woods that night. Knowing he had just moments before our father would be back in his bedroom to confront him about the lie he had fed him, Mickey quickly pulled his lederhosen out of his dresser. While those quirky shorts might have seemed silly to the outside world, they had grown on us for one special reason. The protective leather hide saved our own hides when our father felt obligated to teach us a lesson with the *gürtel*.

I mean, belt.

— 6 —

May 31, 1970
Alamo, Michigan

The sweet aroma of frying pork chops drifted out of the kitchen, reminding me that I still had what was basically a $50,000 Bar left in my jacket. While our weekday menus featured simple creations of chili or goulash, Sunday suppers were served earlier in the day and consisted of baked potatoes and, more often than not, pork chops—peppered and fried up so that they were packed with juice and flavor. Our mother rarely ventured downstairs before noon on any day, so Sunday suppers were usually relaxing and free of drama.

Hanging up my jacket, I noticed the cellar door was ajar and the light on downstairs. Walking down the steps, I peered around the corner into our father's workshop, where two shadows lurked.

"Jesus!" Silvia said, looking up. "You nearly gave me a heart attack."

"What are you two up to?" I asked, genuinely interested in any activity that involved intrigue and trespassing of any sort.

"Shh," Mickey whispered, holding a toolbox open, with Silvia standing beside him. "We found this." He held a dark purple crushed-velvet cloth in his hands, and as he carefully unfolded it, my eyes widened at the sight.

"Wow, can I hold it?"

"Only if you're very careful. Don't worry, I checked the chamber, and it's empty," he whispered, cradling the pistol and displaying it out for us as if it were a Faberge Egg. He then opened the chamber and spun it like the Lone Ranger. He snapped it back shut and handed it to me.

I picked it up gently and pointed it at the wall, pretending to shoot at bad guys. Surprisingly, it was so small that it fit comfortably in my hands. "Why do you think Popi hides a gun down here?"

"I don't know. To protect us, I guess. There aren't any bullets though. Not in the toolbox or anywhere else, so if there are any, they're well hidden.

"Let's hope Mutti's not hiding them," Silvia added, making me suddenly wish I didn't know of the gun's existence.

"Supper's on!" our father called out from the kitchen.

Mickey quickly but carefully folded the gun back up in its velvet blanket. "Don't tell *anyone*," he warned, glaring at both Silvia and me. We nodded, understanding the burden that had just been put upon us.

Scrambling up the stairs, we joined Hanna who was already sitting at the picnic table, which served as our dining room table. She was reading *The Black Stallion* and didn't bother to look up. Our father however shot us a quizzical look. "What trouble were you three getting into?" he asked, smiling, not realizing the impact of his question.

"Nothing," Mickey answered, a little too quickly, triggering Hanna to glance up from her book. "Just hanging."

I walked over to Popi, knowing that I had a quick chore before sitting down with the others, and he handed me a tray which held a plateful of food, silverware, a napkin, and salt and pepper shakers. He smiled at me as I took it from him, and I made my way out of the kitchen and up the stairs.

As I climbed the stairs, the old steps creaked beneath my feet. I caressed the smooth wooden handles of the tray, feeling the heat generating from the hot plate. Our father made this tray in his workshop down in the cellar. The plate covered the word MUTTI, which he had carved into the center of the tray. Also on the tray was a small ceramic vase holding little plastic violets. Suddenly I felt sorry for him, since more times than not, our mother's Sunday suppers went unceremoniously untouched and the flowers unnoticed.

This was only Day Two of our mother's headache, which would likely keep her hidden from us for at least another day. Halfway up the stairs, I stopped to swipe a bite of the buttery baked potato. Our father always made sure that her potatoes were carefully peeled, revealing no remnants of skin, and topped with a mound of sweet salted butter.

"Knock, knock," I said, pushing the door open with my elbow. Leaving the light off, I waited for my eyes to adjust to the darkness. A curled-up form on the bed slowly came into focus, hidden under a German feather comforter pulled up to her neck. Her dark hair fell in a tangled mess over her face, making her look much older than her forty-three years. I stood over her with the tray in my hands, looking at her, not with hate or pity, just watching her. She was just over five feet tall and proud that she weighed only a hundred pounds, but she looked even smaller than me curled up under the blanket.

"Mutti," I whispered. "Your supper's here." She didn't respond, forcing me to repeat myself. "Mutti?" I twirled the plastic violet between my fingers and rolled my eyes at the idea of our mother sleeping yet another day away.

"I see you rolling your eyes," she said coldly, staring at me through her stringy bangs.

"Your supper's here," I said cheerfully, trying to distract her. "It smells really good. Popi fried up pork chops, just the way you like them."

"Take it away. I don't want to eat." She closed her eyes and added, "I hope you get headaches like this one day, and then you'll see."

A shiver shot up my spine as she opened her eyes again and glared at me through her bangs. Without another word, I picked up the tray and left, unable to shake the feeling that I had just been handed a curse.

— 7 —

1940

Eschbach, Baden-Württemberg, Germany

"Crazy old *frau*," Didi mumbled, wringing out the dirty water from the rag into the large metal pail. In the past months, she had grown familiar with her mother's mood swings. She was usually able to navigate around her mother's episodes of violence, but today she wasn't in the mood for this unnatural mother-daughter dance, and she paid the price for not paying attention.

She bent down to mop the remaining water from the kitchen floor, trying to move beyond the throbbing ache in her ear, but the intensity of the pain made it impossible to ignore. Standing up, she reached for a kitchen chair to steady herself, but missed and slipped on the soapy water. As she tried catching herself, she banged her shoulder against the table. Falling to the floor, the side of her head hit the edge of the tabletop, reigniting the sharp pain from the open sore in her ear.

"*Verdammt!*" Didi's mother yelled, lifting her coffee cup. "Look what you made me do. A five-year-old has more grace." Without a glance toward her daughter, who was still sitting on the floor, holding her ear, Didi's mother picked up a cloth napkin and dabbed the spilled coffee from *Der Spiegel* magazine. "Well, don't just lie there. Clean it up. Georg will be here within the hour." Picking up her cup and magazine, she shook her head in disgust and walked out of the room.

Didi closed her eyes with the hope that shutting out the light would lessen the pain, but as she slowly pulled herself up from the floor, she realized that the throbbing in her ear had escalated along with the new ache in her shoulder. She knew that she should have been excited that her father was coming for a visit, but Georg wasn't coming over to see her. After a long evening of drinking, he would sometimes call Didi over to his side. Pulling her hair away from her face, he would look deeply into her eyes, and say something along the line of, "*Nein.* This is most definitely not my daughter." Turning to Didi's mother, he would add, "If you want to marry me, you'll have to do better than this runt." The two would then break out in raucous laughter as Georg tussled Didi's hair before sending her on her way.

Didi rubbed her elbow, grimacing as she touched the raw skin, the result of skidding across the linoleum. She tried to be angry, but the pain deadened her rage. *Just clean the floor*, she told herself, finding it hard to follow her own words of advice. She lifted the rag up from the floor and began mopping up the bucketful of water. She moved slowly, fighting the urge to faint.

A half hour later she mopped up the last of the water and carried the bucket outside, pouring the dirty water onto the lawn. Back inside, she walked down the hallway and paused in front of the small oval mirror that hung next to the coatrack. She barely recognized the face staring back at her—the long dark hair, black as coal, and hanging lifeless. Leaning in, she pulled her hair back from her left ear and turned in an attempt to examine it more closely. The ear was reddened from the most recent blow from her mother and puss confirmed her fear that the wound had become infected. She softly cupped the ear with her hand and felt the rising heat from the swollen mass.

Didi closed her eyes and envisioned herself looking beautiful, with her hair swept up on top of her head like the fashion models in *Der Spiegel*. With a heavy sigh, she pushed her hair forward again, so it covered her ears. Picking up the bucket, she continued down the hall to the cellar door, silently vowing to leave home the minute she was old enough and leave Germany as soon as she possibly could.

And never, ever look back.

— 8 —

June 6, 1970
Alamo, Michigan

I shook my head ever so slightly at the catcher crouching behind home plate. Frustrated, I adjusted my ball cap, touching the English D for good luck. With the catcher's second hand signal, I nodded and wound up, releasing the ball like a bullet. I watched the bat swing harmlessly as the ball screamed into the catcher's mitt.

Only this wasn't Tiger Stadium. And the so-called ball in my hand was actually a big old soggy green walnut.

Rain was forecasted for the day, but it wasn't long before solid gray gave way to white fluffy clouds against a brilliant blue sky. The sun decided to show itself, forcing me to squint as I hurried out the back door, bucket in hand, ready to tackle the horrendous chore handed down by our father. Silvia and Mickey were over by the barn, oblivious to my sinister plan. Picking up a shriveled walnut, I studied the mushy green casing. Why on God's green earth would someone plant walnut trees? Eating the walnuts would make too much sense so we didn't do that. The trees were nothing to look at, shading was minimal, and those damn walnuts grew as large as baseballs, turning into lethal weapons when shot out of the blade of a lawnmower. I rolled the walnut in my hand, wondering if I had the strength to reach my targets, but before I could decide, they both walked into the barn, leaving me with the boring task at hand. Fallen walnuts in

October have a cool green leather-like casing and are easy to throw into the bucket, but the walnuts that survive the winter by burrowing beneath the snow are nasty come May, leaving stains on my hands that even a scrubbing with Comet couldn't remove. I sniffed my hand and scrunched my nose at the stench—like milk that has sat out in the sun for days.

As the youngest, I developed a knack for artfully dodging chores requiring muscle, but on that day my siblings agreed that I was more than capable of picking up walnuts. Sometimes I adored my brother and sisters.

That day, not so much.

The only thing keeping me from flinging my bucketful of walnuts at the two as they walked back out of the barn was my anticipation for the day. Not that a family picnic was anything earth-shattering, but the destination sure was.

"What's your problem?" I shouted up to the bare tree branches hanging overhead, in search of the insistent chattering coming from up above, as a squirrel scolded me for stealing her dinner. I raised my hands in an attempt to block the sun. "Oh, yeah? I dare you to climb down here and say—"

What is it about light fixtures fashioned after wagon-wheels? As I slowly opened my eyes, I found myself looking up at our western-themed chandelier, which was weird because I was just . . . I was just doing something else. A set of snarling teeth jumped up and met me face-to-face. "Get away, Doxy," I said. But as I moved my arm to push our dachshund down from the sofa, a piercing pain shot through the center of my brain, making me close my eyes and wince.

"There you are," our father smiled, looking up from his *Reader's Digest*. "How are you feeling?"

"She's awake!" Silvia shouted, running over to me. She threw her arms around me, triggering yet another jolt straight through my eyes. I let the throbbing subside before speaking.

"I think I'm OK. What am I doing—"

"Mickey and I found you lying on the ground, out cold! Popi figures a walnut fell on you, and you hit your head on the hard ground. You basically took a one, two punch."

"Oh, *schatz*," my mother said, setting her coffee down, and hurrying over to me.

It felt good to have our mother coming to my rescue. She wasn't your typical mom when it came to coddling her children, embracing being atypical in anything requiring a nurturing instinct. So, our mother showing concern for me?

Damn.

She came to me, bent over . . . and picked up Doxy. "Who loves you, *schatz*?" she cooed, giving her favorite family member a nuzzle.

"Popi, is she going to be OK?" Silvia asked, staring at me like she was looking for the television knob so she could change the channel. "She was out for nearly thirty minutes."

"She's fine," our mother answered, setting Doxy back down, and looking back at me. "Get up and go brush your hair, unless you don't want to go to the rest area."

"Are you OK?" Hanna, asked me, after quietly watching from the other side of the room.

"Yeah, I guess so." I reached to the back of my head and found a large knot.

She gave my hair a friendly rub and turned to Silvia and Mickey. "Hey, knuckleheads, my new Frisbee seems to be missing. Have either of you seen it?"

"Come on, knucklehead," Silvia said to me as I slowly sat up. "Let's go look in the backyard."

Silvia was five years older than me, and while we often fought like two rodents in a hamster ball, I shadowed her every move and mirrored her every style, from worn baseball caps to faded Levi's. I stopped at emulating her sad infatuation with the Chicago Cubs, instead opting for the more bankable Tigers, who took the pennant just two years prior. But on this particular day, I followed my own fashion trend of sporting lederhosen.

"Here it is!" Silvia called out, pulling the Frisbee out of the lilac bush. "Watch out!" I ducked, just as the Frisbee flew past my head.

With the Rambler stuffed with six people, one ornery dachshund, and enough food and toys to last through the summer, we finally got the party on the road. Seated up front, I was in such a good mood I didn't even mind that I was sandwiched between our father's Sir Walter Raleigh pipe smoke and our mother's cologne, which based on smell, was a half-gallon of Chanel N°5.

"Mickey, roll up your window," our mother directed while tightening the knot in her scarf to keep the wind from blowing her long hair over her face. Regardless that our destination was a rest stop in Alamo, our mother took care to look her best, sporting her Laura Petrie slacks and black sunglasses that made you believe you were in the presence of Jackie O. Behind her shades, with her sleek black hair peeking out from under the bright orange and yellow silk scarf, she looked more like a Hollywood actress trying to hide from the cameras than a housewife living out no one's fantasy in Alamo, Michigan.

Trapped in the car with no circulation, it didn't take long before I was drowning in a cloud of pipe smoke fighting for dominance with the Chanel N°5. As I plugged my nose, I feared for my life, convinced that this chemical warfare would either kill me or equip me with the immunity of a superhero.

Fortunately, we pulled up to the rest stop twelve minutes later. While those in the backseat jumped out of the car, my father reached past me to open the glove box for his bag of tobacco while my mother pulled down the visor and gazed into the mirror to make sure she was who she imagined herself to be, leaving me trapped and anxious.

Our father was an entire generation older than our mother and never moved with the excitement instilled in the rest of us. By the time I finally escaped from the car, the others were already walking out to the picnic area with their arms full of provisions. I walked around to the back of the car and found the last remaining items—Jarts. Throwing the plastic rings around my neck, I picked up the four Jarts and proceeded to follow the others.

"Silvia!" I yelled, picking up my pace to a jog. "Wait for—"

Suddenly, my foot slammed against a rock that was poking out from the grass. And like a repeat from earlier that morning, I was launched forward, and the Jarts sprang from my hands while I hit the grass, face-down, with a *thud*. I lifted my head, spitting out grass just as Doxy came running toward me, snarling. Remembering that the Jarts were once in my hand, I looked up.

I watched helplessly as the two air missiles came screaming back to earth. *Thump*! One landed inches from Doxy, causing him to yelp in retaliation. As I covered my head in sheer terror, the other Jart barreled straight down and landed with a smack on my butt. Terrified of what I was about to find, I craned my neck to look at my backside, only to find that the Jart had harmlessly bounced off my lederhosen and landed onto the grass. Score another point for those German leather shorts.

"How are you able to survive each day?" Silvia said, shaking her head at me.

With another spit of grass, I gathered up my belongings and walked over to Hanna and Mickey who were arguing.

"This is way too close to the grill, Mickey," Hanna said as she picked up the picnic basket. "Grab that end of the blanket, and let's move it over there where there's more shade."

"But—"

"Plus, it's further away from the parking lot."

"Yeah, but—"

"Trust me. Grab the corners."

As they carried the blanket, I just shook my head, knowing the entire conversation was unnecessary since our mother would be sweeping in—

"Hanna, Mickey, come over here." We all turned as our mother sauntered up. Doxy wagged his tail and ran to greet her. "The blanket needs to be moved over there where there's more sun. We don't want dirt and bugs from the tree landing on top of our food."

Hanna let out a sigh as Mickey put his hands on his hips and shot Hanna a wide grin. They both picked up the blanket and walked it back to its original spot while our mother stood quiet, surveying the area. Her eyes landed on two beautiful picnic tables, both free of carvings and random stickiness left by inconsiderate diners.

"Silvia," she called out. "Help your brother move that picnic table. It needs to go over there. I don't want the smoke from the grill hitting us while we eat." And with that, the party moved ten yards south. No problem, it was still a beautiful day.

As our mother set up the dining area, our father began prepping the grilling station, and I watched as he poured a pile of charcoal briquettes into the bottom of the black iron grill. "Toss me my glove, please," he asked, and I obliged, happy to be his assistant.

"Can you believe it, Popi?" I asked, as he stacked the briquettes into a pyramid. "We're the first ones to use this grill. Why hasn't anyone else grilled out here yet?"

He smiled as he took off his glove. "Well," he said, looking out across the parking lot. "You might have noticed that there's a highway in front of us. This picnic area was made for travelers who are on their way somewhere, maybe Up North, and need to stop and stretch their legs for a bit. We just happen to be lucky enough to have this wonderful new oasis so close to us. How many people can say they live within a stone's throw from the world's most beautiful rest area?"

"What did I tell you about watching where you're going?"

My father and I turned to see Mickey kneeling on the ground, picking up a stack of fallen Dixie Cups. He was helped along by Doxy who grabbed a cup and, with a growl, started tearing into it like it was a squirrel.

"See what you've done?" our mother continued. "You can never do anything right!"

I stood watching as Mickey sighed and slowly picked up the few cups that had stuck together in the stack. Our mother wasn't picky in regard to who was on the receiving end of her discontent, but more often than not, she would zero in on Mickey. Maybe it was the way he insisted on ironing his jeans so that they would look nice for school, or maybe it was the amount of time he spent in front of the bathroom mirror, combing his hair so that his bangs hung just right over his eyes. "Why can't you be more like other boys?" she would ask, yanking the brush out of his hands. Hanna spent enough time in the one bathroom in our house, and our mother didn't appreciate having to share what little availability was left with her only son.

She started toward Mickey, and before I could warn my brother, she shoved him from the back. He fell forward, unable to stop himself from hitting the grass, and landed on a small stack of paper cups. I stopped and cupped my hand over my mouth, scared of what his reaction would be, but without even turning to look at our mother, Mickey brushed himself off and picked up the smashed cups.

"What is taking you so long?" she asked, grabbing his arm, not amused that her antics didn't have the desired effect on him. She tightened her grip, and Mickey flinched while shielding his face with his hand, ready for the next strike.

"Mickey!" our father called out. "Come over here and help me start the grill." He then looked over at me. "Please, run and pick up the cups for your brother."

"Yes sir!" I said, running off, eager to separate the two. As I ran up, our mother gave Mickey's arm one last squeeze before letting go. He flicked his bangs back as he hurried past me.

"Hey!" Silvia called out. I turned to find a Frisbee flying straight toward my head, and I saved myself from another headache by catching it.

"Hey, yourself!" I said, throwing the Frisbee back before picking up the cups and placing them on the picnic table, careful to make sure they wouldn't fall again.

Over in the parking lot, a carload of children poured out of a wood-paneled station wagon as their father leaned against the hood and lit a cigarette before handing it off to his wife and lighting his own. The children ran into the building, laughing and poking at each other the way we all did after spending way too much time in the car, which made me think about what our father had said about rest stops serving as beacons for road-weary travelers. But still, it seemed odd to me that other families living within spittin' distance weren't taking advantage of this incredible place, with a lawn not yet trampled on by thousands of travelers, and a picnic area a skip away from flush toilets. Silvia tossed the Frisbee back to me as our mother smoothed out the wool blanket, making sure that the picnic basket didn't cover up the colorful Hudson's Bay Co. signature stripes.

"Come on, guys," Hanna shouted out to us. "Let's walk around." I tossed the Frisbee over near the blanket, and Silvia, Mickey, and I followed Hanna into the rest area building.

Where once sat two smelly pit toilets now stood a lobby that boasted floor space so large we could have parked our car in there. I marveled at the glossy white tile, not yet dull from scuff marks from a stampede of travelers. In the center of the floor sat an oak display case holding a selection of colorful brochures teasing me with exciting and exotic destination points like the go-cart track on the outskirts of town and the Allegan County Fair. Passing over the brochure featuring a bushel of brilliant red apples on the cover, my eyes landed on a photo of a lone donkey posing for the camera. Dang if he didn't look like he had a smile on his face, telling us all to "Come on down" to the Kalamazoo Nature Center. Pulling the brochure from the stand, I carefully folded it and put it in my pocket.

"Hey," Silvia said, waving Hanna and me over to her. "Come here, you need to see this." She stood in front of a map of Michigan that took up nearly half the wall, and we gazed at the patchwork of cities and highways as she moved her finger across the highway connecting Kalamazoo to Grand Rapids before stopping. "There it is," she said, stepping back so we could see what she had landed on. We leaned in and read the words, You Are Here. "How 'bout them apples? Alamo is finally on the map."

"You guys need to check out the bathrooms," Mickey said, walking out of the men's room, wiping his hands dry with a paper towel. "Man, what a step up. The mirrors in there are huge, and I wasn't even afraid to touch the flush handle!"

As Hanna and Silvia went into the women's restroom, I walked over to Mickey and tugged on his sweatshirt. "Give me fifty cents, Mickey!" I could barely contain my excitement because standing before us was a magnificent red pop machine towering over us like a neon skyscraper. I stared, soaking in the warmth of the bright red light accented with that familiar white wave. This was nothing like the old soda machines found at most gas stations. No, this marvel was lit up like the sun and beckoning to us like the South Haven Lighthouse on Lake Michigan.

"Wow, that's nearly twice the cost of a Coke at the Marathon. You have to share it with me," Mickey said, handing me two quarters.

"Thank you, Mickey," I said, dropping them into the coin slot.

"Get a Spri—"

I hit the Coke button before he could finish, and was treated with the rumbling of churning gears as a bottle rolled down to the mouth of the pop machine. Mickey grabbed the bottle and, with a snap on the machine's bottle opener, took a long slug and wiped his mouth with the back of his hand. "Now, that's the real thing," he smiled, pointing to the bottle in his hand, before handing the cold curvy bottle to me.

As we finished our Coke, people came and went. I wondered where they lived and where they were traveling—maybe they were on their way to the Mackinac Bridge, or perhaps they were Canadians wanting to check out their neighbors to the south. As they hurried to the restrooms without a glance at the large beautiful map or the attractions center, I wanted to pull them aside and show them that a new world awaited them just a brochure away.

"Keep the bottle," Mickey whispered as I tipped the Coke back to catch the last drops. "We want the deposit."

Walking back outside, we approached a couple walking in, making me do a double take. I had seen that woman before.

Her polyester shorts scraped as her knees rubbed together with each step, creating a high-piercing sound similar to the screech of the exercise wheel in a gerbil cage. She looked at me with a scowl, telling me that she probably didn't have children of her own, and was wondering why the one in front of her was running around unleashed.

As the couple passed by, the woman glanced over to the picnic area and spotted our mother placing a red and white checkered tablecloth on the picnic table.

"Good lord, isn't that the Phillips woman?" the woman whispered a bit too loudly to her husband. "Are they really picnicking here?"

As the husband looked over to our mother and laughed, it was all I could do to keep from tripping the old biddy as she brushed by me with the authority of claiming the width of the sidewalk as her real estate. I glanced over at our mother, and at that moment I understood that maybe so-called normal people didn't picnic at their local rest stop. And today I was OK with that.

Everything was new here. While the others walked back to the picnic area, I decided to investigate the shining example of new technology that stood in front of the building. "Get away birds!" I yelled into the sky, running for the phonebooth. "Save the children, they're being attacked!" Channeling Tippi Hendren, I slammed the folding glass doors effortlessly just as a seagull crashed into the glass right in front of my face. "Get away birds!"

Or maybe I was Mary Tyler Moore on assignment, working on a lead story for the evening newscast. I glided my hand along the glass panel, which was still clear, and opened the phone book, surprised to find that it wasn't bloated yet from being left out in every kind of weather. A flash of light hit me as the sun reflected off the chrome of the phone cradle. Lifting the receiver, I twirled the metal cord in my hand and punched a series of buttons before holding the receiver up to my mouth. "Why yes, Mr. Grant, I'm working on the bank robbery story now, and I just might know where the robbers are hiding. I'll get the script to Murray as soon as I get back to the station."

I hung up and savored my quiet time in that glorious phone booth. Finally, I reached for the change lever and moved it up and down several times before sticking my fingers into the change drawer. Bam! I could feel a coin, and, fishing it out, I realized that I had hit the jackpot. One beautiful quarter. Feeling empowered, I stuffed it into my pocket and threw the door open to run back into the sunshine, almost knocking down the same woman who was now walking back out of the building with her husband.

"For the love of God, watch where you're going!" she yelled.

I kept running, embarrassed that I didn't offer up an apology or reply. I knew that woman from somewhere . . .

— 9 —

June 6, 1970
Alamo, Michigan

Alamo was just a stop in the road—a town where excitement came from the screams of the fire department alarm, telling folks throughout the area that another grass fire needed attention. Answering the call, a flurry of volunteer firefighters raced to the station in trucks dolled up with red flashing lights and fire department decals. Moments later, firetrucks squealed out of the station, followed by gawkers, excited to see what unfortunate sad news hid at the end of the chase.

Being a firefighter in Alamo was an honor, and a legacy that many fathers handed down to their sons, and it wasn't uncommon for both father and son to be found fighting fires side by side. While I never saw a female firefighter, it didn't stop me from imagining myself running with a firehose as water sprayed across the rooftops of burning barns.

But fire-chasing in our sleepy town was the exception. More often, days flowed into nights without incident. Lawns needed mowing, dogs got walked, and women looking for a heavy dose of hair spray made an appointment at Treva's Beauty Parlor—where cuts and colors came with a generous side of gossip. Heaven help the woman who didn't get her hair done at Treva's.

". . . and after almost knocking me down, she ran off like a wild child," Luanne added, relishing her time with her girlfriends. "Mark my words, that girl is going to grow up to be just like her mother."

As the others nodded in agreement, Beth sighed and poured herself another cup of coffee from the percolator. She dropped two sugar cubes into her coffee. "I can think of worse people to be," she whispered to herself.

"Well, you can't accuse that family of being boring," Treva smiled, reaching for her shears. "I can't say that it's ever occurred to me to take the kids on a picnic to the rest stop. Did you talk with any of them?

"Other than telling the youngest one that she needed to mind her manners? No. I don't think Larry or Elisabeth saw us. If she did see us, she didn't let on. You think she could ever walk her ass over to me to say hello? She's more likely to take one of those picnic tables home to put in her dining room!"

Treva smiled as she ran a comb through Luanne's hair. "Next thing you know, that family will be pitching a tent and roasting marshmallows at the Marathon."

Luanne let out a snort of laughter.

"What?" Doris asked, lifting the hair dryer back off of her hair. "What did I just miss? Come on, ladies, spill." As the ladies laughed, Doris added, "So I heard that the new rest area finally opened up on the highway." This got the ladies laughing all over again.

"So immature," Doris mumbled as the laughter continued. "Any of you got a light?"

— 10 —

June 6, 1970
Alamo, Michigan

"Allow me, my dear," our father said, digging his lighter out of his pocket to light our mother's cigarette. She inhaled deeply and blew smoke high into the evening air.

After a pleasant afternoon at the rest area, our mother decided that she needed a few things from the grocery store in Kalamazoo. Going into town was usually something our parents enjoyed without the weight of four children, so this bonus adventure was a treat for me. With anticipation, I dug into my pocket and wrapped my fingers around that quarter. I followed the others as we strolled along the front sidewalk of the shopping center, peering into the many storefronts.

"Oh man, there's some kind of grease on my shirt!" Mickey had stopped to look at his reflection in a shop window and was horrified at what looked back at him. He spit on his finger and started frantically rubbing the spot, which only made the smudge larger. "Ugh!"

With Mickey's panic attack, our mother let out a sigh we could all hear. "Stop spitting on your shirt. You can take care of it when we get home."

Unlike our visit to the rest stop earlier in the day, where we were for the most part alone in the picnic area, this place was bustling with people. I could feel our mother tense up as she put her sunglasses back on even though the setting sun was casting a beautiful mix of deep pink against the grey-blue sky. She walked down the sidewalk with the flair of a fashion model—pay no mind to the flock of children trailing behind her.

There was a pay phone just ahead, so I ran ahead of the others, imagining what it would be like to hit pay dirt twice in one day. I cranked the phone's change lever while jamming my fingers into the change drawer. Nothing. No problem—I was already ahead for the day, and it was about to get even better. While the others filed into the grocery store, I stopped just inside the first doors. I had a date with a gumball machine.

The funny thing about gumball machines is that they rarely held gum. With the utmost concentration, I studied the lineup of gumball machines that held Batman rings, plastic cars, and Chicklets before landing on the one that spoke to me. Or rather, I spoke to it.

"Gumby!" I dropped my quarter into the coin slot, and slowly turned the crank. I opened the front metal flap, allowing the clear plastic capsule to roll out into my open palm.

Making my way into the store, I found that my family had scattered in every direction. I hurried past the frozen-food section on my way to the breakfast aisle. With limited time and an unlimited selection of cereal boxes, I made my way down the aisle, grabbing Cap'n Crunch, Freakies, and Quisp. Turning the boxes around, I learned what treasures hid inside.

"There you are," Silvia said. "Hanna told me to find you. Come on."

Freakies box in hand, I followed my sister down the aisle to the magazine section where Hanna was having the same problem I was having in the breakfast aisle.

"I don't have enough money for both. Should I buy *Teen* or *Tiger Beat*?" Hanna held up both magazines to Silvia who studied the covers.

"Do you want to read about other girls or David Cassidy?"

With a nod, Hanna set the *Teen* magazine down. "We should probably find Mutti and Popi. Come on, Mickey."

"Just a sec."

Short on funds, Mickey was trying to devour as much as he could, as he read another article in a magazine called *Rolling Stone*, which made no sense to me at the time since the Rolling Stones were nowhere on the cover. Gracing the cover that week was Little Richard, a colorful flamboyant singer who wore makeup and boldly embraced a feminine persona. Both Mickey and our mother made it a point to catch his regular appearances on the *Mike Douglas Show*. While Mickey lost himself within the pages of the magazine, I picked up the current issue of *Mad* magazine and flipped to the inside back cover, gently bending the page accordion-style to reveal the funny picture within a picture. That wacky *Mad* magazine.

"Let's go, kiddo," Mickey said, putting the magazine back on the rack. "Mutti and Popi are leaving."

We found our parents at the checkout lane where Popi was loading grocery items onto the conveyer belt. I hid my Freakies box behind a package of paper towels and looked longingly at the candy bars dressed in bright colored wrappings, luring unsuspecting shoppers.

"Kids, grab a candy bar," our mother announced as she chose two Peppermint Patties for herself and our father.

"Grab a Snickers Bar for me," Hanna called over to Silvia while I surveyed the overwhelming selection—Mounds, M&Ms, Nestle Crunch, Almond Joy . . .

"Mickey, I said you could pick out a candy bar," our mother called out to Mickey, who was leaning against the wall in front of the check-out lanes.

"No, thanks."

I placed my Reese's onto the conveyer belt, hoping to distract her from Mickey's defiance.

"I'm sorry?"

"I'm not hungry. I don't want one." He folded his hands in front of his chest, but instead of looking defiant, he looked nervous. He flicked his bangs back, but they immediately fell back over his eyes.

"I said, pick out a candy bar."

The rest of us were torn between waiting for our candy bars to be rung up and wanting to leave the store as quickly and quietly as possible. My mother and brother had too many confrontations that started just like this, an argument about nothing at all. And all I could think of was, *Grab a stupid candy bar. I don't care if you're not hungry. Who in the world turns down a candy bar? Just save the stupid thing for later.* Mickey didn't move, and our mother tightened her grip on her handbag.

"All right, is someone going to help me with these bags?" our father asked. Mickey sprang from the window ledge and grabbed two sacks while I picked up a light bag. As we walked out, Mickey ignored our mother's stare, but I couldn't help myself. Our father had one hand free, and, as he walked by her, he touched her back, but she swatted his hand away and followed behind us.

It was dark as we walked through the parking lot. Our mother stood silent as our father unlocked her door, and I crawled in, to sit between them. With the car overflowing with the six of us and a week's worth of groceries, our father pulled out of the parking lot. The light from the streetlamp fell across my mother's face, revealing a faraway look in her eyes. Reaching into my pocket, I pulled out the plastic capsule and gazed at my new prize. As "What's New Pussycat" poured from the radio speaker, I made Gumby dance across my lap.

"Slide over!" Mickey said from the backseat, obviously talking to Silvia since he knew better than to speak to Hanna in that tone. I hadn't heard anything from Hanna since we left the store, making me wonder if she was also aware of our mother's silence.

As Tom Jones serenaded us, I bounced Gumby on my lap. Our

mother reached past me as Silvia snapped back at Mickey with, "It's bad enough that I always have to sit on the hump—"

The music snapped off, making everyone fall quiet.

With the lights of the city behind us, we headed home, with our mother remaining silent. Meanwhile, I tried distracting myself with my new toy, bending his legs back and forth, dancing to the music still in my head. Back and forth.

Burning embers from our father's pipe set off a silhouette of his face in the darkness of our car as we rolled down the backroad, coming up on the stretch between the Twin Lakes. I started humming and raised Gumby up to the dashboard as our mother, without saying a word, leaned over me. Just when I thought that she was about to grab Gumby, she instead reached across me, and latched onto the steering wheel, giving it a strong yank down with one swift movement, throwing the car into an extreme right turn toward one of the lakes.

"What the . . ."

"Did we hit something?"

Hanna stayed quiet, but a dreamy sensation came over me as our father tightened his grip and regained control of the steering wheel.

"Honey, you can't do that," our father said, almost under his breath. "Tell me what's wrong."

This request didn't sit well with our mother, who answered by reaching for the steering wheel again and giving it another hard yank. From the back, I heard yells of, "Jesus Christ!" and "Popi, make her stop!" but still nothing from Hanna.

As we hit gravel, our father tightened his grip on the wheel and maneuvered the car back onto the road. "Damn it, honey. You've got to calm down." Even though he said it calmly, I knew he was losing his patience with our mother. I also knew that telling our mother to calm down wasn't going to go down well.

I bowed my head and started singing quietly to myself. "'Who can turn the world on with her smile? Who can take a nothing day and suddenly make it all seem worthwhile?'"

She didn't move as she gazed out her side window, breathing hard like a racehorse waiting for the gates to open. I closed my eyes and tried picturing Mary Tyler Moore standing on that sidewalk on the Nicollet Mall in downtown Minneapolis, throwing her hat into the air. Rocking back and forth, I kept singing. "'Well, it's you girl, and you should know it. With each glance and every little movement, you show it. Love is—"

Suddenly I felt her pushing against me, and I opened my eyes as she reached past me. In what felt like slow motion, she gave the steering wheel a push, causing the car to cross into the oncoming lane, making the car skid as our father fought to gain control again before maneuvering it back into our lane.

"Oh, come on!"

"Mutti!"

"Damn it," our father said, pulling her hand off the wheel. "Stop it."

I wanted to scream, *Popi, just stop the car!* If it were up to me, I'd lean over, and I would open that passenger door and push—

On cue, our mother opened her door, forcing our father to quickly pull off onto the narrow shoulder of the road. As the car slowed, our mother threw the door open and stepped out, immediately losing her balance. I watched as she fell into the weeds that led down a short embankment, down to the lake. I shut my eyes and cringed, waiting for a thump from running over her. Thankfully, there was no thump, just the door swinging open.

As we kids all instinctively looked back, our mother popped back up, smoothed out her slacks, and proceeded to walk in the direction we were already traveling—heading home on her own terms.

"Good god," our father muttered. A large ugly moth had flown into the car, attracted to the dome light, and it flapped around, throwing us all into the stark reality of our challenge—trying to convince our mother to get back into the car, which I wasn't at all sure was a good idea. Following our father's instruction, I leaned over and pulled the door shut while Mickey grabbed Hanna's *Tiger Beat*, rolled it up and started swatting at the moth.

"Damn it, Mickey, stop it! Use something else!"

"Do you want me to use your jacket?"

Mickey kept swatting at the moth as Hanna grappled to save her magazine. Meanwhile, our father watched our mother walk down the road. His pipe glowed bright as he sucked on the shank, unable to escape the disturbance of the shenanigans going on in the backseat.

She walked at a killer pace. The moment she disappeared beyond the beam of the headlights, our father slid the stick shift into gear. We slowly proceeded down the road, passing our mother, who maintained her pace, never looking our way. He then pulled over shortly ahead of her, rolled down his window, and patiently waited for our mother to catch up.

"Come on, honey. Please get into the car," he pleaded as she came up on us. The ruckus in the backseat had stopped so as not to disturb our father's mission, but our mother passed by without a glance. We watched her until she again reached the darkness beyond the reach of the headlights.

"This is going to go on forever," Silvia grumbled. Our father remained silent, driving past our mother and again offered his sincere assistance on her quest to get home if she would just get in the car.

And without a glance, our mother marched on, leaving us with the only option of playing this game of leapfrog. Again, we watched her walk out of the light, signaling our father to put the car into gear.

After round three, our mother must have grown tired of this perverse game, because as she came up to the car, she walked over to the passenger side, opened her door, and without a word, climbed back into the car. Our father smiled and preceded home, a two-mile trip that seemed like eternity. As we drove along, nobody spoke. Our mother kept her hand off the steering wheel, looking tired, not from the day, but from something bigger. Like she had given up. I started to reach for her, but stopped myself.

She remained in the car as the rest of us quietly unloaded the groceries from the trunk and carried them into the house. I was thankful to be home since our mother couldn't steer the house into a lake. Back inside the house, Mickey turned on the small TV in the kitchen as Hanna lifted a box of ice cream from a grocery bag.

"Yes!" I said, beaming, setting the box of Freakies onto the counter.

"Really? You know its butter pecan."

"Ugh. It's always butter pecan!"

"Because Mutti loves butter pecan," she said without any hint of bitterness as she put the ice cream into the freezer.

"If it could be chocolate, just once. Heck, I would even settle for Neapolitan, even though everyone scoops around the strawberry."

The front door opened abruptly, startling me, and I froze as our mother walked past me to the medicine cabinet that hung above the sink. We all stopped unpacking groceries as she opened the cabinet door. Out of the corner of my eye, I noticed Mickey twitch as our mother turned on the faucet and filled a cup with water.

"Here we go . . ." Hanna whispered.

Our mother turned back to the medicine cabinet and reached for a bottle of pills, which could have been aspirin or the cocktail of medications she took for her schizophrenia, bipolar disorder, and the other medley of conditions doctors had branded her with, which got me thinking about how her medications apparently weren't working so well at the moment. She opened the bottle and filled her hand with a pile of pills.

"Popi!" Hanna called out in a voice an octave higher than normal and a tone I had heard before. "Silvia," Hanna added, with a nod toward me. "Get out of here."

Silvia grabbed my hand, and we hurried out of the kitchen. Passing our father in the living room, I couldn't help but wonder why he took his time taking off his jacket, carefully folding it before placing it on the sofa. He then laid his pipe in the ashtray as Silvia and I made our way upstairs.

Silvia shut the bedroom door behind us, but we could still hear the commotion going on downstairs—a twisted combination of grunts, yells, and random crashes separated by unnatural moments of silence.

"Call the operator," we heard our father call out, followed by Mickey yelling something that I couldn't make out. Silvia frowned, and we both stepped away from the door.

"Let's listen to the radio," I said, wanting to block out the noise. Tuning the dial in search of WOWO, I got nothing but static. While we could occasionally pick up the powerful Indiana station after sunset, on that night, we had to settle for our local pop music DJ.

"Currently number five and screaming up the charts, we've got a little Simon and Garfunkel to carry you into the evening. And I'm Dave Thompson, carrying you through the night!"

Silvia picked up a deck of cards, and I joined her on her bed. As she dealt out the cards, we both quietly sang along to the music, "'You're breaking my heart. You're shaking my confidence daily.'"

My queen beat her seven.

The banging downstairs stopped but I could still hear Hanna talking in an anxious voice. "Silvia," I asked, "why do you think Mickey's helping Popi with Mutti? Why should he care what happens to her after what she does to him every day?"

"I don't know. Maybe because, at the end of the day, we're still family. I don't think Mutti knows what she's doing to us half the time. Have you noticed that she never talks about it later on? Like it never happened."

I nodded like I understood, but the truth is, I didn't.

Silvia's ace took my jack.

As I shuffled the cards, a flash of red light swept over Silvia's face and across the wall. We both jumped up to peer out the window to the driveway below where two men were jumping out of an ambulance as red lights blasted through the darkness. The piercing lights colored the night like a Christmas tree, throwing a beautiful swatch of red across the yard and onto the men as they opened the back door of the ambulance to pull out a gurney. The front door opened below us, and the men with the stretcher disappeared into our house. The red lights continued twirling, announcing to all of Alamo that an ambulance was, once again, visiting the Phillips house. Chatter continued downstairs, but only adult voices. *What are Hanna and Mickey doing? And what about Mutti?*

"Do you think Mutti's dead?" I asked, still staring out the window.

"Nah," Silvia said calmly. "She could take a truckload of pills, and somehow she keeps bouncing back. I don't think Mutti really wants to kill herself. She just wants to be noticed. She's screaming for something. I can't imagine feeling so out of control, that ending everything seems like a solution, but at that point, it must feel like the only option," she continued, pointing out the window where a car was parked alongside our yard. With the headlights off, I couldn't recognize the car, but the moonlight revealed the silhouette of the driver. "If she's looking for attention, this is definitely the way to do it. What a show," Silvia said before walking away from the window. The sound of the front door opening again brought her back to the window, so we could catch the end of her performance.

The same two men walked down the front steps, carrying the stretcher between them, and this time it held a bound-up body. One of the men swung the back door of the ambulance open, and they rolled our mother into the back like bakers sliding bread into an oven. Silvia and I remained quiet as the men shut the door and hopped back into the ambulance.

"They're going to take her to the ER," Silvia said in the tone of a teacher at school addressing her classroom, and I nodded obediently. "That's what Dr. Joe Gannon calls the emergency room on *Medical Center*."

I was simply thankful that it was safe to go downstairs again, and for a short time we would live like normal families on TV. Silvia and I watched the ambulance drive away, those bold red lights disappearing into the night. My attention was suddenly diverted by headlights turning on and the car pulling away, with the driver, no doubt, excited to get home to share this exciting news with their family and friends.

I winced, and touched the back of my head, feeling that familiar knot caused by falling walnuts. Reaching into my back pocket, I pulled out the brochure and looked at the pictures of a snowy owl, trails along a stream, and a cute donkey taking feed from a small boy. We needed to go there soon . . . as a family.

— 11 —

June 18, 1970
Alamo, Michigan

TWO HORSES FOUND. CALL 381-4949 FOR INFORMATION.

"You don't see that every day." Mickey said as we all stared at the piece of paper our father tacked onto the telephone pole at the end of our road. "Missing dog, maybe. A horse, doubtful. Two missing horses? That's a damn story!"

"What if no one responds?" Hanna asked, hopeful but knowing the likelihood of that scenario.

"No one loses two horses and doesn't notice. It's not like a barn cat just wandered off. People notice when they're suddenly short two horses."

"Well, you never know," Hanna said, lifting her chin in defiance. "Maybe the owners never travel down this road."

"Or down D Avenue, or 6th Street, or any of the other dozen places Popi posted these notices," Silvia piped in.

"You never know," Hanna said, ripping the piece of paper off the pole.

But she did know. It wasn't every day you saw a horse strolling down the road, much less two. With help from an open gate, the two escapees saw an opportunity for exploring the world, or at the very least, a part of little ol' Alamo, and they sauntered down the road just as Hanna was watering flowers in the front yard. Seeing this as a gift from heaven, or as she put it, ". . . literally looking a gift-horse in the mouth," she ran into the barn and fashioned up two lovely halters from spare rope. Before we could think about the downside of hiding two horses in the backyard, our new overgrown pets were dining on crab apples and grass while enjoying their vacation getaway. This escapade continued for nearly two weeks until our father happened to wander out back one afternoon and discovered that his children had remodeled the backyard into a makeshift horse ranch.

"Shh!" Mickey said, holding a hand up while turning up the volume on his transistor radio. "Popi's up next."

"I'm George Canter, and this is 'Your Turn'! Where it's your turn to sell that old gun, promote your bake-sale, let us know you lost Fido, and everything in between. Lawrence, you're on the air!"

"This is so cool!" I said, nudging Mickey.

"Good morning. We have two horses that we have found, and we're looking for the owners."

"Wait, I'm sorry. For a minute there, I thought you said you found two horses!"

"That would be right."

We could hear the smile on our father's face, obviously enjoying that he was definitely bringing something new to the show.

"We have two horses, both dark brown, that wandered into our yard two weeks ago, and we're hoping that the owners are listening to your show."

"You've had them for two weeks? I love it! Larry, I have to admit that this is a first. You heard the man, folks. We have two horses that would like to come home! Larry, what number should they call?"

As our father finished up with the announcer, Hanna wadded up the poster in her hands and hung her head. She let out a sigh and whispered, “I guess I’ll get the horses ready. The owners will probably be calling.”

Hanna walked back into the barn as Mickey and Silvia crossed the road, distracted by something. Bored with all of them, I headed toward the house, stopping at the front steps. Getting down on my knees, I whispered, “Thomasina.”

I read somewhere that a pet’s name should never be longer than two syllables. Any longer, and Jonny Quest or Quick Draw McGraw will be slow to learn their name, and slower to respond to it. But I figured that if Thomasina was good enough for the cat in that Disney movie, it was surely good enough for the kitten living under our front-porch steps.

“Thomasina,” I whispered again into the darkness. I crawled further under the porch, searching for that familiar little shadow. Thomasina belonged to a litter born four months earlier at a farm down the road. Barn cats have one job and that is to keep their domicile mouse-free, but apparently Thomasina had dreams of a more meaningful life and wandered over to our house to embark on her new life on the road.

“Thomasina,” I called out again. *Where is that darn cat?* A small crack in the cement steps allowed a single streak of sunlight to stream under the steps, making it hard to see into the corners and forcing me to crawl under the porch on all fours. It was filthy under there—dull gray dirt full of bugs, random bottle caps, broken glass, and what I think used to be a mouse, which had been dead for so long that even Thomasina refused to touch it. Peering around the corner into the hollowed-out bottom of the steps, I saw my old flannel shirt, still crumpled up against the sidewall.

But no cat.

It struck me as strange that she was gone. While she wandered off occasionally like cats do, she never strayed far, appreciative of the milk and leftovers I fed her. She even ate Doxy’s food, unconcerned that she wasn’t a dog.

The only downside was that we did indeed have a dog, and I was nervous that the day was bound to happen when cat meets dog. What I neglected to worry about was our mother discovering Thomasina since that would require her to look under the steps, which seemed highly unlikely, seeing how she rarely ventured out of the house.

But the fact was, Thomasina was missing, and I wondered if she had decided that the adventurous life wasn't for her after all and returned to the barns, ready to get back to work as a mouser. I crawled back out from under the porch, brushing the stale dirt from my Levi's when I looked up and noticed that Silvia and Mickey were still standing across the road, looking down at something in the weeds. Maybe Thomasina wandered over there.

"Hey!" I yelled, walking over to see what had grabbed their attention. "What are you guys looking at?"

Silvia looked up at me, startled, and yelled, "Stop! Don't come over here!"

I stopped. Her expression told me that what I was looking for and what they had found were the same.

Staring up at my bedroom ceiling was something I usually did at night, so in the light of day, I noticed the chip of peeling paint in the shape of Lower Michigan, you know, a mitten. I clutched my stuffed bunny and closed my eyes, hoping that sleep would make the hurt go away.

"Knock, knock."

"Go away," I mumbled, turning to face the wall.

"I was wondering where you went," Silvia said quietly, taking a seat on my bed. "I'm guessing that you know what we were looking at."

I didn't reply.

"I'm really sorry about Thomasina. Popi told us that last night Mutti was in the front porch and heard meows coming from outside. She opened the front door to find Thomasina looking at her from the top step. You know that Mutti hates cats. I guess she called out for Doxy and told him to, 'Go get the cat!' After Popi told her about the horses, she kind of freaked out, and said she didn't want one more dirty farm animal hanging around." Silvia sighed and continued. "Thomasina probably died quickly." She looked down, unsure she believed her own words. "In case you would like to help, Mickey's downstairs making a little marker for Thomasina's grave." I still didn't move. "I guess Mutti saw Thomasina as feral—you know, disposable."

"Is that how she sees us, too?" I asked, turning around to look at Silvia. "Disposable?"

Silvia looked back at me but remained quiet.

"Hey." Mickey was standing in the doorway, holding a piece of plywood. "You OK?"

I sat up and shrugged, squeezing my stuffed rabbit.

"I made this in the workshop," he said, holding up the piece of wood with THOMASINA 1970 painted in black paint. "What do you think? I know it's not fancy but it's something. Thought maybe we could hold a service at the cemetery later."

He was smiling, which made me angry because his smile was contagious, and I wanted to be outraged. Why couldn't they just leave me alone? They both stayed quiet, knowing they could outlast me. Finally, I sighed loudly and nodded.

"Is that a yes?" Mickey asked.

"It's a yes," I said, throwing them a weak smile to show them that as frustrating as they both could be, I appreciated their efforts in trying to lift my spirits.

"All right! I'll set everything up. We'll have the service later tonight." As Mickey turned to leave, he added, "We're going to do this right. Thomasina deserves it."

Silvia looked over at me and rolled her eyes, making me smirk and then laugh. It felt good to laugh.

—

When city kids want to throw a Frisbee around or sneak a smoke with their friends, more than likely, they'll head for the nearest park. But growing up in a town our size, we were forced to be a little more creative, which explained why we spent countless hours riding bikes, blowing smoke rings, and blowing off steam on hot lazy days while sitting on cool tombstones. We didn't mind the occasional gravedigger and random hearse. This place was ours and the best place for burying a body, even a little furry one.

"Wow, Mickey," I whispered, looking at the makeshift gravesite. He had picked out a quiet area next to the old concrete bench located in the far corner of the cemetery. Sticking out of a small plot of turned topsoil was Mickey's plywood marker surrounded by a small batch of flowers.

"I can't believe you put this all together so quickly," I said, bending down to take a closer look at the radiant yellow mums. Looking around the cemetery, I continued, "But I'm afraid to ask you where you got these."

"Best not to then," he answered with a smirk. "They'll never be missed."

Silvia, Mickey, and I sat cross-legged on the grass while Hanna sat on the bench, twirling her long hair in her fingers. Mickey pressed the play button on the cassette recorder, and the service began to the tune of, "Good Morning, Starshine," from *Hair*, a politically-charged musical that introduced the hippie counterculture and sexual revolution of the late 1960s to the masses while also inspiring a popular movie and countless pop songs that later became anthems of the anti-war movement—like "Aquarius," "Hair," and my personal favorite.

"I know you like this song," Mickey said, and I nodded, quietly singing along.

"'Good Morning, Starshine. You lead us along. My love and me as we sing—our early morning singing song! Gliddy glup gloopy, nibby nabby noopy, la la la lo lo, sabba sibby sabba . . .'"

"OK," Hanna said, slapping her hand on the bench as the song finished. "I think I can safely say that is the dumbest song I've ever heard. He really didn't have an extra fifteen minutes to spend on the lyrics to come up with actual words?" Maybe it was the look on my face, because she suddenly realized that she was killing the moment with her insensitive review. "I'm sorry. It's a cute song, really." Looking back at our blank faces, she sighed. "If we're done here—"

"Wait," Silvia said, standing up. "I think we should say something nice about Thomasina."

My only point of reference for post-death nuances was a funeral service held for our Aunt Nola, a crotchety old women who had no use for rambunctious nieces and nephews and spewed venom when forced to converse with us. Not surprisingly, her funeral service was led by a minister who didn't seem to know her—or perhaps did and couldn't voice what he really wanted to say—leaving a sermon limited to Bible passages pertaining to heaven, too many references to his own relationship with God, and generic rhetoric of "what a good Christian Nola was."

Mickey cleared his throat. "We, ah, loved Thomasina. She was a cute kitten, and um, she led a good, well, short life. And we know she will be a cute angel-kitten up in heaven." He looked questioningly at us before finishing with, "Amen."

"Amen," Silvia and I repeated, because that's what the people on the *Hour of Power* always said after Robert Schuller capped off his TV program with a powerful sermon.

"Amen!" Hanna chimed in, standing up and brushing imaginary dirt from her jeans. "Now can I leave? This whole thing is giving me the creeps."

As long shadows slowly covered the cemetery grounds, sucking up the last of the daylight, Hanna left, disappearing into the darkness as she walked down the cemetery lane. "She's just upset that the owners came for the horses," Mickey explained, turning back to me.

Looking at the marker, the pain returned in my chest. "I'll miss you, Thomasina," I whispered as a tear blurred my vision.

"We better head home, too," Mickey said, taking my arm and helping me to my feet. "But, first, let's pump some water for the flowers. The dirt seems a little dry."

Silvia and I followed Mickey to the center of the graveyard. Picking up a rusty pail, I hung the handle of the metal bucket over the spigot while Mickey pumped and pumped until it gargled and water splashed into the bucket.

"Let me carry it," Silvia said, lifting the full bucket.

We stepped deliberately as we made our way back to the gravesite. While the old trees were a pleasure to sit under on a hot day, in the dark those same trees could make a cemetery—

"Shit!" Silvia yelled, dropping the bucket. Water sprayed in her face as the pail crashed to the ground.

"What the—" But before Mickey could finish, he and I saw what spooked Silvia—a large shadowy hunched-over figure walking toward us.

"Come on!" Mickey shouted, grabbing my hand. As we turned to run, we both hit a short gravestone at precisely the same moment and fell in tandem to the ground. "You OK?" he asked, pulling me to my feet. But before I could answer, he looked past me at the figure walking toward us. With a not-so-caring yank, Mickey yelled, "Run!"

We ran. And we kept running, down the lane and down the road, not stopping until we reached the front steps of our house. As the storm door swung slowly shut behind us, Silvia turned the lock, and the three of us stood together, breathing hard. With the porch light still off, we peered out the windows, wondering if he followed us.

"Was that—"

"Oh my god, do you know who that was?" Silvia said between breaths. "It was Old Man Ghouly. In the fricking graveyard! At night! I'm not sure if I peed my pants because I was so scared, or if I'm just wet from the bucket of water."

"Are you sure it was him?" Mickey asked, hanging his jacket on the coat hook.

"Are you kidding me? Who else has a droopy eye like Frankenstein? Even in the dark I could see that creepy eye staring back at me. And the hunched back—I know it was him!" With that declaration she let out an exaggerated shudder. "The only reason we're still alive is that he walks at the pace of a mummy, which is kind of fitting, seeing how we found him in the cemetery."

While Silvia and Mickey continued discussing our great escape, I stood shivering, even though the porch still held the warmth from the day. That was the first time I had ever been so close to Old Man Ghouly, and I sure didn't want our first introduction to be in a graveyard at night. Thinking about the day I had, I gazed out the porch window and down to the front walk, imagining Thomasina sleeping under the steps, curled up on my old flannel shirt. Then I looked up and saw a magnificent explosion of stars.

Starshine.

— 12 —

June 21, 1970
Kalamazoo, Michigan

The smell was driving me bonkers. It took everything I had to keep from crawling onto the rear windowsill of the car where the grocery bag full of buttered popcorn sat, teasing me. I swear our father couldn't find third gear any time his children were anxious to get somewhere.

Finally, it appeared, in glorious flashing illumination—the Douglas Auto Theatre marquee, where a Model-T outlined in neon morphed into a nifty street rod, both images sporting yellow spinning neon wheels. While the street rod was supposed to signify a modern-day counterpoint to the Model-T, the marquee only solidified the theory that drive-ins were on their way to the movie theater graveyard. Still, that sign stood tall as a mesmerizing piece of modern art that I could have stared at it all night long if not for what waited beyond the gates.

"Mutti, did you see my Hot Wheel?" I held it up as our father pulled into a parking spot. "I'm thinking of painting a 53 on the hood and doors."

"Hmm," our mother replied, staring out the window to the family in the car next to us where a mother and father also sat in the front seat. But instead of a backseat filled with too many children, their backseat contained one lone boy who leaned forward to talk with his parents, waving his arms around in great exaggeration.

While the rest of my family were there for the second feature starring an action hero named Steve McQueen costarring with an equally ruggedly handsome mustang, I cared only about the first film of the night—a little Disney movie about a racecar driver's quirky relationship with his Volkswagen Beetle, a car with a mind of its own.

"Is this spot OK, honey?" our father asked, rolling the driver's window down to grab the speaker. Our mother didn't answer, and he lit his pipe, satisfied with his parking selection.

Many people in Kalamazoo were flocking to the new indoor movie theater that recently opened on the other side of town and featured newfangled technology like Sensurround, but even reclining seats couldn't beat the luxury of falling asleep on the back windowsill in your PJs while the others enjoyed the second feature. Outside, kids were starting to gather at the playground by the concession stand.

"Popi, can we—"

"Yes. Get me a Coke, and your mother a coffee." Reaching for his wallet, he pulled out a five and added, "Get yourself something as well,"

Crawling over the front bench seat, I followed the others out of the car.

"Come back before the movie starts!" our mother called out to no one in particular. Her instructions weren't really necessary since none of us wanted to miss a moment of the first feature—a movie so popular, it inspired people across the country to dress up their VW Beetles with racing stripes and the number 53.

"Mr. Kline is furious," Lee said, looking across the street toward the Kline's house. "How someone from this town thought of this prank is surprising, considering the math needed for knowing how to pull it off. It's, well, simply surprising."

We looked back towards the entrance of the school where busses were dropping off children, each one carrying a schoolbag and a look of great surprise as they saw what was blocking their way into the building—a white Volkswagen Beetle, complete with decals and racing stripes. In fact, it was an exact replica of the current celebrity Beetle racing across movie screens across the country. This particular Beetle was also quite the celebrity as it rolled around town, driven by the almost-as-famous Mr. Kline. He was that rare grownup who loved big expensive toys and had the money to buy them. We all loved him, and parents were jealous of him for his effortless way of making them feel their age.

Before the movie even premiered, Mr. Kline bought his own white VW bug, much to the chagrin of his wife who seemed to understand that while the two of them didn't have any children, she did indeed have one. He then dressed up his car with the same racing stripes and decals. On its own, this little car was the spittin' image of its famous friend, but seeing it parked in front of the school on that Monday morning was something else altogether.

When I say, "parked in front of the school," I don't mean it was sitting in the parking lot. I mean it was wedged between the two pillars that stood on either side of the front doors of the school. It was blocking the entrance, with maybe an inch of space between each bumper and the pillars. As the busloads of children stood in front of the blocked entryway, laughing in disbelief, Mr. Kline's car was causing a scene for all the wrong reasons.

"Jenny told me that last night, a group of hooligans rolled it across the street, picked it up, and wedged it between the pillars," Lee said.

I didn't reply, and simply smiled as the vice principal herded a cluster of kids away from the entrance. Yep, this prank was the closest thing to genius since a particular set of monkey bars landed in Alamo Center. I could think of only one person who could work the math required for this art exhibit while also being able to acquire the needed assistance from more-than-willing and able males.

"We better head back to the car," Hanna said, crushing her cigarette into the dirt. "*The Love Bug* will be on soon." As we hid behind the concessions stand, the Pink Panther was getting into and out of shenanigans on the big screen directly above our heads. "Mutti's going to wonder where the heck we are."

Tossing my ice cream sandwich wrapper into the trash barrel, I licked the chocolate off my fingers and followed the others as we wove our way between the many rows of vehicles. Back at our car, we crawled single file into the backseat, chatting with excitement. "See you, losers!" I said, jumping into the front seat, between our parents as Hanna handed our mother her coffee, who took it without a word, making me wonder if we had done something wrong. As the opening credits rolled, I turned my attention to the screen.

"Where were you all?" our mother suddenly asked, staring straight ahead, out the windshield. Because she wasn't looking at anyone in particular, no one offered up an answer, which only made her tense up even more, and her eyes turned black as night. She spun around to look into the backseat. "I said, where were you?"

"We were hanging around the playground," Hanna answered, with a whisper.

"And you didn't come back before the start of the movie. Why?"

My jaw tightened as I stared straight ahead at the movie screen, but my mind was on the others in the backseat. Our mother was still facing the back, and I knew she would be unable to let this moment go, but no one wanted to ruin movie night by fighting back. Even Mickey seemed to know better than to sass back. Just when I thought we might get past it all, our mother lunged back and grabbed the grocery bag full of popcorn, causing it to whip against the backside of the front seat. I turned around just as the ripped bag flew through the air, covering everyone in the backseat with a shower of popcorn.

"What the—!" Silvia yelled.

I looked over at our father, who shook his head while keeping his eyes on the movie screen. Hanna reached down and picked up the ripped paper bag, and the others quietly started putting the spilled contents back into it while eating the popcorn that landed on their laps. I looked out the passenger-side window past my mother and noticed the boy in the next car looking directly at us, apparently more interested in the action going on in the car next to him over what was happening on the big screen. Our eyes met, and he quickly turned away. Meanwhile, my mother turned back toward the film as well, but she was no longer looking at it, but rather, looked far past the screen. Her breathing was quick and shallow, and I could feel her body stiffen beside me.

But as the Love Bug sped across the movie screen, everyone else slowly relaxed, forgetting about the earlier incident other than the fact that the wonderful aroma of buttery popcorn still permeated throughout the car. Settling into my seat, I let the film take me for a ride. As Herbie began the race of his life, I suddenly felt a vibration to my right. I turned as Hanna said excitedly, "Popi, Mutti's having an *anfall*!"

Our mother's body stiffened and thrashed about next to me like a robot that had short-circuited. Ducking beneath her swinging stiff arm, I reached for the Styrofoam cup of coffee that was sitting on the glove box door just as she whacked me across my chest, causing the cup to fly out of my hand, landing squarely in my lap. I closed my eyes as my pants soaked in the contents of the cup. Our father leaned over me to grab a stack of napkins from the glove box as the events going on in our Rambler upstaged the story unfolding on the screen.

Meanwhile, Herbie's antics continued, with laughter pouring out of the cars around us. Our father leaned over me and held a wad of napkins to our mother's mouth as she gargled the spit that had collected in her throat. After several minutes, her body finally started to relax, and the thrashing lessened.

"Hold this, please," my father said to me, and I wrinkled my face as I held the napkins over her mouth, trying not to squirm in my wet clothes. He patted my leg. "Sorry, kids," was all he could muster as he rolled his window down to place the speaker back onto the metal pole. He let out a sigh, flipped on the parking lights, and started the engine.

As I continued holding the napkins in place, I thought about how this evening ended as too many nights did in our family. "Your mother can't help it," was the standard explanation from our father. But, I'm nine, I rationalized. I'm not supposed to understand. Suddenly, I noticed the boy in the next car looking at me again. He didn't turn away this time. Instead, he gave me a half-smile and tilted his head ever so slightly, like he somehow understood what I was going through, and for just a moment I forgot about my wet pants and the embarrassment of holding napkins up to my mother's drooling mouth. As the light from the movie screen flickered and bounced off her face, I caught a glimpse of her left ear, which she usually managed to hide under her hair. It was deformed and smashed against her head.

The sweet smell of coffee with cream and sugar coming from my soggy pants was strong but not enough to mask the odor of urine radiating from my mother, who often wet her pants during epileptic seizures. What a pair we made. As our car pulled away from the parking spot, the boy in the car next to us gave me a small wave, and I waved back, pretending to be just a regular kid in a normal family that decided to go to the movies.

— 13 —

June 27, 1970
Alamo, Michigan

A white stream flew through the air and with a soft *thump*, stuck in the tree, and then as if on cue, fell to the ground on the other side—another textbook toss. Mickey picked up what was left of the roll and repeated with perfect form. "I could do this for a living," he gloated to those of us performing our tasks with a little less pizazz.

I was in charge of the front shrubs and probably spending a little too much time making sure the toilet paper hung to the branches like a string of Christmas lights. Unlike the last time when we bought our ammunition at a convenience store, this two-ply came from our own bathroom, giving our decorating a higher level of sophistication than with the lowly one-ply.

The targeted victim of this front yard makeover was Mickey's friend, Robbie, who I expected had finally caught the eye of Hanna. We knew that he would appreciate the fine art of our efforts. Understanding the fine line between harmless pranks and vandalism kept our nighttime hijinks from escalating into throwing eggs or waxing windows. This was just some harmless mischief.

Halfway through my one roll of toilet paper, a howl pierced through the darkness, nearly knocking me off my feet. Startled, it took me a moment to realize that the howling was coming from a dog, thankfully separated from us by a pane of glass.

"Ditch it!" Hanna yelled, somehow quietly. With one last heave, I let what was left of my roll sail across the top of the shrubs—and right into the face of Mr. Carlson.

If I were a cat, I would have been down one life.

As the front porch light screamed on, my siblings swiftly disappeared into the shadows of the nearest trees and bushes while Silvia let out an, "Oh, shit!" I, however, froze, allowing Mr. Carlson to simply walk over and grab me by the collar of my jacket as a tail-wagging beagle bounded out the door.

"Does anyone wish to collect this one?" Mr. Carlson called out into the darkness as he yanked up on my collar, causing me to stand on my toes.

No response. *Really?*

The chirping of crickets increased as the volume of silence from my siblings also grew. Were they so callous as to assume that this man would never harm such a small child? Probably, but Mr. Carlson knew he simply needed to wait them out.

"Hi, Mr. Carlson," Hanna finally offered up, stepping out from behind a tree. "It's me, Hanna Phillips." And since the jig was up, Mickey and Silvia also came out from the shadows.

With everyone in attendance, Mr. Carlson loosened his grip on me and stepped down from the stoop to access the situation. "Hmmm," he said. Behind him, Mrs. Carlson appeared in the doorway, followed by Robbie, who looked confused, perhaps wondering why his father was talking with his friends so late at night. "So, Hanna," Mr. Carlson continued. "Do your parents know where you all are, and what you're up to?"

In answer, we all looked back toward Hanna's Gremlin, which was parked just beyond the Carlson's yard. Mr. Carlson followed our gaze to see that in the front passenger seat, a lone figure, almost hidden in the dark, was waving back at us.

Mrs. Carlson pushed her husband aside. "Well, go get your mother and get in here," she said enthusiastically. "I'll put some coffee on."

—

"Hello," our mother said, walking up the sidewalk with Hanna as Mr. Carlson waited to greet them.

"Nice to meet you, Mrs.—"

"Didi. It's wonderful to meet you, Mr. Carlson. Please excuse my, what do you call it? My appearance. I wasn't expecting to be invited into such a lovely house!"

I rolled my eyes, thankful that no one was looking at me.

"You call me Rob," Mr. Carlson said warmly. "Aren't you Larry's wife? I thought your name was Elisabeth."

"That's what strangers call me. Didi's a much nicer name, don't you think?"

"I think it's a beautiful name." He reached out and put his hand on our mother's back and escorted her into the house. The rest of us followed and sat down in the living room while our mother and Mr. Carlson continued into the kitchen where Mrs. Carlson was filling a percolator with water.

"Beth, this here is Didi, the mastermind behind the hijinks that took place in our front yard."

"Please, please, sit down," Beth said, gesturing to a kitchen chair, happy to have a guest in the house, even if it was almost midnight. "Honey, get the Archways out of the cupboard." Didi sat down as Rob placed the cookies on a dinner plate and set them on the oak kitchen table before taking a seat himself. "So, Didi," Beth continued, taking a seat between the two. "It's nice to finally get a chance to meet you. I hear you're from Germany."

"*Ja*. I came here after meeting Merle during *der* war. *Sie* have a beautiful home. *Und* these cookies are *wunderbar*."

"Why, thank you, Didi. It's all I can do to keep this house clean. I get absolutely no help from the men in my life. Isn't that right, honey?" She laughed and gave her husband a lighthearted shove.

Mr. Carlson grunted and excused himself, taking a cookie with him.

"I have to tell you how nice it is to have someone to talk to," Beth continued, dropping another sugar cube into her coffee. She glanced at the kitchen doorway. "Rob and I both grew up here—high school sweethearts. It's fine here, but sometimes I wish we lived in a big city where I could meet new people with life experiences that have taken them beyond the four corners of Alamo. You know what I mean? Well, of course you do. Oh, the stories you must have."

Didi smiled and nodded. "*Ja*, a big city. Wouldn't that be something, to be able to walk to a café or buy something at a dress shop that doesn't also sell rakes and fertilizer?"

"Ha! You've got a problem buying clothes at the Otsego Five & Dime? So, how long has it been since you've seen your family? I assume you've been back to Germany for visits."

"*Nein*," Didi paused, not wanting to talk about her mother or the fact that she had made a vow to never go back. "It costs a lot of money to travel overseas, and with four *kinder*, it's difficult to go anywhere."

"Don't I know it."

"Sorry, ladies," Rob said, walking back into the kitchen. "I hate to break up your coffee klatch, but I think it's time for the Phillips kids to head home. Robbie needs to help me at the garage in the morning."

After our goodbyes, we climbed back into the Gremlin. I glanced over to our mother, who was smiling and looking genuinely happy, making me wish the night didn't have to end.

"What nice people!" she said, looking back out toward the house. "And I think that young man likes someone." She pushed gently on Hanna's shoulder, making the rest of us in the backseat laugh. Hanna's shoulders stiffened, and I wondered what she thought of our mother being friends with her new boyfriend's mother. Even I knew that our mother's friendships with other women never ended well.

"He's very handsome," our mother continued. "He takes after his father." As she continued chatting about her new friends, I was content to be sitting on the middle hump in the backseat. I learned something important that night. If you're going to do something illegal or at least, suspect, it helps to bring your mother.

Back home, we followed our mother into the kitchen where she hung her sweater over the back of her chair. "Let's not tell your father what we were up to tonight, OK?" she said. "You'll only get in trouble." She was right about that, but I wondered if that was the only reason why she wanted to keep our adventure a secret. Wouldn't she want to tell our father about meeting the Carlsons?

Mickey gave me a playful shove. "Oh man, when Mr. Carlson caught you, I thought we were all dead."

"You're welcome," our mother teased. She turned on the television, indicating that she wasn't ready for the party to end just yet. Unfortunately, the late-night talk shows were over, leaving us with a TV screen full of loud static. She clicked it off and twirled back to us with a smile. "Do you know what we need? We need music! Johanna, go get your Neil Diamond album."

While Mickey, Silvia and I giggled over our mother's antics, Hanna started to walk away, and stopped. "Mutti, have you taken your pills?"

"Now what do you care about your mother's pills?" She grabbed Mickey's arm and twirled him around to imaginary music, making Mickey laugh. "It's none of your business what I'm taking or not taking." She waved Hanna off and walked over to her cigarette box to pull out a Virginia Slims. Next to the box, sat a lighter shaped like a small pistol. She pulled the trigger and inhaled deeply. "Now go get that album. This party is just getting started!"

— 14 —

June 29, 1970
Alamo, Michigan

Running wild came second-nature to most kids living in Alamo. The only difference between other kids and us is that we had the luxury of owning wooded land just a skip from our house. This was where we spent our days—building campfires, picking wild strawberries, and picking at gnats hiding under our hair. With the campsite located deep within the woods, there was only one trail leading to our sanctuary—walking the rails.

"I feel like a hobo!"

"Most hobos aren't pulled in a wagon by a very gracious brother." Mickey replied to me, not appreciating the extra forty-eight pounds that had jumped into the Radio Flyer already brimming with camping equipment.

The railroad tracks that passed through our little town were a natural extension to our yard, leading us to the woods and far beyond. Well, beyond Alamo, anyway.

The week prior, armed with bologna sandwiches and a package of Ritz Crackers, the four of us followed the rails to the town of Mentha, which, in its heyday, had the distinction of being the mint capital of the world before a disease wiped out the sweet aromatic crop. Mickey claimed that Mentha was just a short walk away and worth exploring, but after eight long miles we discovered that the "village that used to be" didn't offer much more than Alamo, with the exception that Mentha still had an honest-to-goodness train depot, complete with snack counter and clean bathrooms. Weary from our travels, we collapsed on the long wooden benches, thankful for the coolness generated from the large slow-spinning ceiling fan.

The man working behind the glassed-in booth, who had been ignoring us since we came in, finally lifted his head, and with the excitement of a fat cat laying in the sunny spot in the kitchen, made an announcement over the intercom. "The 12:45 from Kalamazoo will be arriving in ten minutes. Next stop . . . Bloomingdale."

His announcement would have made sense had there been anyone in addition to us in the lobby. The fact that we were parentless should have tipped him off we were there simply to steal the cool air. As he repeated his line with even less enthusiasm, we all looked at each other.

"Are you thinking what I'm thinking?" Silvia asked, sitting up from the bench.

"Let's do it!" Mickey answered, jumping up.

I followed them out the door with a sign that hung overhead reading, BLOOMINGDALE – WEST / KALAMAZOO – EAST.

"Seriously?" Hanna sighed. "We see trains every day."

"Not ones that do this!" I explained, running onto the train platform. With the sun directly above our heads, we paced, excited that we were about to see something that hadn't happened in Alamo since before I was born.

A train stopping.

With the familiar whistle from the approaching train, we all whistled back, laughing at the thought of hopping on the train and taking it to Bloomingdale. But we quieted down as the train approached, the conductor blowing the whistle continuously as the brakes squealed and the train eased to a stop. A young man in a uniform and cap hopped off and set the steps, and we watched, excited to see what type of people traveled by train. Would they be wearing suits and fancy dresses?

After a few moments we learned precisely who traveled to Mentha by way of the rails as one lone man in overalls, holding a Bible, stepped down and paused to take out a handkerchief to wipe his sweaty brow. As he made his way across the platform, he nodded at us, and we nodded back a hello. One hundred years ago, Alamo had its own train depot located right across from our house, and we often played on the cement foundation that still peeked out from under the weeds and dirt. So besides the drinking fountain and clean bathrooms, Mentha had something else that our town didn't have—a reason for the train to stop.

While the train sat at the station, Silvia and I ran down the tracks and placed two pennies each on the rails. As the train engine started back up, I couldn't help but think about the warning Silvia once shared with me—stories of trains falling off tracks due to the foolish pranks of children putting coins on the tracks. I shook off the memory, convincing myself that Silvia was just feeding me another tale. *Right?*

With the blow of a whistle, the train inched forward, and I held my breath as the conductor approached the two of us. Inscribed along the bottom of his window, in what looked like the scribbling of an artist using a jackknife, were the words, NORTH STAR. As Silvia and I ran alongside, we pumped our arms wildly until the conductor answered back with another blow of the whistle.

"Shoot, I don't see my pennies," Silvia said, walking along the tracks after the train was long gone, on its way to Bloomingdale. "The train must have sucked them up. How about you? Anything?"

A kid could spend a quarter plus one penny at the Chicago Museum of Science and Industry to smash a penny by turning a crank in a machine, or a kid with half a brain and a neighboring train track could flatten a penny the old-fashioned way. "I got one!" I shouted, picking up the oblong coin, still hot from being fresh off the presses. "Woo hoo, I got a smashed penny!"

There are those who claim that no matter where you stand in America, you can hear the whistles of a train. I'm not sure if that's true, but we were certainly blessed in that not only did we hear the train on a daily basis, it passed right by our house, and right alongside our woods.

Now, with it hanging from my neck attached to a small chain, I rubbed my smashed penny for good luck while Mickey laid down the axe and tossed a large stick into the fire. Silvia slid a marshmallow through the top of a long tree branch whittled down to a sharp spear while Hanna and I sat on the adjoining bench. It was a clear night, and while the majestic maple trees hid the flurry of stars overhead, we felt the serenity of the quiet summer night broken only by the soothing symphony of crickets and tree frogs, with the occasional rustle of leaves generated by a random nocturnal rodent.

"So, what are you going to do next summer, Hanna?" Mickey asked as he poked at the burning embers. "You know, after you graduate."

"I know what I'm not going to do. I'm not going to stick around here a minute longer than I have to." Sensing that her declaration was having a negative effect on the rest of us, she steered her response in a more positive direction. "Don't worry. I'm not going far. They're building a new department store at the mall. It's going to have everything from record albums and makeup to sleeping bags and swimsuits. And clothes. When I get a job there, I bet I'll get a discount on everything, including stuff for you guys! It's supposed to be open by September. I'll get an apartment nearby so you can visit any time you want."

"Don't you want to live with us anymore?" I asked quietly.

Hanna leaned into me and gave me a squeeze. "Oh honey, I won't be going far. It's time for me to go off on my own soon. Mickey and Silvia will still be here for you."

"I can't wait until I'm eighteen," Silvia said, blowing on her flaming marshmallow. "Maybe you can get me a job there after you've been there a while. I hear McDonald's is always hiring. That'd be cool." She bit off the burnt shell and returned the naked marshmallow to the fire. "So, why do you think Popi doesn't just wind up and let Mutti have it? You know, she has it coming to her. Jesus, I won't be staying a minute longer than I have to."

"Thanks a lot, jerk," I replied.

"That's not what I—"

"I know it's hard to understand," Hanna interrupted. "Mutti's sick. And I don't mean just the epilepsy."

"She's crazy."

"Stop that. It's not that simple. It's hard to explain, but she can't help herself. She gets all wound up and doesn't know how to turn it off. I think the medications help, but they tend to just make her thoughts foggy, and who wants to walk around in a fog all day long? I know it's easy to blame her, but it's not her fault. She's dealing with the cards she was dealt, just like we are."

"I want a new deck," Silvia said, making Hanna roll her eyes.

"I don't care how sick she is. I'm tired of being a punching bag," Mickey said, popping an uncooked marshmallow into his mouth.

"I know you are," Hanna whispered. "Popi was hoping that the shock therapy would help—"

"And it obviously didn't," Mickey finished. "When I finally get out of here, I'm going to go a lot farther than Kalamazoo. Did you know that if you work at Cedar Point in Ohio, they put you up and pay for your meals and everything? I'm going to work in the entertainment area with the singers and dancers." He twisted his neck with a jerk, unaware of his movements. "Heck, I'd even bus tables to work there. Anywhere would be better than this place."

"That's a long way from here," I said, not liking where this conversation was going. "I don't want to talk about this anymore."

"It's OK," Hanna said. "Nobody's leaving for a long time. Let's make a pact. No matter where we end up, we'll never lose track of each other. All for one—"

"And one for all," Mickey, Silvia, and I said in unison.

The next morning, I woke to the friendly aroma of a smoldering campfire. Crawling out of the pup tent, I rubbed my eyes and sat down on the bench next to Mickey. I looked around at our campground, appreciating the work we had put forth in making it our own—with a makeshift outhouse, water pump, and a large plywood floor for our tent. But what made that place so special to us was that adults never bothered us when we were out there. In fact, I don't ever recall our mother setting foot in the woods. This was our place, and while our father occasionally made an appearance, I believe he understood that we needed a place to call our own. He used the barn and his workshop in the cellar as his own refuge.

Homemade benches surrounded the fire pit, and it felt good to sit, watching the flames of fire lick the fresh twigs I tossed into the pit. With the sun almost straight up, Mickey stirred up the smoldering embers while I went in search of a roasting stick, since breakfast would have to be an encore performance of marshmallows.

"'Won't you look down upon me, Jesus, you've got to help me make a stand. You've just got to see me through another day . . .'"

Hanna sang along with James Taylor, while Mickey adjusted the tuner on the radio, trying to fix the crackling of the music. Hanna's radio wasn't the old-fashioned square kind like the one that sat on our father's workbench. This one was round—a blue plastic ball with an attached chrome chain that looked more like a leash for this wonderful musical pet. Mickey continued to turn the silver knob.

With WLS finally tuned in, we settled in for the breakfast of champions. With a marshmallow hanging at the end of my stick, I searched until I found the sweet spot in the fire pit where there were no visible flames, but the needed orange glow of burning ashes. Rotating my stick, I was about to lift the marshmallow when it suddenly caught fire, forcing me to blow out the torching mass. Crunching through the black shell to the warm soft center, I lazily watched the flames burn out, leaving ashes glowing red under the high-noon sun.

"Hey! Put down breakfast and help us out over here."

Mickey sighed, knowing that he was sadly outnumbered by three demanding sisters. As he lifted the Coleman lantern off the tree branch behind us, I got up to help roll up sleeping bags.

"Bringing you the hits and past-hits all day long! Gotta love the Beatles' 'Drive my Car.' For those of you shopping for a used car, we have this public service announcement. When buying a used car, punch the buttons on the radio. If all the stations are rock and roll, there's a good chance the transmission is shot. There you have it, little Tommy! Let's shift gears now with a little Carly Simon."

As Larry Lujack continued from behind the microphone, a familiar song ramped up.

"*'You walked into the party like you were walking onto a yacht. Your hat strategically dipped below one eye, your scarf it was apricot . . .'*"

I sang along, hitting my sleeping bag to the beat. "'You had one eye in the mirror as you watched yourself go by . . .'"

"Gavotte," Mickey corrected.

"What?"

"Gavotte. It's, 'As you watched yourself gavotte.'"

"Gavotte? That's not a word!"

"It is, too. I read the lyrics in *Rolling Stone*. Gavotte is French for dance or something like that."

"Now you're just making crap up. Why don't you just gavotte over there and leave me alone?"

"Ha ha, very funny. Gavotte is a real word. I asked Popi what it meant, and he's the one who told me. And you know that if Popi says it's French, it's French."

"Yeah," Silvia said, butting in. "I'm with Mickey on this one. You know that Popi's a Mensa member and the smartest man in town."

"Did you know that Carly Simon is dating James Taylor?" Hanna said, picking up the marshmallow bag.

"Hmm. Let me guess, *Tiger Beat*?" Mickey asked.

"I love 'Fire and Rain'! It's my favorite James Taylor song," I added, not wanting to admit that it was the only song I could think of by him.

"Fire!" Hanna said, correcting me, I thought.

"I think the title is, 'Fire and Rain.'"

"No! Fire!" she repeated, pointing behind us.

While we were all busy gavotting, the campfire did what campfires do—it kept burning. It took only a moment for a dry twig to ignite and fall out of the fire pit, landing gently onto the surrounding grass that was already dead from the campfire's heat. And it took only another few seconds for the fire to spread throughout our campsite, ignoring our sudden attention and our failed effort to snuff it out with our screams and stomping sneakers.

"Run and get Popi!" Hanna yelled to Mickey, who paused for just a moment, contemplating the toll of bringing our father into the current situation. He then nodded and took off running as fast as his feet would take him, leaving the rest of us to grab what we could and to run from the fire that was growing at frightening speed and spreading like . . . well, like wildfire. Sleeping bags and radio in hand, we ran from the woods and down the railroad tracks without stopping until we reached our yard.

On that day we were thankful that the volunteer fire department was just down the road from us. It took only minutes before firetrucks were screaming down the lane and crashing through our woods, running over saplings and crushing wildflowers along the way. We watched from the safety of our yard as hoses were unrolled and a flood of water cascaded through the air, saving a large chunk of the woods and saving our asses from our father, who remained surprisingly calm as he watched our woods go up in flames.

After more than an hour of gulping streams of water, the woods finally spit its last smoke ring as the firemen rolled up their hoses and rolled out—leaving a steaming mess of broken trees and four scared children. As the first of the firetrucks passed by us on its way back to the station, I turned around to look up at our parents' bedroom window where the curtains remained tightly closed. It had been only a week since our TP-ing adventure, and our mother crashed hard the following morning. As she lay on the floor after her third epileptic seizure, our father managed to get a handful of pills down her throat and carried her to bed, where she had remained for the past week.

Our father walked up behind us and put his hand on my shoulder as we watched the last firetruck roll out of the woods. "Your mother doesn't need to know about this one," he said, before turning and walking away.

She never did.

— 15 —

July 2, 1970
Alamo, Michigan

"Come on, you've already had two. Split that one with me," Silvia tried rationalizing as Mickey grabbed the last Johnnycake from the basket. Corn muffins were staples around the kitchen picnic table, especially when they accompanied our father's homemade chili. We were sitting down to dinner as the local weatherman teased the next day's forecast, letting us know that rain was finally on its way.

"You're going to want to grab your raincoats before heading off to work tomorrow morning. And in answer to the question, Can bees fly in the rain? Not without their yellow jackets!"

I rolled my eyes as the weatherman slapped a magnetic raincloud on the map behind him for emphasis, and blew on my spoonful of chili, bored with the conversations on TV and around our kitchen table.

"You haven't even finished your chili," Mickey shot back, loud enough so that our parents could hear his argument, perhaps hoping that they would agree with him, but they were both listening to Walter Cronkite as he introduced the top story of the day—a remembrance being held on the grounds of Kent State University, honoring the students killed during the protests of the Vietnam War.

"Oh, come on," Silvia pleaded, reaching for the muffin. "You already had your two." As Silvia reached across the table, Mickey pulled his arm back, keeping the muffin basket just out of her reach, and as he did so, the muffin fell softly onto the floor.

"Jerk," Silvia said, giving Mickey a shove.

Mickey made a face at Silvia before bending down to pick it up, but realized it had rolled beyond his reach. Our mother, without a word, got up out of her chair and picked up the muffin, gently placing it on Mickey's plate.

"Thanks, Mutti, but—"

Before Mickey could finish, our mother slapped him across the back of his head, causing him to knock over his bowl of chili. Tomato sauce ran down the length of the table, seeping between the planks of wood before splattering as it hit the floor. Mickey and Silvia scrambled to sop up the spilled chili with paper napkins while I sat still, too stunned to help.

Then she hit him again. He turned in anger, trying to speak but she kept slapping him as he cowered, trying to shield his head with his arms.

"Stop it!" I screamed. Tears rolled down my cheeks as I stood up. "Stop it!"

But our mother didn't stop. In fact, my screams seemed to fuel her energy. I wanted Mickey to turn around and smack her so hard that she wouldn't know what hit her. If I had that gun from the basement in my hand . . .

"Popi!" Silvia yelled as the hitting continued, with Mickey shrinking deeper onto the picnic bench. "Popi, do something!"

Our father got up and walked to the phone and dialed zero for the operator. After several seconds, he spoke calmly into the receiver. "Yes, please send an ambulance. My wife is out of control, and I need help." He paused before adding, "2625 Hart Drive. Yes, that'll be good. Thank you."

Meanwhile our mother's blows increased in force and speed. She took a swing and landed directly on Mickey's nose. I shrieked as blood squirted from his nostrils. After hanging up the phone our father walked over to our mother and grabbed her from behind, finally stopping the hitting. But like a wild animal caught in a trap, she screamed and thrashed about, trying to free herself from our father's bear-hug.

"Hit her, Popi!" Silvia yelled, wanting our mother to pay for what she had done to our brother—not just for that day but for every day. "Slug her!"

But that wasn't our father's way. He kept his hold on her and said to all of us, "Pick up your things and put them in the sink, and please go outside."

Silvia grabbed Mickey's bowl, and, as Mickey ran out the back door, Silvia and I quickly cleared the table.

"Let's go," Silvia said, grabbing a handful of paper towels on her way out the door. I started to follow, but stopped to look back at our father who had wrestled our mother to the floor. As he held onto her, he started doing something I had never seen him do before.

"*Du bist mein Ubahn, mein einziger Ubahn . . .*" He was singing softly to our mother, a tune I recognized as "You Are My Sunshine." He continued singing, even as our mother gathered strength in her screams.

I followed Silvia out the door.

The sun was out, and I let myself exhale before taking a long breath. I could smell the sweet scent of lilac, and it had a calming effect on me. Mickey was waiting for us at the barn, and Silvia handed him the wad of paper towels. He carefully unfolded them and refolded them into two squares, one for cleaning up the blood already on him, and the other for stopping the bleeding. As he tilted his head back, we didn't speak.

We settled onto the loading dock of the barn, unsure of what to do next. Hanna was spending the day in South Haven at the beach with Robbie. I was glad that she wasn't a part of this, but still, I felt lost without her. The only thing I was sure of was that I wasn't going back into the house. Trying to relax, I took in another long breath of air. Even from across the yard, I could still detect a hint of lilac. But it wasn't long before we heard the familiar blaring of sirens, and I sprang to attention as the ambulance drove up the street and turned into our driveway, red lights barely visible in the bright sunlight. It was odd having the ambulance visiting in the middle of the day since our mother's moods generally spiraled out of control under the blanket of the night. Two men in white jumpsuits climbed out, one of them holding a white garment in his hands. They hurried to our front door, and the driver knocked, but didn't wait for anyone to answer before stepping inside.

The yelling continued from within the house, soon followed by the opening of the back door, with our mother racing down the back steps like she was being chased by a swarm of hornets.

"Damn!" Silvia said, jumping to her feet. Mickey didn't move, and we watched as the two men bounded out the door after our mother and tackled her to the ground in the middle of the yard. The driver struggled to hold our mother while his partner forced her arms into a straitjacket. He then rolled her over and pushed her face into the grass as the other man fastened the back of the jacket. They then hoisted her up onto her feet like a rag doll and wrapped the extra-long sleeves around her chest, locking them behind her. With a snap of the lock, she fell silent, knowing the fight was over.

How many people get to say they've worn a straitjacket? I imagine that being unable to use your arms would really mess with your balance. And if you happen to fall while bound in a straitjacket, you're going down like a sack of potatoes. As all of this went through my head, I realized that most kids would be horrified at the sight of their mother being hauled away in a straitjacket. Should I have been crying? As the men escorted our mother to the ambulance, I felt . . .

Relieved.

". . . and I couldn't care less! She's fucking crazy! She's fucking out of control, and I hope they put her away for good this time! We don't deserve a mother like that—no one does!" Mickey stopped and removed the cloth from his nose to check if the bleeding had stopped. In a much quieter voice he added, "Who does that? Normal mothers don't do that."

"Wait 'til Hanna hears about this one," Silvia said, her eyes riveted to the show our mother was putting on for us. If nothing else, our mother was entertaining.

A car came up the road, and as it approached our yard, it slowed down. The woman in the passenger seat peered out her window, her eyes wide and her mouth hanging open as she watched our mother, still in her straitjacket, strolling to the ambulance like she was just going out to get the mail. If our mother's arms weren't wrapped around herself, I imagine she would have waved to the passing car.

And in case the image of our mother in a straitjacket wasn't jarring enough for the woman in the passing car, there was that black, red, and yellow striped flag waving behind her. It was the week before Independence Day, and while American flags were gently waving in front yards throughout our town, our mother decided she needed to display her cultural pride, just twenty-five years after the fall of Nazi Germany.

". . . to be free! I'm miserable in this hell-hole and a day doesn't go by when I don't dream of getting out of here." Mickey jumped from the deck and watched as the men helped our mother step into the side door of the ambulance. "And I will never ever look back."

— 16 —

1942

Eschbach, Baden-Württemberg, Germany

"*Ist* that all *sie* have?" the nun asked, looking down at the old battered suitcase that once belonged to Didi's mother but was currently stuffed with Didi's clothes. It was the parting gift from her mother, who stood beside her daughter on the front stoop of the orphanage.

With her hand on her daughter's shoulder, Didi's mother looked disconnected from the moment. "Now don't give them a hard time. You'll be fine here. I would walk you in but the meter's running. This will be good for you." She kissed her daughter on her forehead and scurried down the sidewalk back to the taxi waiting in the driveway.

The nun looked past Didi, down the lane, and watched Didi's mother climb into the taxi. "Can't get out of here fast enough," she mumbled as the taxi backed out of the driveway. Looking back at Didi who was still holding the suitcase and gazing down at her feet, the nun took the suitcase from her and waved Didi into the building. "Well, come in. It's freezing out here. I'll show you to the room you'll be sharing with the other girls. Not very private but you'll be comfortable. I am Sister Ruth. Do as you're told, and we'll get along just fine. We've got a couple of drawers for your clothes and toiletries. You'll like the . . ."

Didi stopped listening as they climbed the staircase. It was a long car ride over to the orphanage, the first time she had ever been in a taxi, which she normally would have enjoyed, but never in her wildest dreams had she envisioned such a big occasion being eclipsed by a destination such as this.

"As far as orphanages go, you'll find this isn't bad," Sister Ruth continued as she placed the suitcase onto a small bed. Seeing that Didi wasn't going to keep up with her side of the conversation, she added, "Those two open drawers over there are yours. Put your belongings in there. The water closet is down the hall, third door on the left. It's lunch time so wash up and join us downstairs when you're ready." She started to leave but stopped and turned back. "You're on dishwashing duty this week so don't be long."

A train whistle blew in the distance, shaking Didi out of her fog. She pushed her suitcase aside and sat on the bed, her bed. The springs sagged beneath her as she looked around at the walls that held nothing but a painting of Jesus nailed to a cross, with blood dripping from his hands and feet. Not exactly the vision you want before falling asleep. It seemed ironic to be now living in a Catholic home. While her mother regularly wore a cross around her neck and treasured her ceramic Virgin Mary, Didi couldn't recall the last time they attended Sunday Mass. As she looked around, she noticed all of the beds, about a dozen in all. She closed her eyes, letting the tears roll down her cheeks, not bothering to wipe them away.

"*Guten Tag,*" called out a girl who appeared in the doorway and looked to be about thirteen, Didi's own age. "Lunch is almost over but we've saved a plate for you, so you'll have to hurry. You sure don't want to skip lunch here because you'll soon find that meals are the highlight of your day." Hungry for any sort of positive attention, Didi stood up and followed the girl down the hall. "And if Sister Ruth asks, you washed your hands, unless you want a ruler across your knuckles."

"*Sitzen* here," a second nun ordered, pointing to two empty chairs as the two girls entered the dining room. She was younger than Sister Ruth, and Didi wondered what life-changing event happened to this woman earlier in her life that made her want to abandon the traditions of love, marriage, and babies in exchange for the lonely sacrificial life of eternal bliss with the Lord. Did she grow up in a religious household and realize early on that following God was her calling, or did a lover reject her affection, leading her to the conclusion that Jesus was the only man who would never turn on her? As Didi sat down, her new friend took a seat beside her.

"That's Sister Trudy," Didi's friend whispered. "She's nicer than Sister Ruth." And in an even quieter voice she added, "But don't let her fool you. The nuns here have no outlet for all their pent-up sexual energy, so it gets rechanneled as rage. They all have two moods here, angry and angrier." She snickered at her joke, and Didi couldn't help but smile despite the lingering pain in her chest.

Lunch was Braunschweiger on pumpernickel bread, and Didi took a few small bites of her sandwich. She pushed the peas and carrots around on her plate while the other girls laughed and argued over who had the prettiest hair. As they finished their lunches, Sister Trudy rose from her chair in the corner of the room. "Pick up your plates. Those of you on dish duty, follow me into the kitchen." She clapped her hands for emphasis with a final, "Come along."

Following Sister Trudy into the kitchen, each girl scraped the leftovers off her plate into a garbage can. As plates, cups, and forks were placed into the large industrial-sized sink, Didi's friend and another girl prepared the area for washing. Didi recognized the other girl as being the one who was chosen for having the most beautiful hair. She looked older than most of the other girls, probably closer to sixteen. Didi stood to the side and waited for instructions.

"Here," the older girl said, tossing a towel at her. "You can dry with Mari. Set everything on the table over there." Didi nodded and grabbed a wet pot from the drying rack and began drying.

"Don't talk much, do you?" Mari said, grabbing a plate and running her towel over it with two swipes before setting it on the table. Grabbing another plate, she asked, "So, are you lost or broken?"

"Excuse me?"

"Don't be so rude," the older girl scolded. "She just got here and doesn't appreciate your humor yet." Looking back at Didi, she added, "Mari is trying to ask you if you're here because your parents are dead or because you're not wanted?"

"My father's not around most of the time," Didi mumbled, not wanting to share that her parents had never married and had never even lived with each other. "And my mother can't deal with me right now. You know, with her problems. I won't be here too long. My mother promised that she'll be back for me soon. This is just temporary."

As Mari opened her mouth to say something, the older girl turned from the sink and shot her a stern look. Mari went back to drying a large pot.

"Anyway, I . . . I guess I'm what you call broken."

"I'm broken, too," Mari said, with a small smile. "Don't just stand there, keep drying. When we're done here, we can go outside, and I'll show you around. If you like music . . ."

As Mari talked, Didi reached for a wet plate and realized too late that the plate was still shining from soap suds. Before she could tighten her grasp, it slipped between her fingers, and she watched helplessly as the plate dropped and shattered onto the hardwood floor. The other girls jumped back but Didi stood frozen with embarrassment. A shadow loomed over her, and she felt a sudden burning sensation across her back that dropped her to her knees.

"Pick up your mess," Sister Ruth said calmly, twirling the switch in her hand. "You will now have dish duty for dinner as well this week. There will be no tears here," she added, noticing that Didi had closed her eyes. "You can cry when your job here is done. The dustpan is hanging on the wall over there."

After Sister Ruth left, the other girls remained silent and went back to cleaning as Didi scooted along on her knees, sweeping up the shards of ceramic that had jumped to every corner of the kitchen. She closed her eyes and opened them again, wishing that this was just a bad dream, but as her knee landed on a sharp piece, she winced, realizing that this was indeed very real.

As she swept, a fog slowly rolled through her head, and the voices of her new friends dimmed in volume and clarity. Her thoughts continued to blur, becoming thick and paralyzing. She looked at her hand, which was shaking—her whole body shaking. As her bones locked, her thoughts faded away, saving her from the pain of her body slamming onto the floor.

"You'll do anything to get out of dish duty, won't you?"

Didi sat up in her bed and immediately held her hand up against her forehead. Her head was aching, and her arm was sore. A large bruise on her forearm reminded her of what took place earlier. She looked around the room where long shadows were falling across the floor, telling her that it must be evening. Mari was sitting on a nearby bed, grinning at her. Didi shut her eyes for a moment trying to connect the pieces of the day, with this funny girl who, for whatever reason, hadn't run off screaming yet.

Mari continued smiling at her. "You OK? You've been sleeping for a few hours now. We've already had dinner, but we thought you might be hungry, so Sister Trudy saved you a plate. Can you get up?"

Didi started to answer but the dryness in her mouth blocked her words. She looked down and noticed that she was wearing different slacks, not a surprise since she usually wet her pants when she had a seizure. Embarrassed, Didi looked back at Mari.

"It's OK," Mari said. "We're all misfits here. We'll get through this together, right? This place is just a stupid stop on the way to better things. We're going to make it."

Didi thought back to how the day began—her mother was unusually quiet all morning, and when Didi finished breakfast she walked into the living room and found her mother staring out the front window. A suitcase sat on the floor next to her, which puzzled Didi since she wasn't aware of any upcoming travel plans. "It'll be for just a short time while I figure things out," her mother said, still looking out the window. "Your father isn't ready for a family yet, but I know he loves me, and I think this is for the best." Didi was too confused to do anything but stare at her mother.

The taxi ride went without conversation, and, standing on the front stoop of the orphanage, Didi watched her mother walk away without looking back. The suitcase, the taxi ride, the switch across the back all led to this. Despite the pounding in her head she looked back at her new friend.

And smiled.

— 17 —

July 22, 1970

Alamo, Michigan

"Did you hear the latest about Larry's wife?" Treva asked, having held on to this juicy bit of gossip for as long as she could, waiting for Beth who finally walked in for the girls' afternoon coffee.

"Let me guess," Doris said, taking a long drag of her cigarette and blowing the smoke into the fumes of hairspray that already hung in the air. "She finally made an appointment with you to get her hair done?"

"No. Now, *that* would actually be unbelievable," Treva said, adding tape to the back of a poster featuring a young lady sporting a bouffant hairdo. She held up the poster and leaned into the other girls. "You know the Duncans who live about a mile north of Wolfe Lake?" The women nodded. "Well, Susan Duncan has a friend whose daughter works at the Plainwell Sanitarium, who told her that Elisabeth Phillips is staying there."

"Really?" Luanne asked as she studied her hair in the mirror before adding a spritz of hair spray. "Are you sure? Well, I can't say that I'm surprised. I always thought she was a little off. She hides in her house, and never comes out, like she's too good for us. We're just small-town country rednecks that she can't be bothered with."

"Wait, I'm not done," Treva continued, pressing the poster against the wall and smoothing it out with her hand. "Apparently she tried to kill one of her children and then tried to commit suicide by taking a bunch of pills."

"Oh my god," Beth said, putting her hand to her mouth. She set the spoon down and took a seat in the salon chair and stared at Treva. "Is she OK now?"

"OK? Well, I'm not sure anyone staying in a mental institution can be called OK. And this isn't the first time she's been there. Susan says that she's even spent time in the Kalamazoo Insane Asylum."

"Are you serious?" Luanne asked, still looking at herself in the mirror, trying to tame a wild curl.

"And, hang on ladies; I saved the best for last." Treva dipped her comb into the blue cleansing solution and dried it off, savoring that she had everyone's attention. "Last winter, she went through electro-shock therapy over at the mental institution in Detroit."

"Christ," Doris said. "Where the hell is my Juicy Fruit?" She pulled a pack of gum from her purse and folded the stick of gum before popping it into her mouth. "Jesus, she's got to be mixed up good. I imagine that her poor husband is practically raising those children by himself."

"You got that right," Treva said. "I can't imagine what that poor husband puts up with, living with that crazy woman. Although, it does kind of explain why those children are as wild as Luanne's unruly curl. Stop fussing with your hair, dear. I'll get to it in a moment."

"What about what that poor woman is dealing with?" Beth asked, setting her coffee cup down on the counter. "Do any of us know what she's going through?" She sighed and looked away from her friends. "I know I can't even imagine what it must feel like to be so far from home and so lost."

— 18 —

July 22, 1970
Plainwell, Michigan

"Step closer so I can see you," our mother called down from behind the bars that separated us from her, and signified the reality of our visit. "I wish I could bring you in here to meet my friends. It's been very relaxing, like a resort!" our mother smiled down at us. "How are you, my little *liebelein*?" she cooed, looking directly at me, which only made me burrow deeper into Hanna's arms.

"We're glad you're doing well," Hanna shouted up to the window. Silvia and I nodded, not knowing what else to do, since asking our mother how she spent her day didn't seem like the kind of question to ask someone behind bars. In fact, all two stories of the windows at the Plainwell Sanitarium were covered in bars, which made me wonder just how much fun was really happening inside this imaginary summer camp.

Our mother had first arrived at the sanitarium a few weeks prior, and she insisted that this place was much nicer than the Kalamazoo Insane Asylum. While the mature maple trees, park benches, and the rose bushes at the front entrance painted a picture of bliss, the bars on the windows told quite another story. But our mother insisted that staying at the sanitarium was her idea, and we went along with it because arguing with her didn't seem like a good idea.

"We made purple and blue picture frames today with felt flowers," she said, trying to see past the bars. I tried envisioning our mother at the arts and crafts table, because craft time was something that didn't happen at our house. While I daydreamed, our mother chatted nonstop, with sudden pauses where she just looked down at us, causing me to squirm and look away. Her smile never diminished, which made me wonder if they had her on a new pill or two.

Then she would ramp up again, telling us how she was getting better and that she would be coming home any day. Hanna carried the weight of the conversation from our end while I concentrated on trying to see past her, into the room, but all I could see was darkness. She suddenly turned back and called out, "Wendy! Come meet my children." A woman appeared at the window and gave us a disturbingly large grin without saying a word, and I could see that she was missing a tooth. "Wendy and I have become great friends, haven't we, Wendy?" our mother continued, giving her new friend a squeeze. At least the sanitarium gave the illusion of being a happy place. "Wendy doesn't have any children, so I told her that she can visit with us soon. You'll love her!" Even Hanna was at a loss for a proper response to this announcement and simply offered up a smile. "Wendy can't wait to visit, isn't that right, Wendy?"

We all knew that our mother would be coming home eventually, and I was just relieved that it was still down the road.

"I'll be home soon," she promised as we waved and mumbled our goodbyes. Walking back to Hanna's car, she called out after us, "I'll see you soon! Before you know it, we'll all be on our way to Tahquamenon Falls!"

— 19 —

August 8, 1970
Tahquamenon Falls, Northern Michigan

Maybe my father oversold the idea, but more likely, I just wasn't listening. In any case, as he turned into the driveway, honking and waving while towing our brand-new camper behind him, my heart sank as I realized that "camper" didn't mean "trailer," as in a tiny house on wheels, equipped with cute little windows and a micro-sized bathroom. When I was told that it was silver, I pictured one of those sleek Airstreams with the metallic rounded roof, so shiny that it could blind you with the reflection of the sun. No, this wasn't one of those by a long shot. Fortunately, no one was looking at me as they ran to get a closer look at that quirky contraption.

It couldn't have been more than five feet wide, six feet long, and less than two feet tall. I looked around at our family, which consisted of two parents, three nearly grown kids, and me, and I shook my head. Someone was going to have to explain to me how this was going to work.

"It's simple," my father boasted, as if reading my mind. He waved his hands toward the camper, like a ringmaster introducing the lion tamer. "Mickey," he called out. "I need your help with this." Our father and Mickey lifted the top off, and with help from metal poles and a mile of canvas, the pop-up camper came to life, and with it, my understanding of the definition of "pop-up camper."

While it was definitely no Airstream, it was large enough to accommodate a small family—and a step up from our tent, literally, since you had to step up to get into it. The novelty of camping off the ground was enticing as I pictured our entire family dry and laughing in the camper as we weathered the occasional rainstorm. It was still basically a tent from the midsection up, but this tent came with an honest to goodness real floor, a fold-out dining table, and two full-sized beds. *Wait, two?* As it slowly dawned on me that the whole family wouldn't be sleeping here, I held on to hope that at least some of us would.

"Oh, I forgot something," our father added. He returned to the car and pulled out a box. "We can't go camping without this." And with that, he turned the box to show off the beautiful photo on the side—a whole family huddled around a black and white TV that was small enough to fit in our fancy new camper. *Oh my god, camping with a TV? This camping trip just went high class!*

"Ugh! We're not even close to the Mackinac Bridge," I sighed as we drove past the WELCOME TO CADILLAC sign. Technically we were still in the Lower Peninsula but the pine benches lining the sidewalk, and the PASTIES SOLD HERE neon sign flickering in the diner window told us that we were at least getting closer to being up north.

"There's a McDonald's up ahead," our father informed us as he handed the gas station attendant a five. "Should we stop for dinner?" which, of course, was an unnecessary question. After we parked, Mickey led Doxy to a grassy area behind the dumpsters while the rest of us hurried for the outdoor restrooms. As I looked across the parking lot, I saw it. If this had been a movie, I swear the angels would have been singing during this scene.

A McDonald's with indoor dining and restrooms that were *inside*!

I ran ahead of the others, not stopping until I stood in the center of the lobby. Spinning around, I took it all in as the overhead fluorescent lights hummed and lit up the room like it was the middle of the day. The dining area was decorated with rows of red hard-plastic tables with bright yellow chairs and benches. And in the center of the lobby, stood a life-sized plastic Ronald McDonald.

It was McBeautiful.

"You need to go to the bathroom before you eat," my mother said, wiping her hands with a paper towel. As I ran past her, she added, "And don't forget to wash your hands."

I returned to find everyone ordering at the counter. "What do you want, honey?" our father asked, gazing up to the glowing menu board. "Would you like your Filet-O-Fish?"

"They're talking about me," our mother said.

"Who is?" our father asked, looking around and seeing no one but a young couple discussing their menu options.

"They are," our mother replied defiantly. "What are you looking at?" she added, looking at the unsuspecting woman.

"Honey, no one's looking at you except for me, constantly overwhelmed by your beauty." He put his hand on her shoulder and asked again, "Do you want fish or—"

"I don't care! Get me anything," our mother snapped, brushing his hand off, and continuing to glare at the woman who was still standing at the counter, oblivious that she had attracted our mother's attention. Our mother grabbed a wad of paper napkins and made her way to the lobby to wipe down a bench.

"And here we go," Hanna mumbled as we watched our mother wipe down her seat even though it looked spotless. We picked up our trays of food and headed to the dining area.

Silvia sat next to me at a booth, sliding across the beautiful plastic bench. Apparently not impressed with the Ronald McDonald in the lobby, our parents sat at their own table. Our father tried to engage our mother with witty banter, but finally gave up, and they continued to eat in silence.

Meanwhile, the couple from earlier made the unfortunate decision to sit within shooting distance of our mother, and it took only a moment for our mother to lock on her target. "Some people should mind their own business," our mother said to our father in a voice that had no problem traveling toward her intended targets. "Was *ist ihr* problem?" Even though the couple had no idea what our mother was talking about, her antics had the desired effect on her audience, with the woman glancing at her and then back to her companion who simply shook his head. "*Ich würde gerne wissen, was sie bei uns suchen!*" my mother barked in response.

"Please tell me this isn't happening," Silvia whispered as Hanna lowered her head and rubbed her forehead. Hanna wanted to leave, and I just wanted our mother to shut up so we could eat in a restaurant like a normal family.

Now the man and woman *were* looking at our mother and whispering to each other, causing our mother to ramp up the volume of her accusations. The teenager behind the counter stopped cleaning to watch, and I dipped two fries at once into my ketchup, knowing that we would be finishing our meals in the car.

"Let's go, kids," our father said, shoving the last of his hamburger into his mouth. "We've got a long drive still ahead of us." He crinkled the wrapper up into a small ball, and stood up as we started rewrapping what was left of our food.

At least in Cadillac, no one knew us.

With the car pointed north, we rolled on, the monotony broken up by tourist signs informing us that Mystery Spot was only four, three, two more exits away. Finally, as the sun began to set, we pulled into the glorious tourist town of Mackinaw City for bathroom breaks and our first foray into a world where black bears were the staple design on sweatshirts, welcome signs, and wool blankets.

As we were herded back into the car, I sucked on my miniature souvenir corncob pipe, thinking that I might sneak some tobacco later on for a little flavor. In the distance, the lights of the Mackinac Bridge flickered against the twilight sky, welcoming us to St. Ignace and the Northern (Upper) Peninsula. In order to get to the UP, travelers must cross the Mighty Mac.

"Drive on the grate, Popi!" I yelled from the back as I looked out to Lake Michigan on my left and Lake Huron to my right. Our father obliged, merging into the right lane. I leaned against the window, trying to see past the grates down into the water far below, but all I could see was darkness.

"I hate you," Hanna muttered to me as she bore a hole into the headrest in front of her with her eyes, making me feel only a little guilty for teasing her.

"Only four more miles," Mickey whispered in Hanna's ear, making her scrunch up her face even tighter.

Driving on the grates of a bridge makes an eerie hum, and if someone is the least bit nervous about driving on a bridge that is nearly five miles long, the loud vibrating drone generated from the rubber of the tires caressing the metal grates can put that someone on the ceiling of the car, where we regularly scraped Hanna from each time we crossed the Mackinac Bridge.

Three dollars and fifty cents later, we made it to the other side of the bridge and pulled into a rest area, where we would be spending the night. As much fun as the ride Up North is, we were still a family of six wedged into one Rambler, without funds for hotel accommodations.

Along with three semis, we settled in for the night at the far end of the parking lot. With my sleeping bag in hand, I followed my siblings to a grassy area away from the lights. Despite the mid-August warmth during the day, I pulled my sleeping bag up around my chin to trap my body heat during the coolness of the night. Gazing at the soft glow of the blue and green lights that ran along the arches of the bridge, I stayed quiet while the others laughed and told stories.

"See the Big Dipper?" Mickey asked, pointing to a bright cluster of stars. I nodded, and he continued, sweeping his finger across the sky. "If you draw an imaginary line up from the front of the pan, it points to the North Star."

"Oh, yeah," Silvia said, pointing. "I see it!"

"And did you know that the North Star is actually the tip of the handle of the Little Dipper? You'll notice that it's harder to see because it's upside down, and the stars aren't quite as bright." As he traced the path of the Little Dipper constellation I squinted, trying to find the constellation. "Do you see it?"

"Yeah, I think so," I lied, not wanting to ruin the moment.

"Can you do me a favor?" Mickey asked, looking at me, and then up to the sky. "Any time you feel lost, I want you to remember tonight. Just find the North Star and remember how it has helped so many find their way. We can make it our star, too. And if you think really hard, it'll make me look up too, and then you won't be alone. You know, all for one . . ."

"And one for all," Silvia, Hanna, and I whispered.

With the lights of the bridge serving as a wondrous nightlight, the others kept chatting and joking while I closed my eyes to rest them for just a moment.

"Turn right!" Hanna called out from the back corner of the lot as our father backed the camper into what we had collectively agreed was the best lot in the Lower Falls campground. I threw my jacket on, excited to explore our new surroundings. The campground was still quiet, with only a smattering of campers milling about. I closed my eyes and inhaled, taking in the symphony of delightful indulgences for the senses—from sizzling bacon to coffee made over campfires and Coleman stoves.

As our father worked at leveling the camper, our mother focused her attention on the picnic table. *Is it good here or perhaps, directly under the awning? Or over there . . .*

"Come on, Mickey," Silvia said, holding the pup tent. "Grab the stakes." She and Mickey began the task of finding a patch of ground free of protruding roots and sharp rocks sticking out of the dirt while I watched a boy pedal by our campsite on his way to the restrooms.

Because there was no way to tie four bicycles onto the top of a camper already overflowing with coolers and folding chairs, I considered myself lucky that my bike made the trip. "Give me a minute, and I'll get it down for you," my father said to me as he set my bike free from its restraints. But as he set the bungee cords into the trunk, he picked up the lantern and left, apparently distracted with setting up camp. *No problem,* I told myself. *I'll just drag the bike down, myself. How hard can it be? I just need to hoist myself . . .*

I meant to jump up onto the camper, but I immediately slid back down the rear-end, slicing my knee against the edge of the metal sign our father had screwed onto the back side. The sign read, FORGET ALAMO, which was a play on the slogan, *Remember the Alamo.* It was supposed to be ironic but the problem with that logic was that no one living beyond a four-mile radius knew of our town's existence, making the sign simply confusing to other travelers.

"Ow! Son of a . . ." Falling back, I landed hard on my butt. Grabbing my injured knee, I winced with pain and slowly removed my hand. My Levi's now revealed, not only a clean three-inch cut, but also a gouge that was spurting a gurgling fountain of blood, and with each pump, I could feel the pain shoot through my entire body. Wiping away tears, I hobbled to the picnic table in search of something to help stop the bleeding and grabbed the first suitable thing I saw—a dishtowel. The bleeding stopped with the constant pressure, but the pain was nearly unbearable, and my tears kept flowing, mixing with the blood and dirt as I tried to wipe them away. Bent over on the bench, I pressed the dishtowel even harder against my leg.

Slap!

The hard slap to the side of my head made me lose my balance, causing the bloody towel to fall to the ground. I turned quickly to see my mother glaring at me. "What do you think you're doing with my good dishtowel?"

I cupped my hand over my cheek, which was burning hot. "I . . . I cut myself," I stammered, showing her my wound, which was now exposed to the open air and forming a pool of blood.

"Well, you might as well keep using it now," she said, looking past me to the camper that was coming to life as our father blanketed the metal poles with the canvas tent.

"It's OK," Silvia said, taking a seat next to me. She picked up the dishtowel, shook the dirt off, and folded it in half. "Here, this part is clean."

Hanna walked up and lifted the dishcloth from my knee. "Ouch! You need a Band Aid. Wait right here, and I'll find the first aid kit." She hurried off and started rummaging through the car trunk. Meanwhile, Silvia stayed by my side and put her arm around my shoulders while I removed the cloth, entranced by the blood flow that would bubble up when given a breath of fresh air.

"It must really hurt," Silvia said, keeping her arm locked around me as I wiped the stream of blood, which was lessening in strength.

"It's not just that," I said, wiping my nose with my sleeve before placing the towel back on the wound and pressing harder to stop the throbbing. "These are the only pants I brought. I'm going to have to wear shorts for the rest of our vacation." I started crying again, unable to stop.

"No you're not. We'll just have to patch these up. They'll look cool when we're done. Don't worry about it." She gave me a hard squeeze and almost toppled me over, just to make sure I didn't get the false impression that she was going soft on me.

Unaware that his youngest child was bleeding to death, our father poked his head out from the inside of the camper. "I need someone to make the rounds for firewood."

"We got it!" Hanna answered back, handing me a large Band-Aid.

This morning campground ritual entailed collecting the leftover firewood from newly vacant campsites. It's a learned skill, and I followed Hanna and Silvia, tightly securing the dishtowel around my leg. In stealth mode, we glided through the lots swiftly and silently. Two boys down the lane spotted our operation, and suddenly we had fierce competition.

"You two go that way and check out those sites. I'm going that way," Hanna said, pointing one lane over. Seeing that the boys were separating as well, she added, "Hurry!" Silvia and I sprang into action, running across the empty sites in search of nature's currency.

Holding a small bundle of firewood, Silvia and I stopped at a site where a family was breaking down camp. As the father hitched up the camper to the truck, the mother noticed us, and seeing our bundle, made a calculation on why we were loitering in front of their lot.

"Good morning," she said, with a smile. "You two would help me a lot if you could take this firewood we obviously won't be needing anymore." As Silvia thanked the lady, I started for the firepit, ready to fill my arms. "Excuse me," the mother said, seeing me limping, with the towel still wrapped around my leg. "Are you all right? Come here. Let me take a look at that." Not used to having an adult pay attention to me, I looked over to Silvia, who nodded her approval.

"I'm a nurse, so you came to the right place," she said motioning for me to take a seat at the picnic table. "Can you roll up your pantleg?" As I obliged, this woman, who kindly offered up her firewood suddenly turned into an angel as she brought out an emergency kit that could have treated an entire football team. In the next several minutes, she cleaned my cut and wrapped it with a mile of gauze. I wanted to throw my arms around her, but instead, remained still as she patted my knee and smiled back at me. "You're lucky your knee doesn't need stitches," she continued, digging into the kit. "But I think we can put this thread and needle to work in a different way."

Soon after, with armfuls of firewood, Silvia and I returned to our site to find our mother sweeping dirt from the plastic-grass carpet laid out in front of the camper while pointing out to our father that the owl lights were hanging crooked on the camper awning.

"Nice job," Hanna said, seeing the stack of firewood now lying next to our firepit. She then looked down at my jeans, and with a quizzical look, asked, "Who in the world sewed up your pants?"

As a truck passed by our site, the woman in the front seat waved at me, and I answered back with a large wave and smile. "Long story," I said, taking off for the camper.

"Wipe your feet," my mother called out after me as I unzipped the front flaps. Stepping into the camper, I was taken aback as to how nicely our home-away-from-home was decked out inside. The Melitta coffeemaker was set up on the table alongside our mother's pistol cigarette lighter. And sitting on the end of the table was that beautiful portable TV. I lifted the pistol from its cradle and shot a flame.

While our father called this, "our camper," I realized that this was in actuality, our parent's camper, and any time I would be spending inside these canvas walls would be rare and fleeting. Digging into a grocery bag, I pushed the *National Enquirer* aside to uncover the bright blue canister. While it was apparent that I would be spending little time in the camper, I could sure eat all the damn cheese balls. With my hands and mouth full of orange crunch, I turned toward the clear vinyl window, aimed, and shot another flame.

—

"I got the marshmallows," I garbled, thinly disguising the fact that one had landed in my mouth. After a quiet evening around the campfire, and a morning with wild blueberries floating atop cereal served in individual-sized snack-pack boxes doing double-duty as make-shift bowls, it was finally time to check out the finest tourist destination in all of the Upper Peninsula. And the competition was fierce, with many wonderful places to be discovered—quaint towns like Paradise and Escanaba with souvenir shops selling moccasins and sweatshirts with snappy sayings like, "Mosquito—The UP State Bird," and the stone-covered shores of White Fish Point where one can find solitude and, perhaps, a Petoskey Stone. And for our father, the Soo Locks at Sault Ste. Marie where people spend countless hours watching the locks fill with water so that ships can pass through the channel, taking them from Lake Huron to Lake Superior. And yes, watching water rise is as boring as it sounds.

But the water we were rushing to was anything but boring.

"Keep up!" Silvia yelled as she ran past me and down one of the many back-trails dusted with sand and pine needles. Shifting into a full-out run, I struggled to keep up with my siblings and was thankful when we bunched up again at the top of a cliff. Mickey took my hand and helped me down the jagged rocks and through the swamp on our way to the falls. We knew the back trails by heart and continued through the forest, which eventually led us to the public trails lined with soft pine needles and eager tourists.

It was our second morning at Tahquamenon State Park, but it felt like it had taken us forever to finally get to the place that mattered most to me. Our parents were meeting up with us by car, so we only had a limited time to get to—

"Hurry up," Hanna called out from farther up the trail. "We don't want Mutti and Popi to beat us!"

The idea of losing a race to a car didn't really concern me, but I picked up my pace and stayed only a few steps back as we made our way down the trail, which led to the main entrance of the falls. I ran under the familiar archway created by a tree that fell long before any of us were born, letting my hand glide along the smooth bent trunk, shiny from the thousands of people who had also run their hands along this beautiful, natural doorway. We continued, running down steps carved out from the roots of more fallen trees. With the Tahquamenon River to my right, I picked up speed, knowing that I was close to reaching the trailhead conveniently located just a skip from my sole reason for being here.

"Come here, guys," Hanna called out, standing in front of the stone wall overlooking the falls. "Don't worry. We'll get there," she said to me with a wink, letting me know she understood.

Another family had gathered ahead of us to have their picture taken in front of the scenic overlook, and we stood back to give them room as the father snapped the photo. The family smiled on command and left after a quick look over the stone wall. This overlook is where all families started their visit and where many posed for their official vacation photo. I squeezed between my siblings, and Mickey hoisted me up, allowing me to peer out over the stone ledge. Caramel-colored water rushed far below us, in the magnificent Tahquamenon River.

"It looks like root beer," I remarked. "Even the white foam looks like the head on a cool glass of root beer."

"It really does," Silvia agreed. "What causes it to look that way?"

"I remember Popi saying that it's created by the acid from the pine needles dropping into the water," Mickey said. "See over there? Way over there. That's the fourth set of falls. The churning of water from the falls and rapids helps create the foam, or as you call it, the head of a root beer."

"OK, let's go check out the souvenir shop," Hanna said as Mickey set me back down. "I hear a root beer float calling my name."

Before she even finished this suggestion, I was halfway down the path leading to the Lower Falls Souvenir Shop, my whole reason for being on that particular day. I was already envisioning the chocolate ice cream cone that would soon be in my hand. But, this would only be after walking down every aisle first, checking out the endless selection of jackknives, T-shirts, and cedar boxes with clever sayings like, "We don't swim in your toilet so don't pee in our pool." I'm not sure why anyone would want a pretty box with that on it but if they did, they would find it here.

"Yoo-hoo!"

No! With a roll of my eyes, I turned away from the cedar door to see our mother sauntering up the path with all the brashness of Audrey Hepburn dunking her donut into her coffee in front of the Tiffany's window. As if on cue, she adjusted her sunglasses and placed a Virginia Slims to her lips, and, without skipping a beat, our father whipped his lighter out and had a flame licking the tip of her cigarette before she could ask for a light. As our mother took a long drag, it occurred to me that those sunglasses and cigarette weren't the only things our mother and the main character in *Breakfast at Tiffany's* had in common. In sync with our mother's movements, our father snapped shut the lid of his Zippo, snapping me back to reality.

You could tell our father was proud to have this exotic German by his side and content standing in the shadow of our mother's spotlight. Our father was a simple man—sporting the same crewcut he acquired in the army and wearing his everyday-uniform of industrial-strength cotton slacks found only in the hardware department at Sears. But with this woman on his arm, our father walked a little taller, which at fifty-seven made him look younger than the sixteen years he had on our mother.

They just looked good together.

"Come on," our father called out to us. "You know what we need a picture of." While the novice to Tahquamenon might believe that we headed to the scenic overlook, we knew what our father was really requesting, and we all ran over to pose in front of the large wooden sign in the parking lot that welcomed all visitors to the Lower Falls, while instructing them: TAKE NOTHING BUT PICTURES, LEAVE NOTHING BUT FOOTPRINTS.

I dashed in front of the sign. "Say, 'Cheese balls,'" my father instructed, perhaps wanting to take a photo of his youngest before the others had time to enter the picture.

And as I was saying, "Balls," Silvia ran into the shot, and he captured the moment.

"All right, kids," our mother said, taking off her sunglasses. "I'd like to get to the island while there is still a good selection of boats."

"Seriously?" I mumbled, looking at the souvenir shop.

"We'll get there, Squirt," Hanna smiled, messing up my hair. She grabbed my hand as we made our way down the steep wooden steps to the docks where a young park ranger with blond shaggy hair and aviator sunglasses was assisting tourists into row boats.

"Welcome to the Lower Tahquamenon Falls State Park!" he said, handing each of us a life jacket. "The Lower Falls actually consists of seven smaller waterfalls, one of which can *only* be seen from the island, which you will have the pleasure of seeing momentarily. And when you're done exploring our wonderful park, don't forget to check out the Upper Falls, located just four miles west of here—a huge waterfall that rivals *only* Niagara Falls in terms of rushing water and visitors east of the Mississippi River! Thank you, sir," the ranger said, accepting the boat rental payment from our father while our mother went in search of the perfect rowboat. This was the *only* time you would find our mother in a boat of any sort, and I understood her hesitancy for watercrafts. Not only did I lack the patience needed for fishing, I felt the tightness of being trapped on a boat—claustrophobia with a chance of drowning.

As Hanna buckled me into a life vest, our mother shook her head and walked away from a rowboat littered with wet papers laying on the boat's floor. Just a few yards away, a young woman let out a raucous laugh as an older woman walked alongside her on the dock. They were both dressed in khaki shorts and serious hiking shoes. My mother spun quickly to face the women, but they had moved on, unaware that they had attracted our mother's attention.

"How about this one?" the park ranger asked the women, motioning to the boat directly in front of our mother.

"This one is as good as any," the young woman answered. "Give me your hand, Mom," she continued, stepping into the boat, and extending her hand.

"Am I invisible?" Our mother asked loudly, turning around, with her arms outstretched. "*Was sie suchen bei?*" she then called out to our father who was busy exchanging our mother's lifejacket for one that didn't look like it had spent twenty years baking under the sun.

As our mother strapped on her imaginary gloves, Hanna steered me away from the boxing ring into a nearby scrappy rowboat. With Silvia at the oars, Mickey shoved us off from the dock and toward the small island. Looking back, I couldn't help but feel a little sad that we had left our father with the challenge of luring our mother away from the women, and I wondered if he would be successful in pulling her back from that dark place she had a habit of visiting.

Stretching my leg out, I marveled at the handicraft of the woman who patched me up the day before. With extra gauze in my shorts pocket, I thought about that woman, wondering who she might be saving at that moment with her angelic heroism.

It was nearly high noon as we drifted across the river, and I leaned back, soaking in the warmth from the sun peeking out from behind the clouds. With Silvia rowing, I dragged my hand in the water, creating my own little current, and as we drifted into shore, Mickey jumped out and pulled us onto the dock. Climbing out, I looked back across the river to see if our parents were on their way or if we would be enjoying the island without them. With the sun directly overhead against a clear blue sky, I held my hand over my eyes, scanning the few boats coming toward us.

"There they are," I said, spotting a faded yellow rowboat halfway across the river. But as the boat came into view, it appeared that our father had stopped rowing toward us, and instead, had started rowing slowly upriver.

"Where the heck are they going?" Hanna asked.

"Maybe they've had enough of us," Silvia said. "I know I would row as fast as I could to get away from us."

"Son of a gun, would you look at that," Mickey said, pointing.

I squinted to see our father moving to sit next to our mother, who, in turn, scooted to where he had been sitting, and started rowing! *Our* mother, who couldn't drive a car, and who I had never even seen on a bicycle, was rowing the boat as our father coached her on how to dip the oars. They were laughing, and we watched in silence, knowing that we were witnessing a rare personal moment between our parents, something that didn't happen often in a family our size.

Looking across the water, I did a quick inventory of the boats coming our way and let out a breath of relief, seeing that the women who inadvertently ignited my mother's dark mood were not island-bound. Our mother had stopped rowing, allowing the boat to drift downriver. Shortly after, our father once again took command of the oars, and the two of them made their way towards us.

"Tag, you're it!" I yelled happily, pushing past Silvia as I ran up the wooden steps to the first series of waterfalls that outline the island. Tossing my sneakers onto the grass, I waded into the shallow water to catch the minnows as they warmed themselves in the pockets of water that collect on the rocks.

— 20 —

1942

Eschbach, Baden-Württemberg, Germany

"Slow down, girl!" Didi called out, following Mari down one of the many trails behind the church. "What in the world can be so urgent that we have to run?"

"You'll see," Mari said, turning her head without slowing her pace. "In fact, the only way you will believe it is to see it with your own eyes. Come on, pick up your step!"

Didi started jogging, trying to keep up with her excited friend who insisted that she knew of a secret that would ". . . knock your socks off!" Didi pulled at the front of her blouse, which was already wet with humidity and sticking to her stomach even though it was still morning. As they ran down the trail, she admired the colorful flowers and trimmed hedges, suddenly appreciating the effort they had put in earlier in the spring, working in the gardens. Life at the convent hadn't been easy but she had to admit to herself that it wasn't without its upside. Once she figured out the system of the Catholic Church, it became easier for her to navigate around the trouble spots. She learned to steer around the individual quirks of the nuns who were quick with the slap of a ruler and not at all above assigning toilet cleaning duty to girls who sassed back, and she acquired the skill of blending into the shadows when in the presence of all other adults living and working under the roofs of the church and convent, knowing that other girls that were more popular were also more apt to be assigned chores and asked favors.

And then there was Mari, who not only made the last year bearable, but also surprisingly pleasant. In between sneaking out at night to walk with cute boys under the streetlights in town and sneaking smokes in the garden out back, life at the home wasn't horrible. Still, at night as Didi lay in her bed, she wondered when her mother might be ready to pick her up. Surely her mother occasionally thought of her, too, but then, again, maybe she didn't.

"Shh," Mari said, turning around.

They kept walking, slowing to a more deliberate pace, with Didi following, smiling and shaking her head, wondering where their adventure would take them this time. Carelessly, Didi stepped on a twig, triggering a loud snap and a stern look from Mari.

"I know, I know, be quiet," Didi whispered.

Finally, the trail opened up into to a wooded area, and Mari stopped next to a row of tall hedges and waved Didi over to stand next to her. Still confused, Didi did as she was told while Mari separated the branches, holding them apart. As she stepped back, she motioned Didi to lean in closer.

"Who is that?" Didi whispered, seeing what looked like two people lying on the grass. The man was on top of someone and tugging at his own trousers. He sat up for a moment to yank his pants down, exposing his very white rear-end, and revealing the woman lying under him.

"Oh my god!" Didi whispered, not ready to believe what was happening right in front of her. She let the branches spring back into place as she turned to look at Mari in disbelief, who was sporting a wide grin. "Sister Trudy and Father Heinrich?"

Mari nodded. "I told you this was big," she whispered.

Didi parted the branches again and looked through the opening just as Father Heinrich laid back down on Sister Trudy. After several movements and adjustments, he started raising and lowering his body in jerky movements. The only sounds Didi could hear were the grunts coming from Father Heinrich each time he came down on Sister Trudy, and Didi watched, engrossed in the peep show. She knew that she should probably turn away, but she had never seen anything at the film house that went beyond heavy petting and found this scene both fascinating and titillating.

She kept watching, her breath matching the rhythm of Father Heinrich's movements until he let out a low moan and settled onto Sister Trudy, who lay beneath him without any movement. The act certainly didn't seem as romantic as Didi had imagined it would.

With one last kiss, Father Heinrich lifted himself off Sister Trudy and stood to pull up his trousers. Sister Trudy just as quickly, pulled up her undergarments, and smoothed out her frock, carefully wiping the back of her dress to make sure it was free of dirt and grass. As Father Heinrich zipped up his trousers, he lifted his gaze and looked out across the garden toward the hedges, and he landed on a pair of eyes looking back at him.

"Oh *scheisse!*" Didi shrieked, letting the branches snap shut. She grabbed Mari's hand. "Run!"

"Ha! That's what you get for being a sex peeper," Mari laughed as they ran down the trails back to the home. "You know that watching is one of the deadly sins. You'll finally have something interesting to say at confession."

"Oh, hush, and keep up!"

They didn't slow their pace until they reached the back steps, hurrying through the back kitchen where several girls were preparing lunch.

"Oh, the stories we will tell our *kinder*!" Mari laughed, stopping to catch her breath.

"Ah, no! We are taking this to our graves, do you hear me?" Didi replied. "What I'm not taking to my grave is that visual. Bleach in my eyes won't erase that vision!"

Mari looked past Didi, through the back window. "Follow me, and quick!" She grabbed Didi and dragged her through the kitchen and into the sitting room. "Grab a book, sit down, and look like you're reading!"

Didi did as she was told, and Mari grabbed a book as well and sat on the braided rug just as they heard the backdoor opening.

Suddenly, Sister Ruth appeared in the front doorway of the sitting room, making Didi visibly jump in her chair.

"Skittish today, are we?"

"Beautiful morning, Sister Ruth," Mari jumped in, relieving Didi of having to fumble over her own words.

"Hmmm," Sister Ruth replied, apparently not trusting the innocent scene laid out before her. "Clean up for lunch. You have chores and studying to do this afternoon." With that, Sister Ruth turned to leave, but before Didi could exhale, Sister Trudy hurriedly entered from the kitchen, her eyes darting around the room as she subconsciously smoothed out her habit.

"Ah, Sister Trudy," Sister Ruth said, looking over her cohort curiously. "I've been looking for you. We need to go over this afternoon's study plan. Have you seen Father Heinrich?"

All three instinctively looked up at Sister Ruth, and Sister Trudy responded a bit too quickly with, "Of course not. Why would I know where Father Heinrich is? I haven't seen him all morning."

"Very well, I wasn't accusing you of having run off with him," she chuckled. "I simply wondered if you had run into him on your errands today."

Mari coughed as she stifled a laugh while Didi remained quiet, wishing that everyone would just go away.

"Yes, ma'am. And, no, ma'am, I have not," Sister Trudy responded, slowing her delivery, and lowering her voice in a concentrated effort to sound more casual. "Well, if you'll excuse me, I have studies to tend to—"

"Wait," Sister Ruth added as Sister Trudy walked past her. "You have something dangling from your hair." She reached for the object and pulled it off of Sister Trudy. "Just a twig."

Mari let out another cough, waving off everyone's stare with a, "Got to get a glass of water."

After the two girls were alone again in the room, Didi shot Mari a glare. "Seriously, could you have been more obvious?"

Mari laughed it off. "Oh, don't be so paranoid. I don't think Father Heinrich knows who the heck was watching them in action. We were too far away. You're safe. The last thing on Sister Trudy's mind is us. She's too busy trying to protect her own ass. Sister Ruth made her so nervous, she didn't even know we were in the room."

"Do you think Father Heinrich and Sister Trudy love each other?" Didi asked, putting the book back on the shelf.

"No. Well, maybe Sister Trudy is in love. Men don't have any real feelings for women. Why do you think you and I are in this god-forsaken place? If men care about anyone other than themselves, they have a peculiar way of showing it." Mari slammed her book shut and stood up. "That's it for our show. Let's go wash up—I'm hungry."

Didi let Mari's words sink in as she started to follow her out of the room. While it was her mother who dropped her off at this place, her father certainly did nothing to stop her actions, preferring to not get involved in the trivial actions of his girlfriend's daughter. Didi spent many nights looking at the ceiling, wondering if he missed her and knowing all too well the answer to that question. Still, she fantasized about her father walking through the front doors with the announcement that he was taking her home.

She then heard the opening of the front door, followed by heavy footsteps walking through the front room. Suddenly, a dark form filled the doorway leading into the sitting room.

Father Heinrich looked around the room, and just when Didi looked back at him, he turned his gaze toward her—and their eyes locked, sending a shiver up Didi's back.

— 21 —

August 20, 1970
Alamo, Michigan

"Silvia?"

She answered with a short snort, telling me that she didn't hear the noise that I heard. Maybe I was dreaming. Nope, there it was again.

We went to bed an hour earlier, which of course is different from actually going to sleep. Silvia was the perfect roommate, and while I don't recall ever being tucked in by my mother, Silvia invented a colorful story involving a family of rabbits that frolicked in and out of trouble. Most nights she shared their adventures with me until I fell asleep. Her stories always had happy endings, and while she claimed they were bedtime stories, she became increasingly frustrated with me for falling asleep without letting her know, leaving her with the challenge of trying to figure out when exactly I nodded off so we could pick up at the same point the following night.

But I was awake that night.

I blinked, trying to shake the sleep away, but all I could see were the beautiful stars and planets shining off Silvia's black-velvet poster. The ultraviolet light also highlighted the lint on my blanket like a million brilliant stars, making me wonder when my blanket last saw the inside of the wash machine.

Still half-awake, I slowly recognized the noises coming from downstairs—voices. And one in particular was the voice of a man, and not our father, who had already left for work. This voice was bold with vociferous laughing, which wasn't at all like our father, who chuckled at the most.

"Silvia."

Still nothing. Wanting to know why our mother was having a party this time of night, and more important, why I wasn't invited, I climbed over my stuffed animals and crawled out of bed. Through the darkness, I tiptoed down the hall and down the staircase to the bottom step. Hiding in the shadows and crouched against the wall, I pulled Mickey's old T-shirt over my knees. As the talking in the room continued, I peeked around the corner.

"You have no place being here, this time of night." Hanna said defiantly. She was in her nightgown and standing in the middle of the living room. Hanna's bedroom was located downstairs so she must have been awakened by the same man's voice that I heard. But I couldn't see who she was scolding. Her voice was different, higher than usual, and with her arms folded across her chest, she looked small, standing there.

And where was our mother?

"Don't be silly, Johanna," our mother snapped. "He just happened to stop by and we're chatting. Now, go back to bed."

"That's right, we're just chatting," the man replied, letting out a laugh that I vaguely remembered. Stretching as far as I could, I peered around the corner to see that the man was sitting on our couch, with our mother right beside him. There was a shadow falling across his face, but I recognized him from the night we went TP-ing. But what was Robbie's dad doing here?

"I don't care," Hanna challenged, and it was all I could do to stay hidden in the dark. I wanted to jump up and yell, *Bam! You heard her, she said scram!*

Hanna's voice was shaking as she stood her ground, with her arms still tightly crossed in front of her. "Our father isn't home, and you shouldn't be here." She was quiet for a while before finally adding, "You need to leave."

Mr. Carlson let out another laugh and grabbed our mother's hand. "It's getting late," he said, like leaving was his idea, and he got up to grab his jacket from the end of the sofa. Hanna didn't move as he walked to the front door. He stopped and gave Hanna a smile. "Robbie doesn't need to know about this."

He then shifted his focus past Hanna, toward my direction, startling me as I wrapped my arms tight around my knees, trying to make myself invisible. He winked, a wink I'm not sure was intended for me or Hanna, and it triggered a shiver from deep inside me.

Finally, he turned, opened the door and left.

Hanna turned to our mother. "You can't leave anything alone, can you? Crazy to think that you could let me be happy about one thing. I can't believe you had to ruin this, too."

Our mother didn't reply, and with the sound of a car starting, Hanna walked to the front door and locked it. I ducked back into the shadows as Hanna, without another word, returned to her bedroom. Our mother walked out of the living room as well, and shortly after, I heard the click of the TV turning on in the kitchen. I listened to Johnny Carson cracking jokes to the audience while Ed McMahon laughed loudly every five to ten seconds. I didn't care for his laugh, either. I quietly made my way upstairs back to bed.

Hanna would be graduating soon and moving out. I hated thinking about it, but I just couldn't help it.

— 22 —

1944

Eschbach, Baden-Württemberg, Germany

Seeing how she didn't go on any shopping excursions during her two years at the orphanage, Didi had no problem fitting all of her clothes and personal items back into her suitcase. With a snap of the buckles, she lifted the suitcase off the bed and smoothed out her blanket for the last time. She looked around the room at the dozen other beds, all neatly made, with shoes carefully lined up under each one. As she looked over at the far wall, she suddenly stopped. She was puzzled, not at what she saw, but at what she didn't see—that disturbing picture of Jesus on the cross. It hadn't grown on her during her stay, and she still found it an uncomfortable image to fall asleep to at night. Still, the nuns obviously felt that this was the image that the girls should carry with them into their dreams, so where was it, and why did she care?

"Damn picture," she mumbled.

"You'll be flushed straight down to hell for saying things like that," Mari said, standing in the doorway.

"I'm glad you're here," Didi said quietly, turning around to face her friend. "I know this should be a happy day, but—"

"Don't you dare," Mari interrupted, putting her scolding finger up to Didi's mouth. "This is a great day!"

"But I wish you were coming with me. My dear, I don't know what I'm going to do without you."

"I have a feeling that you're going to be just fine," Mari smiled, taking a seat on the bed. "The bigger question is, what the hell am I going to do? We've all gotten a little used to you and your crazy ways." She paused and added in a softer voice while flattening out a wrinkle in the blanket, "With you here, I actually started feeling a little less broken. I guess you were my glue."

"Now it's my turn to say don't you dare," Didi scolded, taking Mari's face in her hands. "You are the most unbroken person I know, and if anything, *you* saved *my* life. And don't lose sight of the fact that you're going to be out of this godforsaken place in no time."

"I know, a step behind you. June just seems so far from now. My sixteenth birthday can't come soon enough. Maybe, before then, I'll get lucky and have a long-lost uncle show up here to take me home. Your aunt and uncle won't mind one more kid, will they?" She laughed, knowing that she was suggesting the unthinkable. "I'm just glad you're not serving your full sentence. It's good to have family, no matter where they come from."

"Look, it's not like I'll be a million miles away. We'll meet for lunch at the Bauer Corner Diner."

Mari lifted her head and straightened her posture. "You're right, and I will be out of here faster than Sister Ruth can say, '*Essen* your peas!' It's safe to say that I will never eat peas again."

Mari laughed as Didi gave her a soft smile and held her hand. "I'm going to miss you," Didi whispered, throwing her arm around her friend, and leaning her head atop Mari's shoulder.

"Oh, one last thing," Mari said, jumping up. Walking to her dresser, she picked up a small item wrapped in tissue paper and presented it to Didi. "So, you won't forget me."

"You know I won't." Didi pulled back the tissue paper. "Oh, Mari, you can't," she said, seeing the Christmas ornament that Mari painted during an art project with all the other girls before Christmas dinner last month. A delicate light blue bulb with a white cross painted on a glitter of snow, and "Mari" painted at the bottom.

"I insist. A bit ironic, don't you think, that the nuns had us making Christmas gifts? If we had someone to give gifts to, would we even be here?"

Didi raised an eyebrow and nodded. The ornament she made was already packed. She had planned on giving it to her aunt, but as she started to open her suitcase, Mari stopped her.

"Stop. You can give it to me when I get out of this place. Deal?"

"Deal."

"Promise you'll write?"

"Every week." Didi stood up and brushed Mari's blonde curly hair back over her shoulder to get a good look into her eyes. "You'll be out of here before you know it, and as soon as you are, we're going to go out on the town to celebrate." With that, Didi pulled her friend up and gave her another hug, longer this time, afraid to let go.

"Didi," Sister Ruth called out from the bottom of the stairs. "Your family is here, *mach schnell!*"

"Six short months," Mari smiled, picking up the suitcase and handing it to Didi. "And stop crying like a baby," she scolded, in her best Sister Ruth voice. "You will cry on your own time!" With a forced smile, she pushed her friend forward. "Go on, get out of here."

"Six short months," Didi called out as she walked down the hallway.

She picked up her pace as she ran down the stairs, eager to greet the visitors waiting for her. It was a chilly day, which explained Tante Lisi's thick wool coat, and shawl wound tightly around her neck, making her look larger than her actual petite size. Her uncle stood next to her aunt, with one arm draped lightly around her shoulder.

He brightened with a wide grin as his niece appeared on the staircase. Tante Lisi offered up her usual tight smile, careful not to reveal too much emotion, knowing that her husband would be displaying enough excitement for the both of them. "*Guten morgen!*" he said, reaching for Didi's suitcase so her arms would be free for hugs.

"Good morning," she replied with a grin as Onkel Otto wrapped his arms around her. Didi collapsed in his embrace and started to sob, which brought out a lighthearted chuckle from him.

"*Ach du lieber,* we didn't realize you loved us so much! Or would you be just as happy if the mailman was picking you up?" He winked at Didi's aunt and Sister Ruth, who both returned a look of annoyance. "There, there, everything *ist* going to be just fine." After a while, Didi pulled away from her uncle's embrace and wiped her eyes and cheeks with her shirt sleeve.

"Here," he whispered, pulling a handkerchief from his coat pocket, and handing it to her. "I'm sorry that your mother hasn't been there for you, but we're here now. And you're going to be OK." Looking at the one suitcase, he asked, "Is that all you have?"

Didi looked down at the suitcase that held all of her belongings and let out a laugh. "Yes, I'm afraid that's it."

"Get your coat," instructed Tante Lisi, motioning to the row of hooks holding an assortment of coats, sweaters, and scarves. Didi obliged and put her wool coat on. Turning to Sister Ruth, she paused, unsure of how to say goodbye.

"Be safe, Didi," Sister Ruth said, standing stoic, saving Didi from an emotional goodbye. "And do as you're told. I don't want to see you back here."

"Yes, ma'am," Didi said with a smile.

"Give me your hands." As Didi obliged, Sister Ruth held her hands tightly. "When you came here, you were scared of your own shadow. In the short time you've lived with us, I have seen you grow into a young lady with heart, strength, and perseverance. With the Lord by your side, you will not only make it in this world, you will make a difference. Don't let anyone tell you different. Do you hear me?"

"Yes."

"Yes, who?"

"Yes, Sister Ruth," Didi smiled.

Sister Ruth then picked up a small package wrapped in butcher paper from a shelf behind her, and handed it to Didi. "Take this. It will help you find your way. Now go, you'll be fine." Sister Ruth released Didi's hands and returned to her stoic stance.

"Time to go, ladies." Onkel Otto picked up Didi's suitcase and walked Didi and Tante Lisi to the door. Pausing, Didi looked back toward the staircase, hoping for one last glance of her friend, but the stairwell was empty. *Six short months*, she told herself.

With her suitcase beside her, Didi settled into the back of the auto. Glancing into the rearview mirror from the driver's seat, her uncle noticed Didi unwrapping the gift from Sister Ruth, revealing a book of blank pages bound in a soft leather cover. "I imagine you have plenty to write about, eh, Didi?"

Didi offered up a small smile but remained silent. She had dreamed of the day when she would finally escape the orphanage, but something changed along the way. It turned out that the people she feared most weren't monsters after all, and the kinships she built with the other girls were true, even though they came and went without logic or clarity, which only added to the heartbreak. As the car pulled out of the driveway, she lifted the smooth leather cover up against her cheek, not wanting to look back at the home, and not wanting to see if Mari was looking out the window.

As Didi rested her arm on her suitcase, she suddenly noticed a hard bump, and as she ran her fingers along the raised leather, she wondered what was making the dent since she had nothing but clothes lying on top. She unzipped the suitcase and lifted the flap. Sitting on top of her belongings was a picture. That damn picture.

She let out a small laugh and closed her eyes.

— 23 —

August 25, 1970
Alamo, Michigan

"Stop!" I yelled in excitement as Hanna took her fingers off the silver horse that came to a rest on Baltic Avenue. "That'll be $120!" I knew the others were stringing me along by giving me ownership of this low-income stretch of purple properties, but I didn't care as Hanna handed me my beige and aqua-colored Monopoly money.

"Who wants pudding?" our mother called out, closing her magazine and standing up.

"Me!" I shouted along with the others. As our mother brought out the instant pudding mix and milk, Mickey rolled double fours and landed on Free Parking.

"Yeah, baby!"

"Oh man," Silvia groaned. "I never land on that. Watch, I'll land on it now, since there's no cash on it anymore. "Stop," she added, smiling as Mickey's next roll was a three. "That'll be $200!"

Our father had already left for work, and since our mother came downstairs only a few hours earlier, this time of night was more like mid-afternoon for her. "We have Chocolate Fudge and Banana. Can you think of a reason why we shouldn't have both?" our mother asked, plugging in the hand mixer.

"No reason, I can see!" Mickey yelled.

"Come on, baby, roll me an eight," Silvia said, shaking the dice in her hands. She let them roll. "Yeah, baby!"

"Are you kidding me?" Mickey said as Silvia jumped over Park Place and Boardwalk, landing on Community Chest. "Pass Go," she said, extending her hand out to Mickey who also served as banker. "Collect $200!"

"Mickey," our mother called out as she poured milk into the mixing bowl of pudding mix. "Would you please help me and get the parfait glasses down?"

"Yep," he answered, getting up from the picnic table. "No skipping over my properties while I'm gone," he warned, pointing his finger at all of us. He walked over to the cupboard, and reached for them on the top shelf.

"Use the stepstool," our mother urged. "I think we need some actual bananas in the pudding. You kids go through bananas quicker than a bunch of monkeys. Mickey, be careful," she added, seeing that he insisted on grabbing each one without help. As he set them on the counter, she continued. "So, tell me about this Robbie boy, Johanna. Are you two crazy in love yet?"

"She's not in love, but she is crazy," I said.

"Just roll," Hanna said, not amused.

Still on his tiptoes, Mickey reached for the last of the parfait glasses and placed it on the counter. Meanwhile, our mother walked over to Hanna and grabbed her sides, tickling her. "Oh, come on. You know you like that boy. I saw the way you looked at him at the Carlson's house."

Hanna laughed and tried to squirm away from our mother's tickles. As she wiggled, she playfully slapped at our mother's hands, sending a long fingernail flying across the room. Our mother let out a howl as she stepped back, stunned. The rest of us stopped as well, too scared to move as our mother shook her injured hand wildly, and with the other, she slapped Hanna across her back, making Hanna fall forward onto the game board, sending pieces flying across the table and onto the floor.

"Mutti, stop!" Hanna yelled, standing up. "I didn't mean to do that. I was just—"

"I know you meant to do exactly that! You're a tramp, you know that? Do you really think that boy likes you for your brains?"

"Stop it, Mutti!" Silvia blurted out as Hanna tried pushing our mother away from her, which only drew another slap. Then, another. Silvia and I instinctively jumped away from the picnic table as Mickey grabbed our mother from behind in an attempt to stop the slaps but that only made her angrier, like a cornered lion lashing out at the zookeeper.

"Run! Get out of here," Mickey yelled as our mother punched him in the gut with her elbow. He let go of her and followed us out of the kitchen and through the front door.

"Get out! And don't you ever come back!" our mother screamed, throwing a parfait glass at the wall as the front porch door swung shut behind us.

While the days in late August are beautiful when the sun is shining down, under a nearly full moon, I felt cold and naked as we stood together, Mickey breathing hard and Hanna rubbing her arm where our mother had scratched her. A car traveled up the road, and we watched it as it drove by.

"So, what do we do now?" Hanna asked. "My car keys are in my bedroom." She cupped her hands on top of her head and looked toward the house. "And I'm not going back in."

"Is it unlocked?" Silvia asked.

"Yeah, why?"

"Well, we can sit in the safety of a locked car, or we can wait out here for Mutti to come screaming out of the house, wielding a knife like the posterchild for *Psycho*."

"Good point," Mickey said. He quietly opened the car door and jumped in, turning off the dome light.

On most nights, it was easy to appreciate the yard light that our father installed at the end of our driveway. It gave us extra play time on summer evenings long after the fireflies disappeared, and it provided us with security after he went off to work the third shift each weeknight. But on that night, the yard light was not our friend. Coupled with the bright-as-day moonlight, it only illuminated our presence in Hanna's Gremlin, forcing us to crouch even further into the seats and floorboards. After what felt like an hour, I cricked my neck and stretched out my leg. "Hanna," I asked. "How long have we been in here?

"About ten minutes, honey," she said, giving me a squeeze.

With the exception of an occasional tree frog and the constant hum of chirping crickets, the night was still, so when we heard the familiar creak of the opening of the back-porch door, my heart pounded. I swear it was what caused Hanna to whisper, "Shh," as she pushed me closer to the floor. Mickey lifted his head up ever so slightly to peer out the windshield. Looking . . . listening . . .

Hanna reached over me and locked the car, providing a sense of safety but also making me feel trapped should our mother have the bright idea to simply peer into the car window for her darling children. I weighed our options, one being to go back outside since we all ran faster than our mother and could keep a safe distance from her. If we had the car key, we could just—

"I know you're out there!" our mother shouted into the night, which was strangely comforting for we could tell that she was yelling from the back door, a safe distance away. Mickey ducked down and hit his head on the steering wheel with a loud thud.

"Shit," he mumbled.

"Be quiet," Hanna warned while I tried to calm the thumping in my chest. I looked up at Hanna's face, illuminated by the yard light. While I had never been surprised by her courage in protecting us, looking at her now, with her tightened mouth and her eyes darting about, I understood that she was scared, just like me. At any moment, our mother's face could appear in the car window.

"You can't get away from me! I know where your father keeps the gun, and I will find you!" And with that, we heard the shutting of the back door.

"Oh my god, she knows!" Mickey said.

"Knows what?" Hanna asked.

"The gun. She knows about the gun." He turned to look at Hanna. "We found it in Popi's toolbox in the cellar. Shit, she knows about the gun!"

"But Mickey," I said, "There are no bullets. Remember? We checked, and it's empty."

"What if she knows where the bullets are?" Silvia added.

"Stop it," I said, not wanting to hear any more about the gun. "Just stop talking." I was trying to figure out how our mother even knew about it since she rarely ventured into the cellar, and I had never seen her tinkering in Popi's work area. Maybe she snooped like we did when everyone else was out of the house.

"She's in the cellar." Mickey reported, and we all popped our heads up to see that the cellar windows were lit. "Oh man, she's getting the gun!"

"She won't find it," Hanna said, trying to reassure us. "And even if she does, we know there aren't any bullets." With that, Hanna stretched, and I snuggled against her, trying to get comfortable. This current situation made me wonder why our father chose to have a gun in a house, knowing how unstable our mother was. *Why would he do that to us?* And that got me thinking about Mickey, Silvia, and Hanna, all older than me by many years. *What was I going to do when they grew up and moved out, leaving me behind?*

Another five minutes passed before Mickey announced that the cellar light had turned off. With none of us moving, we listened, waiting for the back door to open again, but it remained shut, and we started to relax. It was after midnight, but I couldn't sleep.

"Do you think she gave up?" Silvia asked. "I feel like she'd be tapping on the car window with the gun by now, if she actually found it." She paused. "I got it. Mickey, go out there and peek into the house. Hopefully, Johnny Carson made her forget that she wants us all dead."

"Me? Why me? Shit, I'm not stepping out of this car. If she sees a male face peering at her through the window, who knows what she'll do. I know, let's send the one she's least likely to shoot." He turned around to look at me.

"Oh, come on!" I moaned, tired of being the most expendable and just . . . tired.

"He's got a point," Silvia pointed out. "The youngest one is automatically the cutest, and the least likely one that Mutti will take a shot at. It makes the most sense to send the youngest."

"Oh, I get it," I said, angry that it appeared I didn't have a vote on this. "Go ahead and send the one who's only been on the planet for nine years! No one will miss the fourth kid! We'll just make another one!"

"Shh!" Hanna said, obviously tired of the whole thing. "No one's leaving this car. Let's all get comfortable. It's going to be a long night."

Mickey reclined the driver's seat and yawned. Suddenly he started singing softly, "Just got home from Illinois. Locked the front door, oh boy. Got to sit down and take a rest on the porch. Imagination sets in. Pretty soon I'm singin'—"

The rest of us joined in on the chorus. "Doo, doo, doo, lookin' out my back door."

— 24 —

1944

Eschbach, Baden-Württemberg, Germany

"Did you get them?" Didi asked, spotting Mari wading out from the crowd of theatergoers. "Damn it!" Didi said, detecting a frown on Mari's face. "I knew we weren't going to be able to snag the good tickets. I can't believe we're stuck having to watch *Feinde*, because we all need to be reminded why invading everyone is good for Deutschland."

"Shh . . ." Mari whispered, looking around. "I'm sure the propaganda film is quite enlightening, but I'm afraid we won't have time to see it." She smiled and brought her hand around from behind her back to reveal two movie tickets.

"We're going to see *Nightclub Hostess*? That's *wunderbar*! Wait," Didi added, thinking about the likelihood of getting the two tickets on opening night, when most movie houses were only showing government-driven films designed to increase patriotism for Nazi occupation. "Fess up, how in the world did you pull it off?" Mari replied with a smirk, making Didi look at her friend skeptically. "Please tell me you didn't make a date with the guy in the ticket booth in exchange for these."

"All right, I won't tell you. But, he has a friend, so I'm afraid we both have a date after the movie." Mari laughed.

Didi sighed and shook her head. "My dear friend, I can't decide if I'm impressed with your ingenuity or scared for you, maybe a little of both." Lowering her voice, she took Mari's hand and added, "He's a little old for you. You need to be more careful. These tickets aren't worth it."

"Don't you worry your little head about my love life," Mari teased, waving the tickets in front of Didi's face. "How I came about these, we'll worry about later. Right now, we have a film to catch." They both laughed as Mari grabbed Didi's arm and led her into the lobby. "Since I got the tickets, you're getting the popcorn!"

As Didi walked to the concessions counter, she weaved between the crowds of people streaming through the lobby. The film house was only two years old, and Didi admired the rich mahogany paneling. Above the crowds, she noticed a poster for *Nightclub Hostess*, featuring an etching of film star Michéle Morgan, wrapped in a striking blue scarf that perfectly framed her flowing fire-red hair.

Oh, to be her, Didi thought. *What it must be like to be loved by so many, by anyone, really. I should dye my hair that gorgeous color. Then the world will take notice.*

"May I help you?" the lady behind the counter asked.

"Um, yes," Didi answered, embarrassed to be caught daydreaming. She stepped up to the counter. "Two popcorns and two Fantas, please."

Trying to balance everything in her hands, Didi found Mari and quickly handed her a popcorn and soda. "I got you your own so that you'll keep your hands out of mine," Didi said, smiling. "Come on, the propaganda shorts should be over by now."

Two hours later, the girls walked out of the theater with empty popcorn bags and full of conversation. Chatting without care, Didi didn't notice the two men leaning against the wall, watching them.

"Good evening, ladies," the man Didi remembered from the ticket booth said, stepping in front of them. "Did you enjoy the film?"

Mari grabbed Didi's arm and answered with, "Why, yes we did. It was very good."

"Good? Is that all I get for my incredible generosity? *Nightclub Hostess* is a fantastic film!" The man leaned in close to Mari and asked, "Is this your friend? I hope you two ladies are looking forward to a night on the town you will never forget. Let me introduce myself. Name's Karl. And this here's my friend, Gunter."

Gunter nodded, stuffing his hands in his jacket pocket. "Ladies."

Didi looked at their two suitors, offering no hint of a smile. Instead, she tightened her grip on Mari's arm.

"Nice to meet you, Gunter," Mari said. "So where are you two taking us for dinner? Just so you know, we can't stay out too late."

"Sweetie, this date has only just begun." He winked at his friend, and added, "After you, ladies."

As the four walked out of the movie house, Didi leaned into Mari and whispered, "I don't like this, Mari. My Onkel Otto won't be happy if I'm out late again. We don't have to do this, let's just go home."

"You'll go home when we say the party's over," Karl said, his smile suddenly turning hard.

"Come on," Mari said to Didi, sounding unsure of herself. "It'll be fine. It's just dinner."

"You'll both be the loveliest ladies in all the city," Karl said, turning his smile back on and spinning in a circle with his arms outstretched toward the sky.

"We'll be all right," Mari whispered, smiling at Didi as she squeezed her hand. "Now let's paint this town red or whatever color suits your fancy."

Didi looked past her friend's smile and detected sadness in her eyes. It had been a year since Mari left the orphanage. She found shelter with a cousin and her husband, but they had three children of their own, and weren't equipped to handle a headstrong teenager. Mari rarely talked about her home situation, and Didi was afraid to ask. As a city bus rolled past them, Didi wished she was on it, heading home. As they stood beneath the marquee, Karl reached for Mari's arm, and instinctively, Mari dropped Didi's hand. Even though Didi had spent many evenings in the city with the sidewalks bustling with people, she never felt so alone.

"You're beautiful," Gunter said, walking beside Didi. She looked over at him, only to realize that he was not looking into her eyes. His eyes were peering down the front of her sweater, making her wish that she had brought a jacket.

Up ahead, Karl and Mari walked arm in arm, with Karl talking and laughing as they ducked into the Silver Stein Tavern. Didi and Gunter followed.

"I just need a little air," Didi said to Gunter as she wobbled out of the bar two hours later. She stopped at a lamp post and leaned against it, trying to steady herself. Closing her eyes, she wondered why she had allowed Karl to tell the waiter that he was her and Mari's guardian, allowing the girls to drink, since the legal drinking age at bars was sixteen when accompanied with a parent.

They're my daughters, she recalled Karl saying when the server looked at Didi with a quizzical eye. Not that the waiter believed him, but he didn't care enough to argue. After all, Nazi Germany had more important things on its mind than reprimanding a teenager for getting a little tipsy. As she braced herself against the post, she regretted playing along. *I just want to go home*, she thought. *Hopefully the buses are still running.*

"The night is still young, sweetie," cooed her date who had sneaked up behind her. His breath was hot against her neck, making her feel ill. "How about a little dancing into the night?"

"I can't," Didi mumbled, moving away. Her hand slid off the lamp post, causing her to stumble. "My aunt and uncle are probably worried that I'm not home yet," she said, holding her head in an attempt to stop the streetlights from swaying. "I don't feel well, and I just want to go home."

"What you are is drunk. Come on, we'll walk to my car, and I'll drive you home." Gunter grabbed Didi's arm to help her up.

"I have to take the bus," Didi said, slurring her words as she pulled away, not wanting to be alone with him. "I have to go." She stumbled away and hurried down the street, knowing that the bus stop was somewhere in that direction. She needed to go home, the place where she knew she was safe. She was even willing to face the inevitable yelling she would be receiving from Tante Lisi, who was a greater force than Onkel Otto when she was wound up. And at that moment, Didi would have given anything to be sitting at the kitchen table with Tante Lisi shouting into her ear, something along the lines of, "Men want one thing, and it's dangerous for you to be out this time of night. Nothing good happens after midnight!"

A taxi drove by, and Didi stopped at the curb and watched the taillights disappear into the night. Everything started to spin, and she closed her eyes. Funny how quickly that fun fuzzy feeling can turn into a bad headache and a knotted stomach. As she stood on the corner, an older couple walked by her, and they stopped talking, conveniently looking away as they passed.

Didi kept walking, but stopped when she came to the realization that the streets were no longer dotted with streetlights. She had no idea where the bus stop was, leaving her to wonder if she was walking in the wrong direction. The pain in her head was escalating, forcing her to stop beside a bench to steady herself. Suddenly her head exploded with heat, and her stomach tightened. She bent over and threw up, trying to avoid messing her clothes but failing.

"Poor little thing. You shouldn't be out here all alone."

This voice was new, and after she was done heaving, she wiped her mouth with the back of her hand and tried to stand but wobbled against the bench. As she attempted to walk away, the man yanked her down onto the bench and put his arm around her back and leaned in close, not caring that he was pressing against the vomit that had landed on her sweater.

"There, there, little *frau*. I'll take care of you," he hissed, placing his hand on her thigh and kissing her neck. The man reeked of sweat, and Didi wasn't sure if the smell of rotten alcohol was coming from him or herself. Either way, it made Didi want to throw up again, but she couldn't move under the weight of the man who had swung his leg over her lap so that he was now facing her. His hand moved under her skirt and up her thigh.

"Please stop!" Didi managed to say as she tried to push him off.

Suddenly the man flew off of her. "Get the fuck out of here!"

Didi closed her eyes and let out a deep breath, wondering what had happened.

"That's it, run, you fucking asshole!"

This new voice actually sounded familiar. Opening her eyes, she looked up to see the man from her earlier date, standing over her. In the distance, the sound of stumbling footsteps disappeared into the night. She couldn't remember his name but was glad to see him at that moment.

"I'm sorry that I let you wander off. These streets turn into a different animal at night." He bent down and gently helped Didi stand up.

Didi tried to gather her thoughts. "Thank you," she said, not knowing what else to say.

"I shouldn't have let you walk these streets alone. It's not safe this time of night."

"Where is . . ." But she stopped, not sure if she needed to throw up again. Suddenly, her head exploded with another wave of heat and she bent down and heaved onto the side of the street.

"That's OK," the man said. "If you can get this all out of your system before we get into my car, I will greatly appreciate it."

"I'm so sorry," Didi said, pulling her hair away from her face. "I'm a mess."

"Don't worry about it. Anyway, I think you were going to ask about your friend. I left them at the bar. Come on," he said, holding her steady as they started to walk. "I'll drive you home. I think you've had enough excitement for one night."

As they drove down the city streets, Didi thought about her aunt and uncle, glad that she had someone to go home to. As angry as they would be with her, she understood that it came from love, and for that, she was grateful. She also knew Mari's cousin would simply shake her head at the sound of the front door opening, and the stumbling of a lone figure trying to find the bathroom before collapsing in bed. Didi hoped that Mari wasn't ruining the one safe shelter she had from the realities of her rough difficult life.

Didi closed her eyes, relieved that the night was coming to a close. Except it was far from over.

— 25 —

September 12, 1970
Allegan, Michigan

Summer was still visible in the rearview mirror, but looking down the highway, I saw nothing but sweet autumn. As we rolled down M-89, we passed a blur of trees already accented with a hint of color. We grew up in a town where the harvest season was celebrated with festivities that brought families together for days and evenings full of blue-ribbon chickens, tractor pulls, cotton candy, and carnival rides that made your head spin and your stomach churn—country-fried heaven.

Slowly, the fields disappeared, replaced with hints of civilization—a car dealership, a Citgo gas station, and a bait-and-tackle shop. Passing a drive-in diner, a wooden sign greeted us with: WELCOME TO ALLEGAN.

"Hmm, I never saw it."

"Saw what?" Mickey asked me.

"The double Ferris wheel. Silvia told me it's so tall that if I look hard enough from the highway, I'll be able to—" I looked over at Silvia, who was stifling a giggle. "I hate you," I said.

As we turned onto the street leading into the fairgrounds, we were met suddenly with bumper to bumper traffic.

"Man, it's going to be dark before we even get there!"

"Oh, I think we'll be OK," our father said, lowering his window and relighting his pipe.

Our mother lowered her visor to check her hair, adding, "It appears the entire population of Allegan decided to go to the fair tonight."

"And lucky us, tonight is the Three Stooges," Hanna added, only somewhat under her breath as she picked a strand of hair off her sweater.

"Bam! Eight o'clock is never going to get here!" I whined.

"Careful, about wishing the evening away," our father laughed. "It'll be Three Stooges time before you know it."

I continued fidgeting in my seat as we drove by a yard where an older man sat in a lawn chair. Lemonade in hand, he appeared to be sleeping, letting his best prospects roll on by. Leaning against his chair was a homemade sign reading: PARKING $3. As we continued down the road, the parking fee reached as high as $5, with some industrious folks being more proactive than others, enticing us with a wave of a stick and shouts of, "Four dollars for premium parking!" I marveled at their ingenuity in profiting from this marvelous event, and applauded them for their luck of living a deep breath away from barn animals and elephant ears.

Finally, it appeared in front of us, like Oz popping out from the endless field of poppies—that majestic entrance that stood over two stories tall, with white and yellow blinking lights that framed a mural of a white stallion and a magician motioning to us with his cane. And in case we didn't already know what the fair was all about, the entrance also featured a humungous picture of a boy and girl devouring cotton candy. It was the Allegan County Fair and I was about to be one with it.

With the car finally parked, I crawled over Mickey and flung the door open, hitting the spongy ground with both feet. I could only imagine that this king-size mud-fest had been a meadow of green and golden grass just three days earlier, before the onslaught of fair-goers and a full day of rain.

"Don't step in the mud puddles," our mother called out. "Grab your jackets and don't take off yet."

I knew she was as excited as the rest of us. Going to the Allegan County Fair was an annual pilgrimage for most everyone from our little town, where the closest thing to a carnival midway was the dunk tank and hay wagon rides at the Alamo Ice Cream Social held behind the volunteer fire department each summer. Allowing the others to catch up, I stopped halfway up the hill and looked up to see the magnificent double Ferris wheel. Closing my eyes, I inhaled, taking in the smells of cow manure, tractor fumes, and fried everything, and I made a mental note to carry this moment in my pocket until the same time next fall.

With the others moving slower than a tractor stuck in mud, I gave up waiting and scrambled up the hill. Slowly, the earth firmed up under my feet as I reached higher ground. My mind was already jumbling with all of the lights, noises, and smells coming at me from every direction—music blaring through cheap speakers on the Twister, kids yelling from the Skydiver as it turned them upside down, and carnival hucksters coaxing teenagers to step closer, with promises of, "A prize every time!"

Over at the grandstand, workers were already setting up folding chairs for the evening with the Three Stooges. I could hardly believe that little ol' me, a nine-year-old from Alamo, Michigan, would be spending the evening with Larry, Moe, and Curly—a trio whose mere mention unfortunately could draw only groans from Hanna, but to me, they were the royalty of comedy. The thought of seeing TV stars *live* was simply unfathomable. On an occasional Saturday afternoon, I would flip through the channels and land on one of their movies or TV shows. In shear slapstick fashion, Mickey shared my appreciation of the talented trio, and taught me the Curly Joe move of flicking his fingers under his chin and a, "Eh, wise guy!"

While I may have been ready to grab our seats at that moment, I remembered my father's words. This was the time for rabbits, french fries, and the Himalaya. As the others finally managed to make their way up the hill, I ran ahead into the 4-H agricultural area and disappeared into the sheep/pig barn.

I wasted little time with the pigs since grown swine look less like Charlotte's Web's "some pig" and more like livestock wearing a dry coating of mud. No Wilburs here, so I moved on and leaned over another pen to stick my hand into the wool of a sheep too busy eating to concern herself with my presence. The wool was so thick and coarse that my fingers didn't even touch her skin, and I wondered if she was even aware that I was petting her. The wool against my fingers felt gritty, making me cringe with the thought of pulling a wool mitten off my hand with my teeth. Two recently sheered sheep were in the next pen, and I marveled at how they looked like completely different animals—skinny little things in need of a wool sweater of their own. I reached in to pet the lamb leaning against the railing, and I was rewarded with a clean cottony feel.

"Be careful," my mother said, from behind me. "Don't let him nibble on your jacket sleeve." I giggled and moved on. There were more animals . . .

"Let's make sure one of these don't follow you home," our father said to Hanna, with a lightness in his voice as we entered the horse barns. After Hanna proceeded to pet every single one, we finally made our way to the barn that I saved for last, the one marked: CHICKENS/RABBITS.

Forcing cuddly rabbits to room with chickens seemed barbaric to me. I held my nose as I walked through the rows of hens and roosters, but the strong odor slipped through my sealed nostrils, making my eyes water. With hardly a hello to the many colorful birds pecking at the chicken wire, I screeched to a halt in front of a cage containing two little rabbits carrying a striking resemblance to Siamese cats. The tag on the cage labeled them as Himalayan rabbits, and as I stuck my fingers through the cage, I was treated to bunnies that were happy for the attention or perhaps too lazy to move away from my touch.

It was still light out as we walked out of the last barn. "Cool your jets," my mother said, grabbing the back of my Barracuda before I could get rolling on all cylinders. "Let's walk the fairgrounds first so we can decide what we want to do next."

While I operated at two speeds, run and stop, my parents had a way of reminding us to take it all in. The two of them walked arm in arm, laughing and smiling as our excitement grew with the anticipation of fresh, deep-fried donuts and elephant ears. My mother seemed calm that evening, perhaps realizing that with the constant buzz of excitement and stimulation everywhere, people were too distracted to be looking at her, so she relaxed and blended in seamlessly with the crowds.

"What do you all say we get something to eat?" our mother announced to the group as we approached a food booth with a flashing marquee that read: FRIES & LEMONADE.

Of course, she was met with cheers from all of us, and our father stepped up to the window with, "Three please."

We continued on, momentarily content with our paper cups brimming with steaming-hot fries, drizzled with malt vinegar and ketchup. Hidden between the food vendors and the arcade strip stood the fun house, teasing me with spinning floors and a chaos of mirrors that reflected bold streaks of lights onto the exhibit across from us. "We'll get to fun stuff," my father promised, seeing my look of eagerness. "Let's finish eating first."

I was so busy shoving a vinegar-soaked fry into my mouth, that at first, I didn't notice the next exhibit. The faded red, blue, and yellow paint on the façade was peeling and more than a few lights needed replacing, but all of that could be forgiven, for all I saw were the boasting words plastered across the top that read: WORLD'S FATTEST MAN 25¢. Several curious onlookers were standing on the platform, peering through a large picture window. *How cool it would be to say you saw the fattest man in the world.* I turned to my father with pleading eyes, drawing a chuckle from him as he reached into his pocket and handed me a quarter. I grabbed it before our mother could warn him that we were wasting money and ran up to a woman who snatched it from me while she chatted with another carny.

Sprinting up the steps, I took my place in line behind a group of four adults. No one spoke, reminding me of the line that formed at the viewing of my aunt's funeral. *Is the fat man even alive?* I thought. *Good lord, what if he's dead?* Finally, the grownups moved along, allowing me to step forward. With great anticipation, I peered into the large picture window, and what I saw in front of me I knew I would never forget.

He was lying on a platform. I say lying because I wasn't sure if he was sitting since there was so much of him. He was naked except for a small towel placed where his privates were hidden. The small towel wasn't really necessary because there were layers of skin hiding any areas that I shouldn't have seen, and it was only there as a respect for modesty. There was so much of him that I was unable to figure out where parts started and ended. The World's Fattest Man didn't look back at us and instead read his *National Enquirer*. The photo on the front page featured a bloated man in terrible shape, a Kennedy, I thought. A plate of cookies and a crowd-pleaser of Coke sat beside him, and he reached for a cookie, devouring it whole. The couple standing alongside me left, leaving me alone on the platform, still fixated on the rolls of fat, each one cascading onto the next, with the belly-rolls flowing into rolls that I could only guess was part of his hip, or thigh—I wasn't sure. Did he ever wear clothes? It was an honest question, since I was pretty sure he was unable to find appropriate attire at Sears or J. C. Penney. And was he able to walk to the bathroom? Even if he could, I assumed that a regular toilet couldn't support his weight. When he was ten, did he ever in his wildest dreams think that this is where he would one day wind up? Being stared at by strangers, one quarter at a time.

As he absentmindedly grabbed another cookie, I wondered why he had resigned himself to being the World's Fattest Man. Did he have a mother who was too wrapped up in her own drama to notice he just finished a package of Oreos in one sitting? Or was his mother hiding in her bedroom as he put on a stained shirt because it was the only one that still fit?

He glanced up and smiled at me, making me realize that I hadn't been staring at a TV screen, but rather a human being. And suddenly I felt ashamed for how I had dehumanized him into a caricature. Which got me to thinking, *Does my mother feel this way when she believes people are staring at her? Does she feel naked and alone?* I smiled back at the man and waved goodbye before joining back up with my family.

As we entered the arcade area, I was smacked with a flurry of flashing lights, stuffed animals in a rainbow of colors, and signs that promised: A WINNER EVERY TIME! From where I stood, it certainly looked simple enough. Just shoot a basketball through the hoop or into the straw basket, toss a ring around the neck of a Coke bottle, or pop a balloon. But I learned moments ago that "a winner every time" didn't necessarily mean the giant Pink Panther hanging overhead. After plucking a yellow rubber duck from a flock swimming around a pool of water, I turned it over to see a #4 imprinted on its belly. Seeing no adults standing behind me, the teenager behind the counter picked up a box marked with a #2 and handed me a plastic whistle.

"There it is!" Silvia said with excitement. The Mouse Game!

This peculiar arcade game was similar to the Color Game, where people place quarters on one of many different colored boxes located around the perimeter of the game. A ball is thrown into the center, which then bounces around before landing on one specific color. But the Mouse Game was unique in that it involved an actual live mouse that was placed into a metal box by the carny who would gently shake it like a pair of dice before opening the box again, causing the mouse to fall onto the center of the spinning wheel, where he would gather his thoughts before running into one of the many holes, each one labeled with a corresponding number. Not how I would want to spend my evening, making me wonder how many mice held the job each day, and how long it would take for their hostile living conditions to eventually warrant the shutting down of this archaic arcade game.

With our bets placed, the mouse was once again dropped onto the center of the spinning wheel, where he quickly disappeared into another hole. "Number 13," the carny called out with all the enthusiasm of a fat house cat being taught to fetch.

No problem, I thought, as the carny handed the winning patron his prize—a large stuffed animal resembling Sylvester the Cat. No plastic whistles hiding in a box at this game. With a quarter in my hand, I circled the counter until I come up on the square marked with the number five. Placing my coin down, I called out, "Come on mouse! Number five, Mr. Mouse! Lucky number, number five!" I had good reason for going with this number. I was born in 1961, and six minus one is five. My birthday month is May, the fifth month, and my birthday is the twenty-third. You do the math.

"Number twenty-three!" the woman called out as she walked around the counter, scooping the random quarters into her palm. No winners.

My father tossed another quarter my way, and I placed it on the five square again, thinking that twenty-three could have been my number but I'm not switching—

"Number twelve!" the woman announced, and I looked over to my right to see that our mother had the winning number and was clapping with celebration.

"It's all yours, honey," she shouted over to me. "Pick out your favorite!"

"The rabbit, please," I said to the woman, who grabbed a hook and plucked the orange rabbit shaped like Bugs Bunny.

Only at a county fair can you pet a bunny in the barns one minute and win an orange Bugs Bunny the next. From the huckster pushing people to let him guess their age for only two dollars, to church people pushing religious pamphlets into the hands of anyone walking by while trying to save them from their sins, it could all be found in this one magical place. Squeezing my furry rabbit, I felt the crinkling of the newspaper stuffing.

"I think we need to head over to the grandstand," our father announced, looking at his watch. "We've got a show to catch."

"Check. Check, check, check," the stagehand spoke into the microphone, looking out into the audience to some invisible source who apparently wasn't happy with the sound level. "Check, Mary had a little lamb. Check, check." As we made our way through the rows of folding chairs on the dirt track, many other families also scrambled for the best view of the stage. Settling into our seats, three rows from the very back, I strained my neck, watching as more stagehands adjusted lights before setting the stage with three bar stools and a matching number of microphone stands. *Oh man, this is going to be good!*

In answer to the setting sun, the lights turned on, illuminating the fairgrounds, and building the anticipation of the crowd. Finally, another stagehand walked to the center of the stage and tapped the microphone before leaning into it and saying, "Are you all ready for a little fun tonight?" He was answered with thunderous applause and cheers, and I stood up on my chair, trying to see who it was everyone was cheering for. As the Three Stooges were introduced, they entered the stage, bringing everyone to their feet and leaving me with the view of a million backsides. The three stars turned on the hilarity as everyone around me laughed at the hijinks exploding on stage. Meanwhile, I watched children, one after the other, leave their seats to run up to the area directly in front of the stage. My father must have noticed them as well because when I turned to look at him, he was smiling at me and nodding his head. Not wasting a second, I jumped from my seat and ran down the aisle to join the multitude of other children who were already enjoying the show from the front row.

And there they were, so close that I could see the stain on Moe's suit jacket and a previously lit cigar sticking out of Larry's pocket. In an attempt to get the best view possible, I climbed up onto the snow fence that separated us from the stage and hung on, mesmerized as I witnessed the Stooges' comic genius blasting before my eyes. Two short hours later, the trio waved goodnight. As the crowd cheered, I ran back to my family to share the incredible news that happened to me while I was watching the Three Stooges up close and personal.

"He talked to me! Larry talked to me!" I shouted to my family.

"Really?" my father replied, surprised that one of them had actually spoken directly with his youngest. "And what did he say?"

"'Get off the fence!'"

For some reason my father couldn't stop laughing, and I laughed with him because this just might have been the coolest night of my life.

With the exhilaration of the show behind us, we headed back to the midway where the lights were shining bright, and the feel of the fairgrounds shifted from families with little kids to teens and adults. The volume of everything increased, and I suddenly felt like I was crashing a private party.

'Hey!" I called out to Jenny who was standing in line for the Ferris wheel with her parents and another girl I recognized from school.

Her friend was popular and had her hair curled in spirals, a byproduct of being friends with a girl whose mom also happens to be the town's beautician. I thought she saw me, but she looked away. "Hey, Jenny! I called out again, waving. Finally, Jenny looked my way, and then appeared to say something to her friend, who looked at me and then over to where our mother was standing with our father. He was lighting a cigarette for our mother who had decided that this was the place to bring out her black rhinestone cigarette holder, which stuck out as much as lederhosen on the Fourth of July.

The two girls giggled before turning away and stepping onto the ride platform. I continued watching them as a middle-aged man in overalls slammed the bar over their laps before tugging at it to make sure it locked. I watched, wondering what it would be like to have someone to talk and laugh with—someone not a brother or sister.

"Why do they both look like Cindy Brady?" Silvia asked, giving me a playful nudge. "Seriously, if you're going to emulate a Brady girl, at least pick Marcia."

"All right, kids," our father said, gathering us all together. "It's been a long night for you all, and it's time for your mother and me to have a little adult time." I turned back as our mother blew a puff of smoke high into the air, making fumes dance with the flickering lights of the midway. "Hanna will be taking you to the car," he continued. "You had a *lot* of fun today, and I need you all to behave while your mother and I attend a show."

"We won't be long!" our mother added, grabbing our father's hand and pulling him down the lane toward the large red-and-white striped tent marked with a big sign that read: ADULTS ONLY. ABSOLUTELY NO ONE UNDER 18 ALLOWED. At the entrance, they were greeted by a woman sitting on a barstool. While our father brought out his wallet, they chatted as the woman kept patting her large Dolly Parton wig, or what I assumed was a wig, since it had a habit of tipping to one side. I stared at the colorful woman, captivated by the many rhinestones on her light blue dance costume accented with shiny pantyhose and high heels. Our father handed money to the woman while our mother said something to her that made them all laugh. A burly man then appeared and opened a second tent flap, causing Silvia, Mickey, and me to lean left, trying to see past our parents, but all I saw were bright lights as the music within grew louder and the tent devoured our parents.

"Come on," Hanna said, yanking me along. "We're not supposed to be here. Where are you guys going?" she called out to Mickey and Silvia who seemed hell-bent on catching a peep—searching the old tent for a hole, any hole. Just as Hanna and I followed them around to the back, another man appeared out of the darkness and shouted, "You kids! Get away, scat!"

Hanna shrieked and herded us away as we giggled and teased her for being afraid of an old man. I swung Bugs around while Hanna took my hand and led us down the hill to our car where I planned on falling asleep, to dream of french fries and friends to share secrets with.

— 26 —

1944

Eschbach, Baden-Württemberg, Germany

After saving her from a night that could have been far worse, her date drove her home without incident. He sped off the moment Didi stepped onto the front stoop, having no desire to being on the receiving end of Onkel Otto's temper, or far more frightening, Tante Lisi's. Didi couldn't argue with his logic. The house was dark except for the light on the front stoop and a lone light coming from within the living room.

Well, Didi thought as she turned the doorknob. *Time to face the music.* She found her uncle asleep on the sofa, and Tante Lisi knitting in her chair.

"I'm sorry—"

"First, are you all right?" Tante Lisi asked as she set her knitting down. She got up from her chair and started toward Didi.

"Ah, yes, but—"

"Do you know what time it is, and how crazy with worry I've been? And I smell alcohol on you. How much have you had to drink? I was scared to death that you were in trouble! You had no right being out this late. In this house, you will act as a lady and be home at a reasonable hour, do you hear me?"

"I think the neighbors hear you," Onkel Otto said, getting up from his chair. "Didi, get to bed. We will discuss this in the morning."

"Yes sir," she replied, relieved to be excused.

As Didi crawled into bed, she thought about the night of drinking and the vague memory of being attacked by a man, only to be rescued by her so-called date. She sat up in bed, suddenly aware of the grumblings in her stomach and the rush of heat rising up her throat. She hurried for the water closet, guessing that it was going to be a long night. Still, she was glad to be home.

It had been over a week since that dreadful night, and while it was strange that Didi hadn't heard from Mari, she was actually relieved that Mari hadn't called those first few days. She could only imagine the choice words Tante Lisi would have shared with her wayward friend if she happened to answer the phone. Tante Lisi didn't care for Mari, calling her "trouble in the making," and frankly, Didi was angry at Mari herself—angry that Mari didn't seem to care that she thoughtlessly threw the two of them into danger by going out with older men they had just met. But most of all, Didi was angry at Mari for her reckless abandon. *You matter*, Didi had said more than once to her friend. *You are not broken so stop acting like you are.*

"*Hello?*"

"Hello, Mrs. Weber? This is Didi. May I speak to Mari?" Silence followed on the other end of the line, making Didi repeat, "Hello?"

Didi thought back about that night and how she left Mari at the bar. She felt guilty about deserting her friend, but she knew that if she hadn't left when she did, things would have gotten out of hand. She recalled Mari's date's insistence on refilling her glass several times, causing her thoughts and vision to blur as the evening progressed, and vaguely, her only other memory was Mari lifting her date's arm from her shoulders, and his insistence on putting it back.

"Are you Mari's friend?" the woman asked, on the other end of the phone.

"Yes, ma'am. I'm Didi." She didn't like this question. Not because she didn't appreciate this woman being concerned for Mari's well-being, but because, as Mari's older cousin, Mrs. Weber took Mari in rather reluctantly after her release from the orphanage. Other than providing a bed and meals, Mrs. Weber didn't involve herself with Mari's affairs.

But something in Mrs. Weber's voice on that phone call gave Didi pause. Silence continued on the other end, and Didi let it play out this time. Finally, the woman spoke.

"Didi, I'm very sorry to tell you this, but Mari died last weekend. She was attacked. The waiter at the bar told us that she had been on a date, and the man took her outside, had his way with her . . ."

She stopped talking, and Didi could tell the woman was searching for words, but it was difficult for Didi to concentrate on what the woman said next. She must be mistaken. *Mari is fine,* Didi told herself. They were together just two weeks ago.

"She apparently tried to fight him off, but the monster just killed her." The woman continued talking. Something about a funeral that had just taken place the day before, but Didi couldn't hear anything anymore.

Didi set the receiver down, took a couple of steps, and broke.

— 27 —

October 5, 1970
Alamo, Michigan

"Hey kiddo," Mickey said without looking up. He was sitting on the sofa, with his long legs sprawled across the coffee table. An open shoebox sat next to him, and he pulled out a narrow sheet of paper.

"This week's Hit Parade?" I asked, taking a seat next to him. I was quite familiar with those sheets of paper. Along with listing the top one-hundred songs, the Billboard Hit Parade also showed where each song stood the previous week, so you could see which songs were climbing their way to number one and the unfortunate songs doing a freefall down the charts. Collecting those colorful pieces of paper was more than a hobby for Mickey—they were his lifeblood. Any time he found Hit Parade sheets in a store, he would swipe the whole stack. Why anyone needed twenty sheets of paper listing "I'll Be There," by the Jackson Five in the top spot was lost on me, but this bit of logic didn't stop Mickey from hoarding those sheets.

I slid the box over and put my feet on the sofa. "August 10, 1968."

"'Hello, I Love You,' by the Doors," he quickly answered.

"Top three, February 8, 1969?"

"Give me a second. OK, third, "Worst that Could Happen," by Brooklyn Bridge. Second, 'Everyday People,' by Sly and the Family Stone."

"And number one?"

"'Crimson and Clover'—"

"By Tommy James and the Shondells," we said together.

"That's a cool song," I said, grabbing the Hit Parade sheet from him. "So, how do I know you're not tricking me by just throwing random songs at me?"

"You know I'm right," he replied. "I know it may seem stupid to everyone else, but someday these are going to be worth a lot of money."

While I wasn't sure about his prediction of riches, he had built an empire of shoeboxes, every one of them stuffed with Billboard Hit Parade sheets.

"Maybe I should start collecting them, too."

"You can look at these any time you want, but only if I'm around." His voice got animated as he added, "And you can always help me build on this collection. Remember, I can never have too many. I'm up to twenty boxes so far. And they go all the way back to July of 1967."

"November 1, 1967."

"'To Sir with Love,' by Lulu."

"'Those schoolgirl days of telling tales and biting nails are gone,'" I started singing.

"'But in my mind, I know they will still live on and on,'" we both sang. "'But how do you thank someone who has taken you from crayons to perfume? It isn't easy, but I'll try!'"

"I love that song," I said quietly.

"Me, too."

We sat in comfortable silence as Mickey continued studying his sheet. He then sighed, placed the sheet back into the box and leaned over the edge of the sofa to pick up something. He frowned as he handed me a 45 record, still in its green Warner Brothers sleeve. "I think Mutti did this. I dug it out of the garbage. I'm sorry."

It was my "Leaving on a Jet Plane" record by the folk group Peter,

Paul and Mary—a trio that produced some of their own songs, but also knew when to take advantage of songwriters like Bob Dylan, Pete Seeger, and a new up and coming hotshot named John Denver. I was able to appreciate the sweet harmony provided by this singing trio, but the one I idolized was Mary Travers, a woman capable of blending her rich voice with others without losing her self-identity. Not only was "Leaving on a Jet Plane" my favorite song, it was my only record.

Not knowing why Mickey was handing it to me, I pulled the record out of its sleeve, to discover that it was broken in half—completely snapped in two and held together only by the green paper label in the center. As I held the broken record in my hands, I looked back up at Mickey, simply not understanding what had happened to my record, and I did what any 9-year-old would do in that situation.

"Oh, don't cry," Mickey said, squeezing my arm. "I'm sorry. Mutti said something about it being a Commie song. I think it's because it makes her think of World War II. You see, Peter, Paul and Mary sing a lot of anti-war songs, so Mutti probably views them as standing up for protesting peace-loving hippies."

Tears rolled down my cheeks as I sank lower in the sofa.

"I'm really sorry." He put his arm around my shoulder as I brought my shirt up to wipe the tears off my cheek.

I had no idea that this song was interpreted by many as being unpatriotic and sympathetic to Vietnam draft dodgers. All I knew was that it was a beautiful song, and I wasn't going to leave my musical trio in the middle of this battle with our mother. With a final sniff, I marched into the kitchen and returned with Scotch tape. Taping up the B side, I sacrificed "House Song," to save that record. It was illogical to tape a record back together and expect it to play, but a mile of tape and one plastic yellow insert later, I quietly slipped into the dining room, and opened the lid of the record player.

"You know it'll never play," Mickey whispered, unable to resist witnessing my musical experiment.

With the volume set on *Low*, I placed the needle on the edge of the record and watched as the record spun and crackled. And then it happened. Ever so quietly, Mary Travers sang to me, "All my bags are packed, I'm ready to go." And with the end of the song, I slipped my non-skipping record back into its sleeve, feeling like a bit of an activist myself.

As I followed Mickey into the kitchen, we heard it—the quiet methodical stepping of someone on the stairs. It was mid-afternoon and probably a good time to go play outside because if our mother was—

"Did I hear the record player?"

I turned around to find our mother standing in the kitchen doorway. I knew there was no good answer to her question.

"Yeah," Mickey answered quickly. "I played one of my records. I put the lid down and made sure I turned it off."

I should have jumped in to admit that I was the one who touched the record player. But I didn't.

"Sit down, Mickey,"

Mickey took a seat at the picnic table, his eye twitching as he watched our mother dig through the kitchen drawer. She smiled, apparently having found what she was looking for, and pulled out the butcher knife—presenting it like a new necklace she just purchased at Gilmore's Department Store. She gazed lovingly at the knife for a few moments before gliding over toward my brother, moving to the beat of a dramatic soundtrack that only she could hear.

Stopping in front of my brother, she leaned forward and put her mouth next to Mickey's ear. "I'm here to help you," she whispered. "I'm going to dig that nervous twitch out of your eye, fixing you once and for all. Do you hear me?"

She was right about Mickey being nervous, and no doubt, she had just managed to pump up the volume on that involuntary twitch two more levels. Mickey looked over to our father, who seemed preoccupied with the day's crossword puzzle, probably wishing that his children could just take it from their mother without talking back and stirring her up. Our father closed the dictionary and picked up his pencil to write down a word. Meanwhile, I stood over the heating vent, trying to be as still as the air.

At that moment, Mickey was likely regretting making that sixteen-mile bike ride to the Plainwell Sanitarium to deliver a bouquet of wildflowers to our mother—beautiful Indian paintbrushes, black-eyed Susans, and daisies. Leaving them at the front desk, he was leery they would actually reach our mother. Turned out, she actually did receive them, and for the next few days after returning home, Mickey was her favorite.

But it didn't last long. It never lasted long.

"For god's sake, Mickey, stop jerking around and sit still," our father warned, apparently having just noticed what was going on three feet from him. Our mother twirled the knife in her hand so that the blade caught the reflection of the afternoon sun streaming in through the kitchen window and the light splashed across her dark eyes. Closing his dictionary, our father looked over to our mother, apparently sizing up the situation. "Sit still" seemed like a weird request in this instance. "Run!" seemed like better advice to give a kid whose mother was coming at him with a butcher knife.

I could hear my heart beating, praying it couldn't be heard from across the room. Perhaps aware of her audience, she brought her face to within inches from Mickey's and slowly raised the knife, and, with the tip of the blade, she gently touched his eye.

Mickey jumped back with a sudden jerk, and before I could yell, "Run, Mickey!" he was up and out the front door. And because I had no desire to see if our mother would look at me for her next form of entertainment, I followed him out the door and down the front steps, where we both stopped to catch our breath while we waited for the door to open again. But the door remained shut. Mickey's eyes darted, scanning his surroundings before he finally exhaled. Hanna and Silvia were by the barn, playing with the bow and arrows. I relaxed, feeling good about being in the sunshine, but I could see that Mickey was still shaking, like the afternoon breeze was blowing right through him.

"Mickey, what did Mutti mean when she said she was going to 'fix you'? What does she think is wrong with you?"

"I don't know," he answered as he looked back toward the front door. "Maybe she can't stand the fact that I don't fit the mold she put me in. People don't like it when you don't fit neatly into the category God assigned to you."

"What?"

He twitched, a shudder that started at his neck and made his shoulders shake. Finally looking at me, he added, "You're too young. Let's forget about Mutti for a while."

It was unusually warm for October—a jeans and sweatshirt kind of day. Most people will say that summer is their favorite season, but I'll take a brisk sunny autumn afternoon any day of the year. The only downside to fall was the occasional arrow that insisted on burying itself in a burst of red, yellow, and orange leaves that had taken over the yard.

Picking up another arrow, Hanna loaded, aimed, and nearly hit the bullseye on our makeshift target leaning against the locust tree. The target was quite ingenious really. Arrows would pierce through the front of the cardboard box only to be caught by the back side. My job was to chase down the arrows that missed their mark. It was the price I paid for getting to shoot Hanna's arrows on occasion and a chore I would have found more enjoyable without the added challenge of Doxy running along beside me, biting my ankles. Damn dog.

Picking up a fallen arrow, I ran my fingers across the vivid pink and yellow feathers on the end of the shaft. As I returned with the arrow, Hanna handed the bow to Mickey, and he stepped up as though he was ready to shoot at the target, but instead, he aimed straight up into the sky, and pulled the string back.

"Run!" he shouted before shooting off the arrow. This was our cue to run for our lives. Taking off, I tripped on something round, catapulting me forward and sending me, face first, onto the grass. Damn walnuts.

While Bow and Arrow Dodgeball probably wasn't our most brilliant idea, it killed time on a lazy afternoon.

"You are such a jackass," Hanna called out to Mickey as she tried to catch her breath.

As the rest of us laughed, I forgot about what had taken place inside the house a short time earlier, so I was surprised to see our mother bursting through the front door, almost knocking Silvia down with her suitcase as she made her way down the sidewalk. I couldn't tell you where that arrow landed because I stopped to watch our mother.

"Mutti, where are you going?" I called out, but she walked by us without even a glance. I expected our father to come out of the house next, but the door remained shut.

Our mother had few friends, and none that I could think of that she could get to by foot, so her options were rather limited. With suitcase in-hand, our mother walked down the street at the pace of someone rushing to an important meeting, and, like a windup toy, she kept going until we lost sight of her.

It wasn't until the sun was close to setting behind the barn, that the front door opened again, and our father made his way to the car, deciding, perhaps, that he had given our mother time to calm down.

"All right you two, get in the car. It's time to get your mother." While I was disappointed at being singled out, I was thankful Silvia was coming along and grateful our father was leaving Mickey out of this.

Silvia jumped into the front passenger seat, and I crawled into the back, behind our father. "I need you two to be on the lookout," he said, rubbing the back of his neck, carefully avoiding the area where a long fresh scratch revealed itself.

As the sun set, our father turned on the headlights, and I stared out the window, wondering what I would do if I actually spotted our mother marching down the road. Would I say anything, or would I look away, pretending that I never saw her? After driving down every road in the area, our father reluctantly turned the car toward home, convinced that our mother must have found cover for the night somewhere.

Mickey was lying on the living room floor watching TV when we walked back into the house. As I swung the door open, he suddenly sat up straight, staring behind us, but as our father shut the door, Mickey exhaled and sat back down, leaning against the front of the sofa. I sat down cross-legged beside him, and together we watched Archie Bunker and Meathead argue about equal rights. Mickey laughed hard at something Archie said, and I laughed with him, relaxed, knowing that the knife drawer wouldn't be opening up again that night.

Three days had passed since our mother ran away from home. Rain had fallen steadily all day into the evening, and the sky had darkened, signaling a storm was coming our way. As Mickey and Silvia sat before the glow of the television, Hanna and I lounged on the sofa, lost within the pages of our books—Hanna engrossed in *Son of the Black Stallion* while I passed the time with *The Ghost of Dibble Hollow,* my latest must-read from the Scholastic flyer. I laid the book on my chest, thinking about what it would be like to be friends with a teenage ghost who actually led a sadder life than me. *The shenanigans we would get into would be endless!* "Who is that?" I asked, looking up, distracted by someone singing on the television.

"Peggy Lee," Mickey answered.

"God, she's awful," Hanna said, looking up from her book. "What's with the gown? Who the hell wears an evening gown while singing a Beatles tune? She looks like she should be performing at the Metropolitan Opera. She should be arrested for slaughtering that song."

"Oh, let it be!" Mickey replied, making Hanna and me groan in unison, and forcing Silvia to swat him with the *TV Guide*.

The phone in the kitchen started ringing, and Mickey turned down the volume as our father rose from his chair in the kitchen. Having a party line, our neighbor's single ring had gone off several times in the last few hours, but this was a double ring, telling us that the call was for us. He picked it up, and for the next two minutes simply listened to whoever was on the other end.

As Ed Sullivan walked onto the stage, I marveled at the dynamics of the two of them on the stage at once—Sullivan's stilted robotic movements mirroring Ms. Lee's wooden performance. Would their children turn out to be Pinocchio? I then turned my attention to our father for signs that it might be our mother on the other end of the phone. Things had been calm in the house, and I wasn't sure what the others were thinking, but I was hoping that it was anyone but her. But watching our father's movements as he hung on the line told me otherwise.

"What do you say, Topo Gigio?" Ed Sullivan asked the Mexican mouse puppet that signed off with him at the end of every episode. *"Eddie, Keesa me goo' night!"* Topo Gigio replied, sticking his cheek out.

"I'm on my way," our father said into the receiver. "Love you too, Spatzi."

And with that, we felt the stormfront rolling in.

— 28 —

1950

Eschbach, Baden-Württemberg, Germany

"I can't believe you thought that going shopping after work was a good idea. If I had known that we would be walking five miles, I would have left my heels at home."

"Oh, hush up," Didi said, laughing at Heidi as she waved at the headlights coming toward them. "If I recall, I wasn't the one who insisted that we go out for a soda to celebrate your purchases!" She laughed again and gave her friend a playful shove.

Didi worked with Heidi at the fabric store, passing the hours helping women pick out fabrics, patterns, and ribbons. As the two consulted and cut, Didi cautiously allowed a friendship to develop between them. Time had put distance between her and the fast-paced life with Mari, and Didi still pushed her memories down on a daily basis until getting through the day became almost bearable. Her friend Heidi had the same mass of beautiful hair that was a challenge to rein in, just as Mari had, but their similarities ended there. Heidi had a quiet demeanor and didn't feel the need to push the boundaries, constantly nudging along the imaginary line of what she couldn't or shouldn't be crossing.

"Hey," Didi said, pointing off into the distance. "Here comes a car. Put your leg out."

"I think it's stopping," Heidi called out as the car slowed.

The car pulled over onto the shoulder of the road, and the driver's window lowered, revealing a handsome man behind the wheel. "*Guten tag*, ladies!" he said with a smile. "May I escort you two lovely ladies to wherever it is you're going?"

"Ooh, an American soldier," Heidi whispered, giving Didi a nudge as the man, dressed in full uniform, climbed out and walked around the car to open the front passenger door. By the way he carried himself, Didi suspected that he knew exactly how he was coming across. Didi spent countless hours going through her *Spiegel* magazines, daydreaming of riding in an American convertible. As she stocked rolls of fabrics in the store, she envisioned herself draped in velvet and on the arm of an American soldier.

And there he stood, his wire-rimmed glasses framing his green eyes, and Didi couldn't help but notice the sun hitting the star medallions neatly fastened on the epaulettes of his starched shirt. His matching brown tie and pressed slacks finished the picture of a man who carried all the swagger of Cary Grant.

"And I do believe he's looking at you," Heidi added, grabbing Didi's hand, and pushing her ahead so that Didi would be sitting between them on the front bench seat.

The soldier shut the passenger door and jumped back behind the steering wheel. As they started down the road, he extended his hand. "Ladies, allow me to introduce myself. My name is Lawrence Merle Phillips, but my friends call me Larry."

"Nice to meet you, Merle," Didi said, teasing.

Didi, at age 23, fell hard for this American soldier who was nearly twice her age. Coming of age in postwar Germany was far from ideal, but this vivacious and headstrong *fräulein* had no problem catching the eye of this dashing soldier, and she set out to capture his heart as well. They soon pulled into Didi's driveway, and Merle jumped out of the car, holding the door open for the young ladies. With Didi's phone number in hand, the American soldier bid them both a good evening, leaving Didi dizzy with excitement. However, convincing Tante Lisi that this significantly older American soldier had nothing but honest intentions when it came to her niece would be quite another thing.

"So, tell me how you plan to explain to your Tante Lisi that you have a date this Friday with an American soldier who is twice your age?" Heidi asked as she and Didi watched the car disappear down the road.

"She has no problem with American soldiers. Well, nothing other than the fact that she might have a little issue with her beautiful innocent niece following one across the ocean, but his age won't matter once she meets him."

"Innocent, my *arsch*," Heidi said, slapping Didi's bottom. "Already writing the end of this romance novel, are we? At least it's a happy ending for you, but what am I going to do at the store without my friend?"

"We're just going to have to find an American soldier for you. Maybe Merle has a friend," Didi smiled, giving her friend a strong hug. "Don't worry. I'm not leaving you."

Friday soon arrived, and Didi paced the living room, waiting for the clock to strike seven. Finally, as the big hand clicked on the twelve, the small door on the face of the clock opened, revealing a tiny man in a traditional felt hat. The little man came out and circled on a track, striking at the air with his mallet once for every hour, a bell chiming with each swing. Just as he took his sixth swing, he was interrupted with a series of sharp knocks on the door.

"Can you get the door?" Didi yelled as she raced up the stairs. "Tell him I'll be down in a minute."

"Well, give him points for punctuality," Onkel Otto laughed, getting up from his chair.

"Hmph," Tante Lisi snorted, not bothering to look up from the sink as she rinsed a bowl. "Just means he's in a hurry to get the date going." She placed the wet bowl onto the drying rack. "Lord, I don't know what's gotten into that girl—bringing strange men she meets on the street into our house. Next thing you know, she'll be bringing home a whole army unit." She wiped her hands on her apron and stepped into the living room to get a look at this American soldier who had caught the attention of her niece.

"*Guten tag*," Merle said as Didi's uncle opened the door.

"Come, come in!" As Merle stepped through the door, Onkel Otto leaned out the doorway and peered down the street, hoping that at least one of his nosy neighbors noticed the handsome American solder pulling into their driveway and walking into their house. It wasn't every day that they entertained a man in uniform, especially the right uniform. "Didi will be down shortly. Probably fixing her hair. Please sit down," he said, gesturing toward the sofa. "Can I get you a glass of water?" He rolled his eyes and corrected himself. "What am I saying? You're a grownup. Would you like a beer?"

"I'm fine right now. Pleasure to meet you, sir," Merle answered, extending his hand out to Didi's uncle. "Didi tells me you're responsible for keeping her on the straight and narrow. It is an honor to meet you."

"I don't know what 'straight and narrow' means, but if it means Didi praised her aunt and me for keeping her from setting the world on fire, I'll accept her compliment," Onkel Otto replied with a huge grin. "Oh! And this is my beautiful wife, Lisi, the one who really keeps Didi 'narrow,' as you say."

"For goodness sake," Tante Lisi said, pushing her husband aside, and realizing that her niece was bending the truth when she said this soldier was "just a few years older." "Give the man some breathing room. What beautiful flowers," she said, spotting the bouquet of flowers in Merle's hands. "Didi will love those."

"Oh these? These are for you," Merle replied, holding the flowers out to Tante Lisi. "But I'm afraid that they cannot begin to match your beauty."

"For, for me?" Tante Lisi stammered, caught off guard by the young man's politeness, but remembering all too well her niece's previous suitors—a parade of young ruffians who grunted their greetings and stared at their watches, praying for her niece to hurry up, to spare them the torture of having to wait in the living room with two old people. "Please, make yourself at home while I find a vase. Otto, for god's sake, get the man a beer."

"Really, water will be fine," Merle smiled, unbuttoning his jacket, and sitting down. "You have a beautiful home." He picked up the quilt that was draped across the back of the sofa and made note of the patches of material in the basket. "Don't tell me this is your gorgeous handiwork?"

Tante Lisi let out a small laugh. "Oh my, yes. I made that old thing ages ago. Let me show you the latest project I'm working on. It's a quilt for Didi," she said, ignoring the surprised comical look directed at her from her husband who had been promised the quilt until that very moment.

"It's beautiful," Merle whispered, holding the soft fabric and delicate stitching between his fingers. Turning it over in his hands, he saw the intricate patches of vibrant colors depicting a variety of flowers and butterflies.

"Well, hello there!"

Merle looked up to see Didi standing at the top of the staircase, while she gazed back at him, admiring how her date managed to win over Tante Lisi at such lightning speed. She was relieved that he looked younger than he did when they met on the side of the road. Maybe it was the clean-shaven face, a change from the rugged stubble he was sporting that day. Or maybe it was the way he was sitting with such straight posture, a sign of respect for her aunt and uncle. His hair was exactly as she remembered, standing straight up and cut short against the scalp. And those green eyes seemed to cut right through her as if he knew her stories and heartbreak.

Smiling, he stood up and walked over to her as she descended the stairs, taking her hand in his. "*Guten* evening, *fräulein*. You look absolutely lovely tonight." As she giggled, he turned back to Didi's uncle. "With your permission, sir, I will be taking your niece out to a show and a bite to eat. I will have her home before midnight."

Tante Lisi waved him off. "You two just have a good time!" She then took hold of her niece's hand and whispered, "You have fun, Didi, but be a good girl. Remember what happened to your friend Mari. Just be careful. And know that you can always find a telephone and call us."

"Yes, ma'am." Without thinking, Didi reached for a curl that had freed itself and dangled in front of her aunt's eyes. The gray seemed to be winning its battle against Tante Lisi's once-dark hair, which was usually up in a bun but now was gently pulled back in a ponytail. She gave Tante Lisi a long hug. "I love you."

"Go on now. You don't want to miss the movie."

"Good night, Onkel Otto," Didi said, grabbing a sweater from the porch hook. Picking up her handbag, Didi looked at the money that Tante Lisi had discreetly tucked into her palm. Smiling as she placed the money into her handbag, she walked through the front door her American soldier held open for her.

Her American soldier.

"Before midnight, just as I promised," Merle said to Didi as he walked her up to the front door. While she was animated and talkative in the car, she was suddenly quiet and nervous about how the date would end. He must have sensed her nervousness, for he leaned in close to her and started to sing an American tune that she was quite familiar with, only, he sang it in German.

"*Du bist mein Ubahn, mein einziger Ubahn. Du macht mich glücklich, wenn der Himmel grau ist!*"

At this, she started laughing, unable to stop.

"Well," Merle said, looking quizzical. "I practiced and practiced that song to impress you. What, pray tell, do you find so humorous?"

Finally, she managed to get it out, "I know you think you're singing, 'You Are My Sunshine,' but you're actually singing, 'You Are My Subway.'"

This got Merle laughing. "My dear, with all my heart, I can honestly say that you are my subway." He then took her hands in his and kissed her ever so lightly on the lips.

— 29 —

October 10, 1970

Alamo, Michigan

"I'll drop them off," I offered, overhearing the conversation my father was having with my mother over the telephone. "I can ride my bike. It's not very far, and I'm not doing nothing."

"Sounds like we have a volunteer," my father said into the receiver. "You'll have them shortly. Have fun with Beth."

He hung up and turned to me. "It's 'I'm not doing anything,'" he corrected, opening my mother's cigarette box. "No double negatives in this house. It's going to be dark soon so don't dawdle. Do you know where the Carlsons live?"

"Yeah, we were there last—" I stopped, not knowing how to finish the sentence. My mother never told our father that she met Beth over a roll of toilet paper. "When we were riding bikes the other day. Gotta go!" I said, grabbing my jacket, and running out the door.

"Don't forget these," he called out, tossing the pack of Virginia Slims to me.

On most Saturday evenings, I would normally be found sprawled out on the sofa in the living room, waiting for the clock to strike eight, but on this day, there was good reason as to why I was frantically pedaling to the Carlsons' house. It was the golden hour, that small window before nightfall when the fields and meadows glow against the setting sun and rabbits wake up after lounging all day in the thickets.

Suddenly, I skidded to a stop and froze. Not far ahead, a tractor had turned the corner and was heading towards me. I recognized that hunched-over figure behind the steering wheel, and as he came closer, I didn't move. While we met earlier in the year in the cemetery, this was the first time that I would come virtually face to face with Old Man Ghouly.

That face.

I was grateful that the setting sun cast shadows across his face. Too frightened to move, I sat still on my bike as the tractor drove slowly past me, with his old collie following closely behind him. I had no idea how old the dog actually was, but as I watched her plod along, with her head bent down so that her snout nearly touched the ground, I made a leap that she was darn old. I'm not sure if Old Man Ghouly drove slowly so that his dog could keep up with him, or if the dog walked slowly to keep from running into the tractor. Either way, they seemed a good match.

Old Man Ghouly's real name was Mr. Cooley but he inherited his nickname because his face drooped horribly on one side, causing his left eye to be about an inch lower, giving him a serious monster face. The talk around town was that he once killed a man, which might explain why his only companion was that old dog of his.

He lived on the outskirts of town and drove his tractor down the road regularly to get to the corn he was growing in the field we owned. We weren't farmers, but our father believed in being a good neighbor so Old Man Ghouly paid us $1 a year to plow our field and grow corn. In exchange, we got all the corn we could eat. There's nothing like fresh Michigan sweet corn smothered in butter and sprinkled with salt. We kids would sit on the back steps and shuck the corn our father would later boil in the big pot on the stove. When camping in the woods, we often tossed the corn cobs, still in their original packaging, into the campfire for an instant dinner.

As the tractor and dog passed, I stayed perfectly still, not relaxing until he was far down the road. Suddenly, I understood how this man could have killed a person, maybe more than one. Feeling good about surviving my second encounter with Old Man Ghouly, I pedaled on.

Soon after, I parked my bike alongside the Carlsons' house and pulled at one of the handlebar grips until it slipped off. Pulling the pack out of my jacket, I let two cigarettes fall into my hand and shoved them into the handlebar before replacing the handlebar grip. *Ammunition for next time I need a favor*, I told myself, putting the pack back into my jacket pocket.

"Knock, knock!" I yelled through the front window screen.

"Come on in, honey!" my mother called out from the living room. "The TV's on."

"Hi, Mrs. Carlson," I said, handing the cigarettes to my mother who looked suspiciously at the open pack before pulling one out. I liked Mrs. Carlson because she was like the mothers I saw on TV who held jobs and still managed to keep their children clean, fed, and loved.

"Sit yourself down. I've got some potato chips somewhere." Mrs. Carlson disappeared into the kitchen just as Mr. Carlson came in from the garage. He saw my mother holding her cigarette and immediately jumped to pick up a lighter from the coffee table.

"Allow me, my lady."

She laughed and held his arm steady as he lit her cigarette.

"That husband of yours shouldn't let you out of his sight. There are hound dogs out there." He smiled and they both laughed again, harder than the joke called for.

"You are the perfect gentleman, Robbie."

"Robbie's my son," he corrected, taking a seat next to my mother on the long sofa.

"Oh, Rob is such a boring name, and not how I would describe you," my mother said with a wink.

"How would you describe him?" Mrs. Carlson asked, staring at her husband as she walked back in from the kitchen. She handed me a Be-Mo Potato Chip canister and took a seat in the La-Z-Boy.

While the grownups continued chatting, I opened the tin and munched on chips, gazing at the many souvenirs that surrounded me, telling me that the Carlsons traveled far beyond the upper peninsula of Michigan. A snow globe featuring a teeny Niagara Falls and a moose statue with the word YELLOWSTONE engraved in the stand sat on a shelf next to a large picture of Mount Rushmore hanging on the wall.

"You like that?" Mr. Carlson asked me.

"Huh? Um, sure."

"You think it's cool now," he said, jumping up from the sofa. "Watch this." With the flip of a switch hidden behind the frame, the entire picture lit up, resembling a gigantic, jarring photo slide. "Pretty special, eh?"

"Um, I can't say I've ever seen anything like it," I answered honestly.

"And if you like that, wait 'til you see this," He hurried over to a cowboy lamp sitting on the end table. "Bought this at the famous Wall Drug." Flipping on the light switch, he added, "Stopped there on our way through the Badlands in South Dakota. Genuine leather. Now, watch."

As instructed, I stared at the lamp, waiting for it to dance or say, "Welcome to South Dakota." Like everything sold at Wall Drug, it was cowboy themed. At the base sat a miniature covered wagon, and on the lampshade was a picture of a cowboy riding a horse. It reminded me of our Hummel lamps back home, which depicted children dancing around the lampstand made to look like the tree's trunk. Except Hummel figurines don't literally dance, which I think is a good thing.

Slowly, the horse and cowboy starting circling the lampshade, speeding up as the lightbulb grew hotter.

"See, the heat from the bulb turns the picture," Mr. Carlson explained, bringing his face within inches of the lampshade, making me wonder if he partook in this ritual every evening.

"Cool," I said as the horse gathered speed. Mr. Carlson seemed to light up as well as we watched the lamp together. He then excused himself from the ladies' coffee klatch and retired into the kitchen, finally allowing me to turn my attention to the TV.

While I used the delivery of the cigarettes as an excuse for visiting, the truth was, I was in that living room for one reason, and I was sitting in front of it. Or rather, it was sitting in front of me—that big beautiful Technicolor television set. Even though color television was introduced in the 1950s, in 1970 they were still as rare in Alamo as a sighting of an ice cream truck (once), and everyone knew who owned one. Curtains remained open in the evening in those select homes so that anyone strolling by couldn't help but see the color TV shimmering in the dark. The rest of us pretended we didn't really care.

We cared.

And in ten minutes I would care even more, because it was Saturday night and the new *Mary Tyler Moore Show* was about to start. If you want an idea of how truly incredible it was to watch the beautiful Mary Tyler Moore on a color TV in a black-and-white world, imagine a wooded meadow in May, covered with wildflowers. Now, picture the wildflowers all being shades of grey, with the exception of a burst of black-eyed Susans. Color televisions are black-eyed Susans in a shades-of-grey wildflower world. Unlike our blah television which sat on a roll-cart, this magnificent piece of furniture was so huge it had to sit on the floor, masquerading as a china cabinet.

The bible of every television aficionado sat on top of the console. I'm speaking, of course, about the *TV Guide*. The previous week, a *TV Guide* reviewer shared his thoughts on this new program about a single professional woman tackling life in the big city. The critic adored Mary Tyler Moore and was infatuated by her studio apartment. Since he had grown accustomed to seeing the show on his black and white TV, he had to imagine what the colors were in her living room, from her sleeper-sofa to the "M" that hung on her wall. In his head, he had envisioned the entire color scheme of her apartment, so when he finally saw the show in all its Technicolor splendor, the actual color scheme of Mary's apartment was far more drab than what he had imagined, and, sorry to say, it just didn't work for him.

Seven minutes . . .

"Color TVs aren't worth it," my mother said, shaking her head. "It looks like their skin is on fire. And look at the sky, such a weird purple. And if you mess with the color control knobs to fix the sky, you end up with yellow people. The whole color TV thing simply won't last because they didn't get it right." And with that, my mother took her black cigarette holder out of her purse and lit up another Virginia Slim.

I knew my mother was absolutely wrong about color TV being a fad, but she did have a point about it being a little off. The images on the screens of many color TVs had a weird glow that didn't look the least bit natural. For a while, people with black and white TV sets were buying this clear plastic sheet that fit over the TV screen, with the top being a blue tint and the bottom a green tint. It was supposed to simulate sky and grass, but it usually just made the people on TV look like they were half blue and half green. It was a really stupid idea.

As my mother changed the topic to the latest turn of events on the *Guiding Light*, I dug my hand into the tin for more chips. Mrs. Carlson and my mother had similar traits—both were on the short side and slim and brunette. Apparently Mr. Carlson had a type. But while Mrs. Carlson often wore long, cotton skirts, my mother preferred slacks and capris, reminding me again of Mary Tyler Moore. But while the new Mary Richards was showing off a more modern look that included bellbottoms and scarves, our mother preferred the more classic stylings of Ms. Moore's Laura Petrie days. Funny, as much as Mutti emulated Mary Tyler Moore, she didn't understand—

"You know why my daughter's here, right? She has to watch that new show starring the wife from the *Dick Van Dyke Show*. I don't know what's so special about her; she's not at all funny. Dick was the hilarious one and the one who should have gotten another TV show."

"'Oh, Rob!'" Beth said, hardly audible through her laughter. "You know . . . my husband and Rob Petrie." She started laughing again, and my mother joined in. It was nice to see her relaxed and enjoying herself with a friend.

I licked my fingers, savoring the mixture of salt and potato chips, and turned my attention back to the TV. My mother was right in that it wasn't a coincidence that I could be found at any one of the select homes in Alamo during opportune moments, one such event being the annual broadcast of the *Wizard of Oz*, a classic that starts out in black and white, but bursts into vivid Technicolor when Dorothy opens the door of her house after landing in the magical Land of Oz.

I was a TV kid, and there were specific times during the day when you would have no problem finding me. All you had to do was peek into the living room to find me sitting cross-legged on the rug, soaking in the warm rays that can only be found in front of a television set.

Just two more minutes . . .

The new McDonald's commercial came on, and I sang along with "You Deserve a Break Today," looking forward to the day when I would be old enough to work at McDonald's even though I noticed that in the commercials, and locally, all the employees were men. I made a vow to myself to work on changing that.

Considering I never had more than two dollars in my pocket at any given moment, it was interesting the number of hours television dedicated to the youngest demographic. But with the avalanche of commercials pushing sugary cereals, toys and soda pop, it was apparent we had substantial input in the buying decisions of many products. This is the only explanation I had for the syndication of Gilligan's Island—a comedy that clearly didn't overestimate the sophistication and overall intelligence of their target audience, and served as my daily after-school babysitter.

With an antenna that picked up only two channels, programming that stimulated the brain wasn't always an option.

Finally . . . the clock hit eight-thirty.

The TV sang to me while my hero danced on the sidewalk and drove her convertible through the streets of Minneapolis. "*Who can turn the world on with her smile? Who can take a nothing day, and suddenly make it all seem worthwhile?*" I sang along quietly, not wanting my mother or Mrs. Carlson to hear me because this was between me and Mary.

"We might just make it after all," I sang, changing the lyrics to include me.

— 30 —

1951
Eschbach, Baden-Württemberg, Germany

"Something on your mind?" Merle asked, watching Didi twirl the straw around in her Coca-Cola glass, creating a whirlpool.

She didn't answer. Instead, she kept staring into her drink as the ice cubes circled. The two of them sat at the end of the soda-fountain counter located on the second floor of the department store.

"The scarf looks good on you," Merle said, giving her a smile. "You do like it, right? We can return it if— "

"It's beautiful, really. I love it," Didi said quietly.

"I hope so," he said, leaning into her. "And I didn't even complain when you made me buy myself new shoes," he added smiling. "Never mind that every purchase I make has to eventually be shipped back to America. You're making my goal of traveling light more difficult. I'm sorry, honey," he continued, seeing that his joking wasn't producing any smiles from Didi.

"You know I'm not leaving for another three months, right, Spatzi?" he continued. It's not good for you to be so focused on that, and not enjoying the here and now." He reached for her hand, and she pulled away.

"I'm late," she whispered, continuing her fixation on the soda in front of her.

"You're . . ." Merle started but stopped himself as he realized what Didi was saying. He sat quiet for a while with no expression on his face, letting the news sink in. "How late are you? I mean, are you sure?"

"Four weeks. That makes me pretty darn sure. But I haven't gone to a doctor yet or told Tante Lisi and Onkel Otto. I know how that will go over."

"OK," he said. "That changes things, but only a little bit." He got up from the stool and stood beside Didi, who finally turned to look at him. "I was planning on this anyway."

He bent down on one knee as Didi's eyes widened. "Oh my god," she gasped, putting her hands to her mouth.

"Oh my god," the soda-jerk from behind the counter repeated, seeing Merle on bended knee. "I love this!"

"Excuse us," Merle said laughing before turning back to Didi.

"Didi, you are the most frustrating headstrong beautiful *fräulein* I have ever met. I am head-over-heels in love with you." He laughed suddenly. "Um . . . I'm not sure your Onkel Otto will appreciate not having the opportunity to give his acceptance."

"Are you sure you want to do this?" Didi asked, grabbing his arm and helping him to his feet.

"What are you talking about? Of course—"

"I mean, you know I'm not like normal girls. I know I'm not right. And epilepsy is hereditary. What if our baby gets it? What if our other children—"

"We'll deal with it."

"You know it won't be easy. Nothing about this is going to be easy. Damn it, Merle, you know I'm broken."

"Stop that nonsense. You are *not* broken. And nothing worth fighting for is ever easy, or so my Sargent tells me. Spatzi, we can do this. I'll put in for more time here so we can get married, and then we'll travel back to the States as a family. You're going to love

America," he said, picking up a napkin from the counter, and wiping a tear rolling down Didi's cheek. "I live in a beautiful house in a little town that you're going to fall in love with. I promise you, Alamo will be everything you dreamed of. Now, where was I?" he said, getting back down on his knee.

"Yes," she said, laughing and crying as she yanked him back up. "Yes, I will."

"Thank god," the soda jerk said, clapping his hands. "Congratulations!"

— 31 —

October 31, 1970
Alamo, Michigan

"You beat a small child out of her last boulder. The power, you must feel," I said, wiping the dirt from my knees and grabbing my marble bag, which was lighter by three marbles. With one swift kick, I obliterated the hole I had dug into the dirt for the game. Bored, I crouched down to pick up a twig, and poked it into another hole in the dirt, teasing an ant lion that popped up from beneath the bottom. *Poor thing. He was expecting a juicy ant and got me.* Flicking the twig away, I jumped onto the barn loading dock, taking a seat next to Silvia.

"Hold out your hand," she said, dropping my marbles into my palm. "Who's your favorite sister, now?" she added, jumping to the ground. "Come on. We need to get ready."

"You're going to want to wear a coat," Hanna said, adjusting my black vinyl cape. "I know it's not the greatest look for your witch costume but the last thing you want to do during trick-or-treating is to quit early because you're freezing, and as soon as that sun sets, you *will* be cold." I grumbled, knowing she was right. While witches weren't known to wear winter parkas, kids running around on Halloween night in Michigan sure did.

As I straightened my cape, Hanna went to help our mother

decorate the front porch for an evening of hovering ghosts, dancing skeletons, and flying bats. Since we lived on the outskirts of town, we were required to provide incentives to entice trick-or-treaters into making the extra effort to travel down our street.

Staring into the mirror, hiding behind my plastic mask and black cape draped over my coat, I looked less like an evil witch and more like the Michelin Man. I pulled at the cape tied around my neck, which was choking me, and walked out the front door, stepping into Halloween magic—a party punctuated with howling ghosts and cackling witches.

Cardboard cutouts of black cats, jack-o'-lanterns, and witches covered the windows, and black and orange crepe paper draped overhead, hanging from one end of the porch to the other. If that wasn't enough to scare the little goblins that would be knocking on our door, my mother set up the record player in the corner to play the scary Halloween record she purchased at Woolworth's. The card table in the other corner of the porch was covered with a festive paper tablecloth and held a tall pitcher of cider, donuts, and a large bowl filled with peanut butter cups and Snickers. And in the rare instance someone was looking for something healthy, a bucket of apples sat beside the table. While the apples added to the ambiance, we always had plenty left on November first.

"How do I look?" our mother asked, twirling her black skirt around and pointing a large wart-covered plastic finger at me.

"You look like a witch," I answered, jealous that, with her green makeup, and minus the bulbous outerwear, she upstaged my witch costume in every way. Over the years, as the foot-traffic to our house grew, so did our mother's role, continuing longer into the night when little kids in costumes slowly morphed into teenagers in much more imaginative costumes or no costumes at all, holding pillowcases. I slid my plastic mask off my face and let it rest on top of my head as I went back inside and sank into the couch, waiting for the sun to set.

And waited . . .

"Let's go!" Mickey finally called out to the rest of us. "We have a lot of houses to hit!"

With that official announcement, I grabbed my plastic jack-o'-lantern bucket and followed the others out the door and down the street, stopping first at the town hall for more cider and donuts before continuing with door knocking and bell ringing in our quest for Milky Ways, Rice Krispies Treats, and popcorn balls.

As the evening rolled into night, I could feel the growing weight of my bucket. After hitting every possible house with a front yard light on, we found ourselves on the edge of town, far beyond the streetlights.

"I've got this," Mickey said, flipping on his flashlight and leading the way. "Let's go this way," he continued, pointing to a small house at the end of a long driveway.

"No way!" Silvia said, and I couldn't have agreed more. "That's Old Man Ghouly's house!"

"Cut it out," Hanna scolded. "It's just Mr. Cooley's house. No one's going to jump out of the bushes. And look, the front porch light is on so he's expecting us." She held her flashlight under her chin and made a scary face.

"Ha, ha," Silvia said, pushing Hanna to the side and following Mickey down the driveway. "No candy is worth this. I wouldn't be surprised if we're the first kids to knock on his door tonight. He's probably handing out poison! Or worse, butterscotch candies."

Hanna noticed that I was lagging behind and grabbed my hand.

"I'm scared, Hanna," I whispered. "He's killed a man. We shouldn't knock on his door at night."

"Oh hush. He's just an old man, and there are four of us. Don't worry. I'll keep you safe," she assured me, holding my hand tighter. Not finding a doorbell, Mickey reached up and knocked on the door three times to be sure we were heard. "All together now," Hanna said.

"Trick or treat!" We stood for several moments, listening for footsteps coming up to the front door but we heard nothing.

"Should I knock again?" Mickey asked.

"No!" Silvia answered. "Let's get out of here." And just as we turned to leave, the door opened, and we turned back to find Old Man Ghouly standing in the doorway, blocking the light from inside so that we could only see the shadow he cast and that droopy eye.

"Well, hello there," he said, looking us over. "Let's see, we have a pirate, a hippie, someone who thinks he's too old to dress up, and a really scary witch!"

"Hi, Mr. Cooley," Hanna said as the rest of us stood quiet, staring at him.

"You're the Phillips kids, aren't you? You tell your father for me that he's a good man." He then turned and, from a small table by the door, picked up a bowl holding an assortment of candy bars. Not penny candy handed out by old people too ashamed to simply leave the front porch light off, and not even the bite-size candy bars that we gave trick-or-treaters. No, these were full-size Milky Ways, 3 Musketeers, and Nestlé Crunches.

"Tell you what," he said. "It's late and you're the first kids to visit me. I don't expect that I'll be getting many more tonight, and I'd like to go to bed. Here, hold out your bags and buckets."

And with that, the monster of Alamo dumped more than twenty large candy bars into our greedy little hands. He smiled as we gushed over his generosity, and I noticed that several feet behind him, his collie stood guard, never taking her eyes off us.

"Thank you, Mr. Cooley. Happy Halloween!" Hanna said as we turned to leave.

"Happy Halloween, Mr. Cooley!" I called out, racing down the driveway and happy to learn that not all monsters were real.

— 32 —

November 7, 1970
Alamo, Michigan

"So, are your women dragging your asses to the church bazaar tonight?" Dale asked with a grin, rolling out from under the car. Our father smiled back while the other men laughed.

The garage door at the Marathon Station remained shut on that chilly morning, and an industrial strength space heater blew a narrow blast of heat into the garage stall. As Dale rolled back under the car, our father took a long drink from his Coke and placed it in the wooden crate with the other empty bottles. Two other men from the north side of town sat in folding chairs, watching Kevin as he topped off the oil.

"Judy says it's the least I can do since I avoid church like the Devil every other day of the year," Kevin said, causing the others to laugh again. "Hey Larry, are we going to see that pretty little edelweiss of yours tonight?"

"I don't think so," he said, smiling. "She's not feeling very well. She gets bad headaches."

"Too bad. Sloppy joes, games for the kids, I'd like to pin the tail on that donkey!" Kevin said with a wink just as the service station bell rang, signaling that someone needed a fill-up. "Duty calls," he added, walking away while our father breathed heavily as he packed his pipe with tobacco.

—

The sign read: BAZAAR / SATURDAY 4–8 P.M.

"Saturday?" I said out loud, peddling past the church message board. "That's today. That's in five hours!" Rising out of my seat, I raced down the road as fast as my one-speed would allow, taking the shortcut through the cemetery. *Just a quick drink*, I told myself, stopping at the water pump. Struggling with the heavy pump handle, I fumbled between pushing down on it and trying to move quickly enough to catch the ice-cold water with my cupped hands, but each time, the water stopped flowing the moment I stopped pumping. After several attempts, I gave up and wandered over to a tombstone that caught my eye. A new gnome sat at attention in front of a freshly dug gravesite—still shiny, and not showing his age by weathering a Michigan winter. The polished headstone stood no more than six inches off the ground. Bending down, I read the inscription.

Always Our Baby
Shelly Marie Randall
October 19, 1970

Just the one date. *A baby that didn't make it through the first day*, I thought, crouching beside the grave. The honking from a flock of Canada geese flying overhead broke the silence as I brushed off a small pile of leaves from the gravestone. Even though it was a brisk day, the sun shining on the fallen leaves revealed magnificent autumn colors, like fireworks fallen to the ground.

Suddenly, I caught the sweet autumn scent of burning leaves, and visually, I followed the trail of smoke to a house across the road where a man was raking leaves. I inhaled, knowing that I would remember that smell long after the season's last bonfire.

Walking back, I skipped across the row of cash register tombstones. We called them that because they were shaped like, well . . . you know. Thinking back to that night last June when we buried Thomasina, I remembered Mr. Cooley standing right about . . . there. With my newfound knowledge, I realized that he wasn't there to scare anyone. *So, what was he doing in the cemetery that night?* I looked at the stone in front of me—a husband and wife. Their last name didn't ring a bell, so I moved on to the next stone.

Cooley Family
Robert John Oct 1, 1899 –
Gwendolyn Rose Jun 18, 1903 – Jan 20, 1933

I stood still, letting the words sink in. Robert John Cooley, born in 1899. There was no date for his death, so he was obviously still alive. Then I looked at the second name: Gwendolyn, who was only thirty years old when she died. I couldn't even imagine Mr. Cooley as a young man with a wife on his arm. My only image of him was that of a hunched-over old man with an even older dog.

I then noticed another line of inscription centered at the bottom of the gravestone.

Our Little Angel

There were no dates to signify the birth or death of this little angel. No date at all, which made we wonder, *Was Gwendolyn with child when she died?* I looked again at Gwendolyn's date of birth—June 18. The same day that Thomasina died, and the night we ran into Mr. Cooley, who was just visiting with his wife on her birthday, even though she had died forty years earlier. I let out a sigh, embarrassed that we screamed and ran when we saw him. Bending down, I wiped away the dirt and twigs that had fallen onto the top of the cash register. Overhead, the sun peeked out from the clouds and warmed my back. Feeling the crunch of the fallen leaves beneath my feet, I walked back to my bike and pedaled down the lane toward home.

"Hey, losers!" I called out to Mickey and Silvia as I turned into our driveway. "The church bazaar is today!"

Neither of them bothered to look up as they continued raking leaves into a pile.

"Yeah, we know," Mickey said, throwing a large plastic bag at me. "And if you help, we just might get there before it's over."

I was glad Mickey went back to raking and didn't see the face I made at him. If there was one thing I hated more than raking leaves, it was bagging them. Large yards with lots of shade were a luxury in the summer, but those same mighty oaks were a mighty pain in my backside when they dumped truckloads of leaves in the fall, or worse yet, after an early snowstorm.

With the last pile of leaves bagged and dumped, the three of us headed into the house just as the sun started its descent. "Wash up and change your shirt," Hanna instructed without a glance to me, as she put away the dishtowel. I looked down at my dirty sweatshirt and headed up to my bedroom to change.

Apparently, long before their fourth child was born, our parents attended the annual church bazaar, but as our family grew in number and size, our mother slowly retreated into the safety of the house. Not interested in holding up his side of the social scene, our father kept his distance from most town functions as well. But he understood that the church bazaar was a special event for his children, and as Hanna cleaned up the sink, our father set a ten-dollar bill on the counter with his usual request. "Don't forget to bring back sloppy joes for your mother and me."

—

"Do you think it's kind of weird that this is only time we go to church?" Mickey asked as we walked up the church steps.

"Weird or not, I'm not giving up my Sundays to sit in a pew just so some old man can preach at me for two hours," Silvia said, pushing past Mickey. "Isn't that why God gave us parents?"

"Yeah," Hanna said in a hushed voice, completely ignoring Silvia. "It is strange to be in here. It feels like we're trespassing, like we don't belong."

"Welcome to church!" I said a bit too loudly to a man and woman walking up the front steps behind us. The man nodded his head and smiled at me as they headed toward the basement stairs.

"Come on," Hanna said. "Let's eat first. I'm hungry."

As the others made their way downstairs, I started to follow, but stopped and waited until they were out of sight. Walking across the front lobby, I peeked into the sanctuary. The lights were off, but I could still see the many rows of pews. A large nondescript wooden cross hung behind the pulpit, and in the far corner, where an organ would normally be, sat an upright piano. The Alamo Congregational Church wasn't rich on funds, so the only extravagance was the recent addition of two stained glass windows. As the light from the parking lot poured through the windows, a vivid splash of color fell across the ordinary wooden pews. I had never set foot in there before, and the mystery of it was intriguing. Our mother, however, felt quite differently about this place. "There is no God," our mother often said. "From what I had to go through when I was a child, if there is a God, I have no intention of wasting my time praying to him. Trust me, I'm doing you all a favor."

So, we never went.

"Psst."

I spun around to find Silvia standing in the doorway.

"What are you doing in here?" she asked.

"I know you were being a smart aleck earlier, but have you ever wondered what it's like to go to church?" I asked in a near whisper.

She walked down the aisle and looked up at the window that depicted Jesus, standing tall and holding his hands out to us. "I went once with some friends. It was pretty boring, actually. You're not missing much."

"Oh."

"Come on, let's go. We're all waiting for you."

As she turned to leave, I remained, standing still for a few moments longer, looking up at Jesus as he appeared to be looking across the room toward the exit sign. Maybe he didn't want to be here either.

Hanna and Mickey were already in line for sloppy joes while several women, who apparently took an active role in the church, were distributing food to the guests—a captive audience. What better way to entice people to join the church than preaching the benefits of worship while people are holding out paper plates, waiting for their sloppy joes?

"You're the Phillips kids, aren't you?" one of the women asked, with a large smile that failed to reflect in her eyes.

"Yes, ma'am," Hanna answered. "I'll take the Bar-B-Q chips, please."

"Well, welcome to our church!" the woman continued, shining in her self-appointed role as the town missionary. "You stay as long as you like!" which seemed like a strange thing to say at a public event.

"Thank you," Hanna said softly, picking up a Dixie Cup of Kool-Aid. Following Hanna, we made our way to the long table covered with a paper tablecloth and sat down.

"Hey, Lee!" I called out, spotting my friend at the adjoining table. He was sitting alone, which wasn't unusual. He sat alone for lunch at school as well. Teachers would often encourage other students to join him, sensing that he was lonely, but I always had a feeling that Lee liked the solitude—preferring to watch the other students from a distance, like Jane Goodall studying the eating habits and social skills of primates as they swung around the lunchroom. Maybe that's why I liked him. "Lee! Come sit with us."

He picked up his plate and sat across from me. Unlike his sister who never missed an opportunity to remind us of her family's wealth, Lee didn't feel the need to stick it in anyone's face. Or more likely, it never occurred to him. Unfortunately, I rarely saw him since he preferred having his face buried in a book, living through the adventures of others over having to experience anything himself. He stayed cleaner that way.

"Hey," he said, nodding to all of us. "Have you played any games yet?"

"Nope." I took a large bite of sloppy joe, letting the juices fall onto the paper plate. "Let's go together." I shoved a handful of chips in my mouth and got up. "I'm feeling lucky!"

Over at the darts game, I started to hand the woman in the folding chair my quarter, but Lee put his hand over my money and lowered my arm.

"Not yet," he said. "Watch."

I rolled my eyes, not having the patience for waiting for anything, let alone something fun. As we stood to the side, two teenagers stepped up and were handed four darts. Bored, I looked away, distracted by other children walking by, making Lee nudge me. "No, watch," he whispered.

So, I watched as the boy studied the board, deciding to aim for the yellow balloon. After missing, he adjusted and threw the dart at the blue balloon, which he nailed. The woman smiled and handed him a cheap balsa wood airplane, which he shoved in his back pocket before handing the remaining two darts to the girl who also scored with her second shot, puncturing the yellow balloon. The woman smiled again and, that time, handed the girl a prize from another box—a beautiful green lucky rabbit's foot.

"And there it is," Lee whispered. "Aim for the yellow balloon."

One purple rabbit's foot later, we made our way to the fishing game where Lee and I started our acquisition of miniature trolls until my pockets were full and I was nearly out of money. With one quarter left in my pocket, I noticed an older man sitting behind a small table that held five plastic cups, all sitting upside down, with a ping-pong ball sitting in front of the cups. The old man wore a scowl on his face, a permanent fixture installed by his wife, who most likely was serving up sloppy joes in the kitchen.

As Lee and I stepped up to the table, the old man slowly raised his head. "Welcome to the 'Now You See It, Now You Don't' magic show," he said, looking past me, and without a hint of a smile. "Pick a cup, any cup. If you find your ping-pong ball, you get your pick of any of these marvelous prizes." Sadly off-beat, he then pointed to four beautiful teddy bears. "If not, you win a sticker."

"OK, we got this," Lee said, confident in his ability to outthink and outwit the old man.

I dug into my pocket and handed the man my money. This was a no-brainer. After all, I had a lucky number. The man lifted one of the cups and let it cover the ping-pong ball. Then, before I had time to register what was going on, he started moving the cups around on the table with the swiftness of a teenager. Again and again, the cups moved around until I felt dizzy from watching. Satisfied that he was about to shake down the kid in front of him, he stopped. And just as abruptly, he returned to his slow robotic delivery.

"Pick a cup, one through five."

"It's the second cup," Lee whispered, not taking his eyes off the cups.

"I think it's the fifth cup," I argued. "I feel good about it being five." Lee shrugged his shoulders, and I turned to the old man with an enthusiastic, "Five."

He lifted the cup to reveal its empty contents. He then lifted the second cup to reveal the ping-pong ball. And for the first time, he smiled as he handed me a sticker of a cross.

"Don't," I warned Lee, stuffing the sticker into my pocket.

Lee smiled and raised his eyebrows. "I didn't say a thing."

"Come on, Lee. It's time to go!"

We both turned to see his sister Jenny standing by the stairs. She walked over and looked across the room, where Mickey was picking out a two-layer chocolate cake. "That's Mummy's cake. She'll be so glad to know her donation is going to a family that needs it. Come on, Lee. It's time to go home."

"See ya, Lee," I said, ignoring Jenny, but thinking about her comment. *We weren't needy, were we?*

A plate of cupcakes and one chocolate cake later, we headed back to the church kitchen for two sloppy joes to go for our parents who, even as heathens, knew how good the food was at the church bazaar. Our mother may not have been God fearing, but I'm sure he feared her, so I can only assume that he didn't mind that she ate his food once a year.

As Hanna placed the two dollars on the counter, the same woman from earlier took the money and said to Hanna, "I can't say I've seen your mother lately. I hope she's doing all right."

Hanna answered with a quiet, "She's not feeling well," and looked down at her shoes, bending down to tighten the laces on one of her sneakers even though it was already tied. Hanna's reply was actually true since our mother was in her bedroom with another one of her headaches.

"Well, I'm so sorry to hear that. You tell your mother that we hope she's feeling better soon."

Hanna nodded in reply, and the woman, deciding that Hanna wasn't going to hold up her end of the conversation, handed her the Styrofoam box while looking over at me, flashing me a smile as phony as the pearls around her neck. I responded by sticking my tongue out before running out of the House of the Lord.

It was dark as we walked home, still giddy from the energy of the games and prizes. "Mutti and Popi are going to love having dessert after dinner," Mickey said, as we bounded up the front steps and into the house. Hanna handed our father the Styrofoam container, and he smiled with amusement as Mickey retold the story of his superior dance moves around the circle of musical chairs.

Our mother was sitting at the picnic table, still wrapped in her robe. Taking a sip from her coffee cup, she stayed quiet while the rest of us chatted and laughed. As our father took two plates out of the cabinet for our mother and himself, Mickey placed the cake on the table.

"I'll get the plates," Silvia called out, opening the cabinet door. With a stack of small plates in her hand, she turned to place them on the table just as our mother casually stood up, reached for the plate holding the cake, and calmly slid it across the table until it fell, hitting the floor with a *thump*, frosting-side down..

"What the hell?" Silvia yelled, causing our mother to spin around.

"We don't take charity," she seethed.

"You had no right to do that!" Silvia challenged, her hands clenched, and her lips, tight. "Mickey spent his allowance on that cake." Doxy ran over to help Hanna clean up the mess on the floor while Silvia put the small plates back, slamming the cupboard door.

With her back to our mother, Silvia didn't notice that our mother had opened the butcher knife drawer until I said, "Silvia, watch out. Mutti's got a knife!"

"I don't care," she said, not bothering to turn around.

"Oh, you'll care," our mother said in a voice that told me there was no going back. "You don't bring garbage into our house, and *you* are going to learn how to speak to me!"

With her eyes locked on Silvia, I knew that she no longer saw the rest of us as I backed away. The cupcakes were still sitting on the table, and I was tempted to grab one and run, but something told me to be still. I put my hands in my back pockets and wrapped my fingers around a slick piece of paper. As I traced the outline of the paper with my thumb, I remembered the cross sticker. I kept tracing the outline. *Think about something else. Think about the church bazaar, Lee outsmarting the woman, the old man outsmarting me, sloppy joes and red trolls . . .*

"Sit down," our mother said quietly to Silvia, pointing to a chair with the tip of her knife. "I said, sit!" she repeated after Silvia failed to respond to her first demand. Silvia looked back at her with a cold stare and sat.

The rest of us didn't move as Silvia sat perfectly still in the chair. Meanwhile, our father set his pipe on an ashtray and sighed. I stood, watching, as our mother looked over toward our father and picked up his lighter. She then stroked Silvia's long straight hair with one hand while holding the lighter in the other. Creating a flame, she took hold of a strand of Silvia's hair and gently caressed it, moving the lighter closer so that the flame almost touched her hair.

Before I had even realized our father had risen from his chair, he took hold of our mother's arm and snatched the Zippo out of her hand. "Kids, go on upstairs. I'll take care of this."

And with that piece of advice, Silvia got up and hurried past our mother, grabbing the cupcakes on her way out of the kitchen, followed closely by Mickey and Hanna. I stayed where I was, and, taking my hand out of my pocket, I looked down at the sticker in my hand. It was a blue cross with ornate swirls, not pretty, too cartoony. I thought about the cross at the front of the sanctuary in the church, and my mother's words. *"And from what I had to go through when I was a child, if there is a God, I have no intention wasting my time praying to him."*

As our mother started screaming, I wadded up the sticker and tossed it onto the floor.

— 33 —

1952

Ellis Island, New York, New York

Driven by a deadline that would eventually lead the soldier back to America, the courtship moved forward at an intense and accelerated speed resulting in a wedding and a beautiful daughter. Both, Didi and her husband felt blessed as they packed for their trip across the ocean—home for Merle and his new family.

Didi watched her breath float away in the crisp afternoon air, and a small sneeze came from the bundle she held in her arms, making her tighten the blanket in the hope of keeping the cold off her little Johanna.

"Can I hold her one more time?" Heidi asked. She accepted the bundle from Didi, and lifted the blanket a little to find the baby gazing back at her. "You're so precious," Heidi cooed. "And so lucky. You're going to love America!"

As the waiting passengers began boarding the train, Didi wiped her tears away and laughed at Heidi who was tickling little Johanna. Merle stood next to a pile of luggage and lit a pipe he had just purchased, giving his new wife the time she needed with her friend and family. The whistle blew, and the conductor announced the final call to board.

In between tears and laughter, Didi hugged her Tante Lisi and Onkel Otto, and started to follow her husband, but stopped for another hug.

"You make that man of yours bring you back here for a visit next summer, do you hear me?" Tante Lisi said as Onkel Otto handed her his handkerchief. "And pictures! Send lots of pictures. We don't want to miss anything. Button your coat up, Didi. I don't want you catching a cold. It's a long trip, and you need to stay healthy for the baby." She took her scarf off and wrapped it around Didi's neck. "*Ich liebe dich.*"

"Don't forget about us," Onkel Otto said, waving, and grabbing his handkerchief back and blowing his nose as Didi finally boarded the train.

"I won't forget any one of you," Didi called out. "I will write every week, and I'll include photos." After the second blow of the whistle, she yelled, "*Ich liebe dich!*"

As the train pulled away from the station, Didi leaned her head against the window and watched as her family and friend slowly disappeared into the landscape. How she wished that Mari was standing on the platform with them. She missed her so much, it hurt. She sighed, knowing that thinking about her did no good, and it wouldn't bring her back. With the baby now sleeping to the soothing rhythm of the rolling train, she let out another long sigh and relaxed. She then reached into the bag leaning against her, pulling out her leather journal and pen.

"I guess now is as good a time as any to write the next chapter," Didi whispered to herself. "I have plenty to write about now."

Days later, with rough waters and seasickness behind her, Didi wearily stepped off *Queen Elizabeth the First* onto Ellis Island, holding Johanna, who slept away while wrapped tightly in her quilt. Pictures from Didi's seventh-grade history book didn't do it justice, she thought as she looked across the water to the majestic statue her husband pointed out to her. As she clung to Johanna and her luggage, she tried to concentrate while her husband explained what they were about to encounter upon arrival to the island. As he continued talking, she nodded, gazing at the magnificent Manhattan skyline that looked close enough to touch.

Didi inched her way down the ship's wet plank with her new daughter swaddled in her arms. They were both protected from the blustery winds by the heavy army coat her husband draped over her. An ornery deckhand motioned them along to another line where a throng of immigrants were already waiting, all excited and anxious to finally be landing on American soil.

"Keep it moving!" another worker directed as the line of people shuffled along. "There are people behind you, and we have hundreds of people to process today. Please keep moving!" He wore a scowl on his face. Didi suspected that he had one goal for the day, and that was to get through the next eight hours with as little contact as possible with all the foreigners.

"Don't let the ornery workers get you down," Merle said as he shifted Didi's small suitcase to his other arm. "They're just jealous that you're with me," he winked.

Having trouble juggling her larger suitcase and little Johanna who was squirming in her arms, Didi let the baby bottle slip out of her coat pocket. It rolled across the dock, prompting a curt command from the deckhand, "Pick it up and move along!"

Still her excitement didn't diminish, because this was America. She gazed across the bay to Liberty Island and stared at the Statue of Liberty so that she would remember how it looked against the rising sun, only to have the moment broken by another worker barking orders at a young boy behind her to stop gawking at the sights and to stay close to his parents. Didi held Johanna tightly against her chest and leaned against her husband, thankful that she was not alone.

"Make sure you have your belongings! You will not be allowed back onto the ship. Keep moving!"

As they were herded into the building, they were greeted by another worker who yelled out, "Americans, to the right! Foreigners, to the left!"

Scared that these instructions would separate her from her husband before even setting foot onto the mainland, Didi grabbed her husband's arm, prompting a laugh. "Don't worry, I'm not going anywhere," he assured her. He stayed in line with her and the other immigrants, knowing that no one would tell an American soldier that he was standing in the wrong line. The line moved as slowly as the hands on the clock. Exhausted, Didi took a seat with other women and their children on one of the many folding chairs set up against the wall while her husband held her place in line. It felt good to sit down. She took her shoe off to rub her heel, which sported a fresh blister.

"Put your shoe back on. We don't need to see your nasty feet."

"*Entschuldigen sie mich?*" Didi asked, startled to find a worker standing in front of her, and forgetting what little English she knew.

"Can't even bother to learn our language, eh?"

Didi looked blankly at the man and then over to the line to see her husband chatting with a young boy waiting with his father. Ignoring the hole in her sock, she pulled her sock back over her aching foot, put her shoe back on, and tied the laces.

"*Willkommen* to America," whispered the old woman sitting next to her, speaking in broken English.

After a long morning of registration, this new American family took a ferry to the mainland where they boarded a bus that would shuttle them to the train station. From the bus window, Didi stared up at the skyscrapers that reached to the heavens, each one taller than the one they just passed. It was early in the afternoon, and the streets were alive with taxis and brave motorists. The sidewalks were crawling with people making their way through the city—dodging trash, tourists, and the occasional rat. Didi pointed out the multitude of colorful flashing signs to Johanna, who preferred the warmth under her mother's coat and slept through the guided tour.

"I wish we had time to take in the sights," Merle said, looking over Didi's shoulder, out the window. "We'll have to make it a point to come back here so that I can take you to the Stork Club. Maybe we'll catch Frank Sinatra, who I hear plays there a lot."

"I would love that."

"It's a date then," he said, closing his eyes. "Wake me up when we're at Penn Station."

Didi couldn't stop looking out the bus window at the blur of delis, nightclubs, and theater marquees. "We'll have to come back here when you're older," she whispered to Johanna. She leaned her head back, looking forward to the last leg of their trip that would take them to her new home in the small town her husband called Alamo. "The Stork Club will wait," she sighed.

The bus pulled into Penn Station, where they joined the masses of people shoving past them. *On their way to work or the theater,* she imagined. Merle set their luggage on a long bench and took a seat, taking Johanna from Didi's arms. "Go look around," he said. "And get me a Coke, please."

Excited to go exploring, Didi climbed the stairs to the second floor and walked over to the railing to stare in wonder at the cathedral ceiling. She drank in the energy of the people rushing about below, everyone in a hurry to get somewhere. She then ducked into a souvenir shop and came out with four postcards and a bottle of Coca-Cola.

"Hurry," her husband motioned to her as she returned. Handing little Johanna back to Didi, he added, "We don't have a lot of time." Following her husband, who carried the bulk of their belongings, she climbed aboard the train, glad to be on the last leg of their long journey that carried them across the ocean and across continents.

Finally settled, she placed her sleeping baby beside her and pulled a postcard and pen out from her coat pocket, excited to tell her friend about landing on Ellis Island and the many wonders of New York City. Selecting the postcard showcasing the Statue of Liberty, she began writing. "Dear Mari, I miss you so!" She stopped suddenly and stared at what she had written. Closing her eyes, she folded the postcard in half and pulled another out and started writing again.

"Dear Heidi, I miss you so. Finally, in New York City! I've seen the Empire State Building, the tallest building on earth." She resisted writing how scared she was, and instead continued with positive thoughts and her excitement for her future as an American. Finishing with, "See you again soon!" Didi then pressed the postcard to her lips and sealed it with a kiss.

— 34 —

December 22, 1970

Alamo, Michigan

There's "winter cold," when you have to keep your wool hat on to keep your earlobes from freezing and falling off, and then there's "Michigan cold," when the snot freezes in your nose every time you inhale, weighing on your lungs like a carton of Camel Cigarettes. And this was Michigan cold.

With my red plastic sled rolled up and tucked under my arm, I looked back at the parking lot, thinking that at least one brave soul would want to conquer the sledding hill. But as the last bus pulled away from the school, I scanned the schoolyard and saw that all the walkers had already skedaddled home.

Sissies.

I can't say I blamed them. Silvia thought I was making an unfortunate decision earlier that morning when she saw me grabbing my sled. It was nice of her to voice her concern for me to be outside for any length of time. She had a habit of looking out for me, seeing how much younger I was. I believe her exact words were, "You're not really going sledding after school, are you? You're such a dunderhead." As I walked across the playground, I realized that perhaps she had a point. The snow crunched beneath my boots as I stomped down with each step, enjoying the loud *crack* as I crashed through the frozen snow.

With not a cloud in sight, the sky was a brilliant blue. Unfortunately, as I learned from our father, while gray overcast days may not be as pretty, clouds helped trap the warmer air. So even though snow that snaps like glass makes for a wonderful backdrop in a Hallmark movie, I was reminded of the downside of frigid temperatures with each breath. Pulling my scarf over my mouth and nose only resulted in more misery as it quickly slipped back down, making my cheeks burn as the crisp air hit my warmed-up skin. I continued across the schoolyard, lifting my feet with each exaggerated step.

"OK, hill," I called out, peering down the steep incline. "It's just you and me." This was a popular sledding hill, and it showed, in the numerous ruts created from other kids and their sleds. With the snow as brittle as it was, I realized that it was "going to be a bumpy ride," as Mickey was fond of saying, unaware he was misquoting the great Betty Davis. Unrolling my sled, I laid it down and grabbed the front rope. Inching up to the edge, I stopped, teetering at the very top of the hill.

It was quiet out, and I sat for a minute, thinking about the upcoming week. Christmas Eve was only two days away, and all holidays brought an added amount of stress to our mother. The ambulance trips were getting commonplace and she had done the gun and knife thing so often that even she was bored with the theatrics.

"Hey."

I nearly jumped out of my snow pants at the sound of a voice behind me. Turning my head didn't work because I was then looking into the inside of my hood, which I finally pushed back. I was shocked to see Chris, another student in fourth grade, but not in my class. He lived north of town, and I rarely saw him outside of school because his mom chauffeured him everywhere. I envisioned her to be one of those TV moms—the kind who wakes her kids up for school with a hot breakfast and throws a scarf around their necks as they head out the door because she insists that it's colder than they think. Sometimes I would watch as Chris's station wagon pulled up to the school. His mom would wave at him as he walked into the building. She loved him—you could just see it on her face.

"Hi." And because I didn't know what else to say, I added, "Cool sled."

He was holding a new orange saucer, and he somehow looked even cuter, all bundled up in his parka and scarf.

"Thanks. It's OK. How's the hill?"

"I don't know. I just got here."

"You're in Miss Neuber's class, aren't you?"

"Yeah, we have recess and gym together."

"That's right. You've got the German mom, right?" I nodded, and he looked down the hill. "All right, time to see what this sled can do. Race you to the bottom!"

And for the next hour, Chris and I conquered that hill as I tried ignoring the pain every time I landed wrong on the hard ruts. Chris even traded sleds with me after a while, and I glided effortlessly and painlessly down the hill on his metal saucer. With each trip, the freezing cold slowly melted away, and I couldn't help but laugh at Chris, who insisted that he was Speed Racer and I was the lovely Penelope Pitstop. I couldn't believe this boy not only knew who I was, but wanted to spend time with me.

After more than a dozen runs, a car horn honked from the direction of the school parking lot. "Shoot," Chris said, out of breath as we reached the top of the hill. "That sure didn't seem like an hour. That's my mom." He turned toward me and said, "Gotta go. It's been fun."

"Hang on. I'm done sledding too. I'll walk with you."

"Umm . . . you better not." The car honked again, and he looked around, not wanting to look at me. "My mom told me that I'm not allowed to hang with you." His voice softened as he added, "It's not about you. Something about your mom." He quickly turned away and started back toward the parking lot. After a few feet, he turned back and waved at me. "See ya at school tomorrow!"

I started to wave goodbye, but stopped myself and stood motionless.

The sun was close to setting, and a cool blue tint bounced off the icy snow, displaying a magnificent light show. With the sound of a car door slamming, I started my walk across the schoolyard. *Silvia is right*, I thought. *I am a dunderhead.* I tried wiping my tears away with my mitten, which only made my face colder. Dragging my sled behind me, I started to run across the parking lot and down the road. A squirrel appeared from behind a plastic Santa, and started running across the yard. I chased it down the snow-covered street until it scurried up an old oak tree.

I kept running, feeling my heart pump with every crash through the brittle snow. The cold stole my breath, making me want to stop, but I kept running.

— 35 —

December 22, 1970
Alamo, Michigan

Back inside our front porch, I shook the snow off and tossed my sled against the wall, not realizing how dark it had gotten until I turned around and looked back outside.

The last person I wanted to see was our mother, and I held out hope that she was still nursing another headache in her bedroom. Entering the kitchen, I found Mickey and Silvia at the picnic table, hunched over a catalog. It felt good to peel off my boots and snow pants. I let them drop on the welcome mat and made my way over to the floor heater, where I collapsed, letting my body thaw as the wonderful hot air warmed my feet and butt. Closing my eyes, I wanted to forget what had happened on the sledding hill. Instead, I would simply turn our mother into the mom from the TV show, the *Partridge Family.* Each day after school, I would find a plate of peanut butter sandwiches waiting for me, with the crust cut off and cut into cute little squares. She'd give me a kiss on the top of my head and ask me how my day went. While I wolfed down the sandwich, I would tell her all about my sledding time with Chris. I would then explain to her how fast metal saucers go in the snow, maybe giving her an idea for Christmas.

I opened my eyes, making Mrs. Partridge and my peanut butter sandwich disappear.

"Hey," Silvia said, looking up from the catalog.

Meanwhile, our mother sat in her chair, turning the pages of a magazine. The sweet aroma of coffee, enhanced with cream and sugar permeated throughout the room. She didn't look up, and I didn't care.

But I probably did.

"Is that the Sears Christmas catalog?" I asked, getting up from the heater, and setting my Deputy Dawg lunch box on the counter. "I want it next," I added, thinking about the popular toys that would be heaven to own. What kid wouldn't want an Easy-Bake Oven, Lite-Brite, or miniature pool table? Every holiday season, I studied both the Sears and J. C. Penney Christmas Catalogs, going through each page of the toy section in the back. What would I buy if I had $100? Maybe the Stingray bicycle with a real gearshift, or better yet, a metal saucer. Christmas Eve couldn't come soon enough.

"So," I said, looking over Mickey's shoulder to a page featuring young men wearing sweaters and ascots. "You guys won't believe what a couple of boys were saying in school today. They were trying to tell everyone in class that there really isn't a Santa Claus. Can you believe that?"

No one answered me with a look of horror that there were children who sadly didn't believe in Santa Claus's existence. Instead, Silvia glanced over at Mickey while our mother let out a sigh and closed her magazine, looking up at me for the first time since I walked in.

"Take a seat," she instructed.

And with all the tenderness of a carpenter nailing down flooring, my mother ripped the magic of Santa Claus out from under me. I stood, silent as Silvia and Mickey stared at me, torn between pity for what I had just been smacked with and guilt for enjoying the show. Pleased that she had gotten the situation over with, our mother turned her attention back to her magazine.

"Oh," my mother said, apparently feeling like she was on a roll and not interested in going through all of this again in four months. "There's no Easter Bunny either."

A holiday double whammy. As I stood in the center of the kitchen, letting this newfound knowledge sink in, Silvia closed up the catalog and with a shrug walked out to the living room.

Mickey got up from the picnic table as well, but stopped to give me a gentle pat on my shoulder. "Sorry, kiddo. Sometimes it's tough growing up," he whispered. When I didn't lift my head to look back up at him, he continued. "We're just going to have to do a better job when we raise our own children, right?" He smiled and gave my shoulder a squeeze, I lifted my head, smiled back at him, and sniffed the snot back into my nose.

Sipping her coffee, my mother didn't seem to notice or care that I was still in the room. At least I had sole possession of the Sears Christmas Catalog, and I flipped through pages filled with women showing off sweaters dripping in rhinestones, young girls in frilly Christmas dresses, and everything from Kenmore dishwashers to Craftsman toolboxes. I kept flipping through the pages, finally landing on the toy section. Rummaging through my book bag, I pulled out a pencil, ready to circle the toys I would be dreaming about until next year's catalog. But I suddenly noticed the large postal box sitting on the picnic table.

"Mutti, is this from Oma and Opa?" But I already knew the answer as I turned the box toward me and found the familiar postage. "Ooh, airmail stamps! It's from Germany! Can we open it? I bet there's Lebkuchen in here!" I tried lifting the box and grunted, finding it much heavier than I expected, causing my mother to let out a soft laugh. This sudden attention made me giggle as she closed her magazine and walked over to the phonebook drawer to pull out a pair of scissors. It was refreshing to see her holding them in a fashion that told me she wasn't thinking about charging at me, *Psycho* style. Instead, she jabbed the scissors into the top of the box and sliced through the tape, separating the flaps with ease.

"It came this morning," she said, pulling out a wad of newspapers used to cushion the valuables hidden inside. "Be careful with those. I want to read them later." As I smoothed out the crumpled paper, my mother reached deep into the box. "Would you look at that," she said, slowly pulling out a dishtowel. Her face brightened as she held it up for me to see. It was a beautiful deep red with white edelweiss sewn along the border. "How did Tante Lisi know I needed new towels?" she whispered, turning the soft cotton-woven cloth in her hands before bringing it up to her face and rubbing it against her cheek. Still smiling, she set it down on the table, and reached back into the box.

"A German calendar!" I exclaimed.

"I'm guessing this is yours," she said, handing the colorful Advent calendar to me as she pulled out three more, setting them on the table. On the cover was a picture of a church sitting in the snow. The dark blue sky was filled with glittery stars, and by tilting the calendar just so, I was able to make the glitter in the sky and snow glisten. Behind each of the twenty-four doors, was a bite of milk chocolate. I found the door marked with a number one, and poked my finger along the perforation, digging for the milk chocolate.

"Don't eat the chocolates all at once," my mother warned, apparently not realizing that the month was practically over, and I had many windows to open. I laughed again as I popped the first chocolate into my mouth. She peered back into the box and slowly pulled out a magazine like it was expensive crystal. She seemed to freeze as she held it in her hands. She flipped through a few of the pages before closing the cover again to study the photo of a small boy with yellow paint splashed across his body. It was a gorgeous vibrant cover, and I think she actually let out a small laugh as she held it gently, like she was holding a newborn.

"Is that a German magazine?" I asked, peering over her shoulder.

She didn't answer right away. Instead, she opened it again. When she finally did answer, she smiled but there was sadness in her eyes.

"Oh, just a magazine I read when I was young—*Der Spiegel*. I spent a lot of my money at the drugstore buying this magazine"

"*Der Spiegel*—that's a cool name. What's it mean?"

"It's German for 'The Mirror,' a reflection of everything going on across the world. I learned all about the American entertainment and fashion world through this magazine." She turned a few more pages before setting it down and saying, with a sigh and a near-whisper, "A lot of good that did me."

She looked back into the box and pulled out a glass ornament. The detail was striking, and she quietly turned it around in her hand, forgetting that I was in the room with her. She brought the bulb closer to her face to study the royal blue cross painted on the front, sitting in a glitter of snow circling the bulb. On the back, she found a name painted at the bottom. She suddenly brought her hand up to her temples and pushed into her skin with her fingers.

"Mari," she whispered.

— 36 —

December 22, 1970
Alamo, Michigan

With everyone downstairs, I took solace in the quiet of my bedroom, sprawled out across the covers so that every limb of my body reached for the four corners of my bed. I thought back to earlier on the sledding hill and I couldn't help but replay that moment. I saw that expression on his face, the same look we received from the staff person at the Plainwell Sanitarium. When asked why we were standing outside of the building, Hanna explained to the woman that we had just been visiting with our mother.

"Oh," she said, standing silent for a moment. "I'm sorry," she added, looking at us like we had just told her our dog died. I didn't want her pity. It was embarrassing then, and embarrassing on the sledding hill. I didn't want people's pity. I just wanted . . .

. . . to be normal.

Slipping my hand under my pillow, I slid the parcel out from its hiding place and ran my fingers across the soft cover—no title or picture, just smooth brown leather. As I flipped through the pages, I noticed the yellowed discoloration of the aged paper. Opening to the first page, I recognized my mother's eloquent handwriting, but the words were written in German, and a mystery to me. I closed the journal and leaned back against the headboard.

Suddenly, surprising but familiar music drifted into the bedroom from downstairs, and I tucked the journal into my pillowcase and listened. Not hearing anything more, I sighed and closed my eyes. I probably should have told my mother that the package from Tante Lisi included this book, but after she walked out of the kitchen, I peeked into the box, wondering if there was anything hiding at the bottom. As I dug through the crumpled newspapers, my fingers wrapped around something, and I pulled out the leather notebook.

There it was again. Darn if it wasn't the sounds from a sweet harmonica. Excited, I leaped from my bed and followed the music down the hall. The music grew stronger as I bounded down the stairs, letting my hands glide over the soft silver garland our mother had draped along the banister.

In the living room, I found Mickey and Silvia standing in front of the sofa, singing "Silent Night." I didn't know those two could sing so well. They stood beside our father who sat on the sofa, accompanying them on his harmonica. Hanna came out of her bedroom as well and stood beside me, and I can only assume she was as shocked as I was with what was unfolding before our eyes.

Completing this surreal picture of Christmas bliss, was our mother, singing along quietly. "*Christ, der Retter ist da ah . . .*" stopping after the second verse to simply listen.

With the finish of the song, I started clapping as Mickey and Silvia took exaggerated bows, when we were suddenly interrupted with two loud crashes occurring, one right after the other. Immediately, our father jumped up from the couch, and I turned around to find our mother lying on the floor, thrashing about. A *LIFE* magazine and an ash tray were on the floor next to her, and Hanna was standing still, perhaps waiting for guidance from Popi.

And I didn't know what to do.

"Hanna, fetch some paper towels. Mickey, get a pillow," our father instructed, moving swiftly while keeping his voice steady. Meanwhile, our mother was kicking and thrashing about. If you didn't know that she was having a seizure, you would have sworn that she was possessed by the devil. Maybe she should have gone to that last church bazaar.

Our father moved the coffee table out of the way, which our mother had apparently hit on the way down, while Hanna hurried back from the kitchen with a fistful of paper towels, and handed them to our father. He then folded each one into a neat square and mopped up her spittle as the thrashing slowly stopped. As she gasped for breath through a mouthful of saliva, I stood still, rubbing the soft fur of my rabbit's foot, which dangled from the front belt-loop of my jeans. Silvia glanced over at me and whispered, "Come on, let's go upstairs."

For the first time that night, I noticed the TV shimmering in the corner. I was missing my favorite Christmas special.

"No, that would not be possible," declared the lion from his throne. *"This island is for toys alone."*

"How do you like that?" Yukon Cornelius said, looking at his pal, Rudolph.

"'Even among misfits you're a misfit,'" Cornelius and I said together.

"See ya, Rudolph," I whispered, turning off the TV.

I followed Silvia up the stairs, leaving our father sitting on the living room floor, cradling our mother in his arms. "You are not broken," he whispered, rocking her back and forth.

We are all broken, I thought to myself.

As Silvia and I climbed the stairs, Mickey called out to us from his room. "Come in here, guys. I have something for you." He shut the door and motioned for us to take a seat on his bed.

"OK, I know it's not Christmas yet, but I thought this might take our minds off what's going on downstairs." He opened the drawer in his desk and handed a neatly wrapped present to each of us. The gifts were flat and about six inches square, making me realize quickly what was hiding under the beautiful red aluminum wrap and dark green bow.

Silvia carefully tore away the giftwrap at the seams while I ripped mine open, and together, we both uncovered our 45 rpm records, complete with yellow tabs stuck in the center hole. Without even reading the song title, I recognized that familiar green Warner Brothers label, and I started crying for the third time that day. Except this was a good cry.

— 37 —

December 22, 1970

Alamo, Michigan

"Treva, you have a nice touch, whether you're styling hair or decorating your shop," Beth said, running her hand along the garland that draped down the door frame. "It looks like a Christmas card in here."

"Why, thank you. Nothing like a little decking the halls to put you into the Christmas spirit," Treva said, sitting in the salon chair. She took a long drag from her cigarette. "Doris, be a dear and hand me that ashtray. Thank you. I swear, everyone wants their hair cut, dyed, or beautified with a permanent right before the holidays, and they all schedule last minute, thinking that I'm just sitting around wishing for the phone to ring. I should charge double for my services this time of year. Seriously, if one more person calls to ask if I can squeeze them in, I'm going to go crazy!"

"Speaking of crazy," Doris said. "I heard some juicy news the other day about the Phillips woman." She took out a pack of gum from her purse, and unwrapped the Juicy Fruit. "Dale told me the other day that it looks like someone has been visiting the Phillips house late at night after Larry goes to work."

"Does he know who?" Treva asked.

"He told me he doesn't know, but something tells me that he's protecting someone. Kevin told him, and when I pressed Dale for what kind of car was at the house, he said he didn't know, and we all know that Dale knows cars."

"Hmm," Treva said. "Well, I can't say it surprises me. I can't believe what Larry puts up with."

"So, you heard it from someone who heard it from someone," Beth said. "Then it must be true." Doris looked at Beth, and then gave Treva a quick glance that told Beth something was left unsaid.

Beth laid the *LIFE* magazine down and got up to pour herself a cup of coffee. "This is the same woman who has tried to kill herself with pills on more than one occasion and has been restrained with straitjackets. Can you imagine? I mean, really, I can only imagine what she must be going through." She walked over to the window and touched the spray-on frost that framed the window as she looked out to see a car crawling down the snow-covered street.

"And what must holidays be like for her?" Beth asked, not expecting an answer. "Speaking from experience, this Christmas is not going to be a happy time in our home." Turning around, she continued, "I don't even know where Robbie is. Can you imagine not knowing where your child is? I haven't heard his voice in two months. And in case you're wondering, no, the pills don't help." Beth knew she was making her friends uncomfortable, and she didn't care. "And where the hell is that sun? I don't think I've seen *that* in two months either."

— 38 —

December 22, 1970
Alamo, Michigan

She didn't remember exactly when she gave up, but the dreams that carried her to America quickly turned to dust when her husband pulled into the driveway, and Didi got her first look at the drab farmhouse complete with a working outhouse, a chicken coop and a built-in mother-in-law who wasn't thrilled about sharing her kitchen with a foreign girl. Nothing in that godforsaken place resembled the America she saw in the pages of *Der Spiegel*. No dance halls or diners—just a rundown village sorely in need of paint.

"Why don't you want to go back to Germany?" her husband used to ask. She would answer with a variety of excuses, ranging from a lack of money to not wanting to travel due to her epilepsy. After a while he stopped asking. What she didn't tell him, was the truth, that if she ever went back to Germany, she could never bring herself to come back.

So, she stayed. Oh, she definitely thought about leaving many times, even taking that first step when she couldn't cope, but with help from a husband who was as endearing as he was frustrating and a handful of pills that dulled the pain and made the fantasies fuzzy, she settled into her life in this horrible little town where the women-folk whispered to each other whenever she dared to leave the house and the men looked at her like a prize to be won.

And slowly, she let go of the memories—of times when she went everywhere with her girlfriends, sneaking into pubs, night clubs, and anywhere she wasn't allowed. Sneaking into places was in her blood. After all, she was lucky enough to escape war-torn Germany with the love of her life.

She just couldn't escape this place.

Out on the front porch, Didi took in a deep breath, taking in the beauty of the Christmas lights strung across the front roof—brilliant red, green, yellow, and blue. The only thing greater than the splendor of those lights was the freezing temperature, so it didn't take long before Didi had to step back into the house for warmth.

"What in the world were you doing out there in your robe?" Merle asked as he pulled a small box out of the drawer in the end table. He opened the box and pulled out his harmonica. He smiled at her and blew out a note. She knew she had every reason to be happy. After all, it was the holiday season, and she just received an incredible gift of foods and gifts from Tanta Lisi. And her poor husband was trying his best to make this Christmas the best one yet with the fresh-cut spruce in the living room decorated with blue and green lights, tinsel, and the glass ornaments from Germany—all for her. But she just couldn't draw the strength to be the appreciative wife—maybe tomorrow.

"Nothing," she said, shaking her head. "I wasn't doing anything. May I ask what you all are up to?" Didi asked, looking back at him and two of her children who had walked into the living room each holding a sheet of paper.

"We have a surprise for you, Spatzi," he smiled, obviously pleased that this trio now had an audience. "Are you ready?" he asked, with a small nod to his children.

Mickey cleared his throat. "We're ready." With a note from the harmonica to set the key, Didi's husband began playing the soulful tune of "Silent Night" as his children sang along.

"Silent night, holy night, all is calm, all is bright. Round yon virgin

Mother and Child . . ." As her two children came to the chorus, Didi quietly sang along. "*Tönt es laut von fern und nah, Christ, der Retter ist da . . . Christ, der Retter ist da.*" She thought back to one Christmas Eve when her mother placed the 78 onto the Victrola turntable and gently set the needle on the record—sending this beautiful haunting tune through the speaker.

Then she thought of Mari, handing her that glass ornament. "So, you won't forget me," Mari had said.

"Jesus, Lord, at thy birth," Silvia and Mickey continued singing. "Jesus, Lord, at thy birth."

Then Didi's thoughts blurred.

She slowly lifted her head from the pillow and tried focusing but saw nothing but darkness. She lay still to allow her eyes to adjust to the darkness and realized that she was on the sofa in the living room. Her mouth was dry, and she felt like she was coming out of a drunken stupor, but she had been through this feeling far too often to not know what happened. Wincing with pain, she placed her hand on the back of her head and found a large bump. As her eyes adjusted to what little light streamed through the window, she slowly sat up and tried to remember the chain of events that landed her on the sofa. *That song*, she thought. *The last thing I remember is singing along with that beautiful song.*

Her quiet surroundings told her that the children must have all gone to bed and her husband off to work. "Ha," she said to herself as the dull pain gathered strength in her head. "Out all this time, and I still have a headache."

With help from the soft glow from the kitchen nightlight, Didi slowly stood, finding that she was still wobbly on her feet as a result of the lingering fallout from her seizure, which had a way of draining everything out of her. She closed her eyes in an attempt to clear the fog in her head, but it didn't help. Taking a few steps, she steadied herself by taking hold of a floor lamp, and slowly, she made her way into the kitchen.

Moonlight spilled through the window, and she stopped to gaze out across the snow, about a foot of it out there. The near-zero temperatures mixed with the nearly full moon resulted in brilliant blue ice that shimmered across the yard. She stood still, soaking in the quiet splendor. A whistle blew in the distance, and she waited for the train to appear, cutting through the snow as it passed by. She smiled at the thought of taking it to Chicago or anywhere that was beyond the stifling small town of Alamo. She then let out a sigh, realizing it was just another dream, and it didn't really matter since she didn't have the strength to go anywhere.

A soft knock on the front door startled Didi out of her thoughts. Whoever it was took the initiative to open the storm door and was standing in their front porch, making her regret not locking the door. Glancing up at the clock, she wondered who would be paying her a call so late at night, but she guessed who it was.

"Good evening!" Rob said as Didi opened the door. He looked quizzically at her before continuing. "Is this a good time? You don't look so good."

"I don't feel so good," Didi answered, opening the door wider. "What could you possibly have told your wife where you were going to at this time of night? Doesn't she get suspicious?"

"You know that old cliché of the husband needing to go out for cigarettes?" he smiled, shutting the door behind him. "Although, it's no lie that something is smoking here."

"Rob, I'm sorry you made the trip, but I really don't feel up for visitors tonight." She backed up, but Rob mirrored her steps and moved in closer. She could smell alcohol on his breath as he burrowed his face into her neck. His body pushed hard against hers, and she pulled away.

"Seriously, Rob, I don't feel up to entertaining tonight. You should really go home to Beth. I don't feel right—"

"Oh come on," he pushed, reaching for her in a way that told her that he wasn't going to take no for an answer. "It's been a long time since anyone paid attention to me, if you know what I mean. With Robbie serving halfway across the world, it's all that matters to my wife. I'm dying inside, Didi. I need you, and I know you need me, too." He took her hand and led her to the couch, pulling her down so that they were sitting close together. "Come on, Didi," he said, leaning into her. "We're just playing around, you and me. You know I'm going to pay a big price for this at home. You can at least make it worth my while."

"I'm . . . I'm not feeling well. Don't you get it?" Didi replied, pushing him off and standing up. The living room swayed as she tried to find her footing. "Nothing is happening tonight. In fact, *nothing* is going to happen. Just go home to your wife. She deserves better." She steadied herself, wishing that the rocking would stop.

"Jesus Christ," Rob mumbled, getting off from the couch. "I don't need this shit. You should know better than to lead a guy on. You look like hell, anyway." He walked out, leaving the front door open. As she heard a car engine start, she walked to the door and locked it.

Walking back into the kitchen, Didi gave a final look out the window, momentarily entranced with the magical falling snow. Turning around, she walked over to the sink and opened the medicine cabinet door, wincing as pain shot through her skull. She reached for a pill bottle and dropped two pills into her palm before walking over to the sink to fill her cup. Popping the pills into her mouth, she gulped a cupful of water. The medicine cabinet door gently swung shut, and she caught her reflection, long matted hair resulting from her own drool. Staring at the face, she no longer recognized it as her own.

Her gaze slowly shifted back down to the open pill bottle still in her hand. She tipped the bottle and opened her palm, allowing the contents to fill her hand. Throwing the pile of pills into her mouth, she took another long drink.

— 39 —

August 5, 2005
Ellis Island, New York, New York

One lonely pill drops into my palm from the travel-size Bayer bottle. "Are you kidding me?" I mumble, pulling the cotton ball out with the hope that one last pill is hiding from me. I toss the empty pill bottle back into my handbag and close my eyes, keeping them shut until I'm rudely interrupted yet again by another announcement over the speakers.

"Looking starboard, or the right side for our landlubber friends, you'll see Liberty Island, home of the majestic Statue of Liberty. This beautiful copper statue is 151 feet in height and was a gift to the United States from the people of France. The statue represents . . ."

As we learn that visitors must climb 354 steps to reach the crown, I slowly open my eyes just as we're passing Liberty Island. Our ferry cuts through the water, teasing me because we're as far as we can possibly be from the nearest pharmacy.

"Another headache?" Jon asks, already knowing the answer as he rubs the back of my neck. "Sorry, honey."

"I'm OK," I say, tossing the pill into my mouth and handing the water bottle back to him. "We're in the city that never sleeps so I'm not going to let a little ol' headache keep me down." In case he doesn't believe my conviction, I throw him a half-hearted smile.

Our ferry is packed with tourists, like sardines in a can, and I'm waiting for the boat to tip as a result of all of the sardines standing on this side of the boat with their smartphones, trying to take a photo of the Statue of Liberty from an angle that a hundred million other tourists haven't already taken. Deciding that Facebook will survive without my photo, I soak in the beauty that stands before us.

Soon after, the engines burst with power as the ferry prepares to dock at Ellis Island, and the sudden noise makes me pinch my temples.

"Another headache, Mom?" Phillip asks, leaning over the railing to look at the people on the lower deck.

"Yeah, but I'll be OK," I say, grabbing his Detroit Tigers ball cap just as it begins to slip off from his head, saving it from being a free souvenir to someone below deck. "What do you think of all this?" I ask, looking out at the immigration building, which spans across the majority of the island. "It's not the Rock 'n' Roller Coaster at Disney World, but—"

"This isn't Disney World. This is . . ."

"Real?"

"Really incredible. Are you excited about finding it?" Phillip asks, taking his cap from me and putting it back on his head backwards.

"Yeah. You know what? I thought this was kind of silly at first, but I guess I'm really looking forward to this. Who knew?" I smile. "Are you going to help me find it?"

"Not leaving here until we do," he answers, echoing his father's words.

Our adventure to Ellis Island started with my discovery of that old worn journal found so many years ago. My mother's journal entries were sporadic, but she shared enough to help me understand the hardship she endured as a child and the demons that continued to haunt her into her early years as an adult. For a year, she wrote regularly, often about her dear friend, Mari, and her life with her Tante Lisi and Onkel Otto. Her writing became less frequent after that night with Mari, but she made a concentrated effort to keep writing after her arrival to America. But soon after the birth of Mickey, she stopped writing in her journal altogether. I suspect her mental condition was deteriorating, and life simply got too overwhelming for her.

While her upbringing explains her mental state, it's hard to present this as the reason or excuse for how she treated her children, especially Mickey. I cannot express my happiness in how my brother was able to move on, enjoying his life with his partner, despite suffering through a childhood that tried its hardest to crush his spirit. He is happy today, just as my sisters are.

"We will be docking on Ellis Island momentarily," announces the ferry's tour-guide over the PA system. *"Opened in 1892, Ellis Island served as a federal immigration station for more than sixty years. Millions of immigrants passed through the island during that time. In fact, it has been estimated that close to 40 percent of all current U.S. citizens can trace at least one of their ancestors to this small historical island. Please be patient and form a uniform line as we disembark. Thank you for sailing with Statue Cruises."*

"All right, let's get in line," Jon announces, packing his camera into his bag. It's all about waiting in lines when you visit New York City—a line for the Empire State Building, a line for buying Broadway tickets, another line for catching the shows, and still more lines for comedy clubs, art museums, and subway tokens.

And I'm OK with all of it.

While Jon and I have been to New York City several times before, this is our first trip with our children and our first time to Ellis Island. There was a time when I wanted nothing to do with my mother's heritage, but as I've grown older, I have come to understand the obstacles that my mother faced—the abuse she endured as a child, and the mental and physical challenges that she struggled with on a daily basis. I have forgiven her, not because she sought my forgiveness but because I understand that forgiveness allows me to move on without bitterness and anger.

The breeze blowing off the New York Bay is cool today despite the fact that it's mid-August. I lean into my husband, trying to find warmth as we stand on the front lawn of Ellis Island in yet another line, waiting to enter the Museum of Immigration.

"You know," Jon says to me. "Your mother and father might have very well walked *right here* nearly seventy years ago. Or . . . here," he continues, grabbing my hand and taking a large side-step. "Or here!"

"Well, it was winter when they landed, so I'm thinking the two of them made a flock of snow angels in the snow." I throw my hands into the air, mimicking the movements. "Or better yet," I say, grabbing Phillip's hat, and spinning in a circle. "Mutti was so excited to land that she threw her beret into the air like this!"

"Yeah, Mom," Tyler says, picking up the cap from the ground, and handing it back to Phillip. "I'm sure that's exactly what happened. Mary Tyler Moore got the idea from your mother." Looking at me, he adds, "I'm glad we're doing this for you, Mom. But, from the stories you've told us, I don't understand why you care about doing any of this for Mutti."

I think for a moment before answering. "I'm not sure either. It's complicated, I guess."

"Well," Tyler continues, looking up at the massive three-story red brick building. "I hope we're able to find some kind of documentation of her arrival. But either way, thanks for taking us here."

I lean over to give him a hug. For added measure, I reach for Phillip. "All right! Don't forget, 'Elisabeth' with an 's,'" I say, looking more at my sons than the magnificent scenery surrounding us. While Tyler inherited the shorter stature of the majority of the Phillips family, Phillip followed the trait of his uncle's height—tall and lanky. At age six, Phillip already matches the height of his older brother. Both boys pull away from me, more interested in checking out the facility than bonding with their overzealous mother.

As we walk into the building, the four of us instinctively look up to the cathedral ceiling, and it is just as I had imagined. The building has been carefully maintained to preserve its original state. There's an earthy smell, making it easy to imagine the history and stories this building contains. The second floor is open, with people leaning over the railing, looking out at the new group of tourists disrupting their personal moment. The brick floor is shiny, and I'm not sure if it's because it's polished on a regular basis or if it slowly acquired its sheen from the millions of footsteps that have walked through this place on the way to great promise.

Roaming through the halls, I can feel the breath of the countless men, women, and children who walked through these rooms long before this became a tourist destination with a café and souvenir shop. Their words hang in the air, and at night, after the tourists have moved on to taking selfies in Times Square, this building takes a breath of relief and comes alive with the presence of hope and the anxious whispers of a million voices.

While Jon and the boys learn about the twelve million immigrants who have passed through these doors in search of a better life, I grow tired of reading statistics and wander off in search of the quieter part of the island that isn't trampled by the masses on a daily basis. Finding an unmarked back door, I open it and I'm greeted with a cool breeze blowing off the water. Brittle cement crumbles under my feet as I make my way down the narrow steps leading down to the lawn.

Despite the Manhattan skyline serving as a backdrop, the grounds are more tranquil, with the silence broken only occasionally by the voice of a wandering tourist. As I explore, I come up on the memorial that spans across the lawn and covers a large portion of the grounds. The structure forms a circle, consisting of many different sections of granite walls that stand nearly four feet tall. A plaque stands at the entrance, and I learn that the American Immigrant Wall of Honor contains over 700,000 names of individuals and families who have traveled to America. Even though the names are alphabetized, a new section is added every several years, leaving me with a multitude of sections starting over alphabetically. I might be here all day looking for her name in a sea of Elisabeths, and the ferry is leaving soon.

Unfolding a paper I had been carrying in my back pocket, I read it one last time.

American Immigrant Wall of Honor
Name: Elisabeth Didi Phillips
Country of Origin: Germany

Folding the paper back up, I start walking, deliberately passing by the first four sections of the wall, stopping as I reached the fifth series of names—lucky number five. Could it be that simple? Walking down the lane, I run my hand along the wall, and despite the warm late-August weather, the granite is cool to the touch.

"We thought you might need a little help."

Startled, I turn around to find Jon and the boys walking up behind me. "I think I might," I say, grabbing Jon's hand and leading them all down the lane past hundreds of columns of names. So many names.

Terney, Taggert, Taft . . . Rantz, Ransom, Ramano . . . Quince, Quincley . . . Thousands of names, and these are just a fraction.

What was Terrance Ransom's story? I can't help but look at each name as my fingers skim across the rows, and I wonder what hopes they carried with them and what became of them and their families. Is there a son or daughter carrying on their heritage, and did America bring them everything they dreamed of accomplishing?

We finally reach the "P"s, and I scan the many columns. Moving my finger down the column, I pass the names Bessie, Coleman, Dora before landing on it—Elisabeth Phillips.

"Well, there it is," Jon whispers, grabbing his camera. "Let me get a photo of you two."

"You know," Tyler says. "You really haven't told us much about Mutti. It would be interesting to know about her time in Germany."

"You're right," I say, smiling for the camera while pointing to my mother's name. "You both *should* know about your grandmother. Did I ever tell you that I'm named after her two best friends from Germany?"

"I always thought Heidimari was a weird name," Phillip says with a smirk.

"No weirder than you!" I say grabbing him and giving him a bear hug until he squirms away.

"Let's get one more photo," Jon says to all of us.

As we smile for the camera, I turn to take one last look at her name etched in stone, among the thousands of others. My parents have long passed, but my mother, quite unintentionally, taught me the importance of embracing life and everything that goes along with it. I understand our father did the best he could trying to protect his children from the woman he adored but couldn't save. I was blessed with a family of siblings who shielded me and nourished me with love, protection, and adventure. And for that, I celebrate.

I imagine my mother looked at her own life quite differently, seeing happiness as being right there, just inches from her grasp, but like the rushing waters of Tahquamenon, it slipped through her fingers.

A gull flies overhead as Jon takes another photo, with the brilliant blue sky and the Manhattan skyline behind us. The whistle blows, and Jon and I both turn to see the line of people waiting to board getting longer.

"All right boys," Jon says. "The last ferry of the day is getting ready to pull out, and I don't think your mother wants to spend the night here."

He's right. I'm looking forward to getting back to the energy of the city. Suddenly I smile, realizing that my headache is gone.

As we board the ferry, leaving Ellis Island behind us, a cool evening breeze picks up, and I grab Phillip's backpack to pull out my sweater. Along with the hoodie, a book falls onto my lap, or rather, a journal. Opening to a random page, I read an entry written so long ago by a girl who had no idea what adventures were waiting for her. It's in German, but with my limited knowledge of the language, I am able to understand the essence of the words written in longhand. The penmanship is flawless, with each letter crafted with a precise hand.

January 15, 1944—I miss Mari so much. I knew that I would have mixed feelings about leaving the orphanage, but I had no idea just how much it would hurt. It turns out that the saying, a broken heart, is not just a figure of speech because my heart actually aches like I'm having a heart attack. And while I knew I would miss Mari and the other girls, even I'm surprised that I miss those damn nuns. Even Sister Ruth.

Of course, I haven't heard from my mother since she dropped me off at the orphanage. Not even a phone call. Tante Lisi told me that I should be thankful to be where I am and to not sulk about what I cannot change. But I can't help but wonder. Does my mother ever think about me?

January 22, 1945—The phone rang today, and something told me that it was finally my mother, calling to see if I'm OK. I stood motionless as Onkel Otto picked up the receiver, but it was just a friend of his from work. I've thought about calling her because maybe she feels bad about leaving me at the orphanage and she's afraid that I'm mad at her. Tante Lisi tells me that my mother's not worth worrying about. I know she means well, and most of the time I'm fine knowing that my mother doesn't give a shit about me. I don't give a shit about her, either. Someday, I'm going to get married to someone rich, and go far, far away from here. I don't need anyone.

I shut the journal and close my eyes, taking in the significance of the day. As I put the journal back in the backpack, I notice the post-cards I purchased earlier in the gift shop and I pull those out. Even though it's likely that we'll beat them home, I promised my siblings that they would be receiving official New York City postcards. While Jon takes more photos of the Statue of Liberty against the skyline, I quietly take in the warmth of the setting sun. Sandwiched between an older woman who is bickering with her husband about the money they have already spent on their trip because the man likes his whis-key sours with every meal and a teenage girl who hasn't looked up from her phone since we boarded the ferry, I pull a pen from out of my handbag and begin writing.

"Mom," Phillip whispers, tugging on my jacket. He points over to a man sitting across the aisle from us. He's a large man, with a white neatly trimmed beard. He's wearing cargo shorts, and carries a tired look on his face. I imagine he's heading back to his hotel room after this excursion to rest up before the evening activities. You don't come to this city only to skip the nightlife, when the city truly comes alive. "That man looks like Santa Claus."

"Hmm," I say, leaning into Phillip. "You never know. Santa proba-bly grows a little tired of living in his snow-globe up north. After all, some say that his heritage started in Germany, and this is the City of Immigrants."

As my son continues to stare at Santa Claus, I stare at both of my sons with more love than I can muster.

It isn't long before we're pulling up to the docks at Battery Park just as I'm placing a stamp on the last of my postcards. The city lights grow brighter as we make our way off the ferry and through the park. We've been walking everywhere on this trip, and next on our agenda is Times Square at night. A buzz in my pocket reminds me that my phone is nearly drained of power. "Damn, 11 percent," I say, looking at the small screen. "You know that the moment my phone dies, Cher is going to walk by." Noticing that my family is ignoring me, I add, "And she'll be naked." Still nothing.

As we walk through Battery Park, I notice a mailbox by the gift shop. "Keep walking, guys," I say, shoving my phone back into my pocket. "I'll catch up!"

The gift shop is closed but a streetlamp glows nearby, casting a shadow over the front of the small shop. It's an interesting contrast to the vision I remember from earlier in the day when thousands of people stood in line for their once-in-a-lifetime trip to the Statue of Liberty and Ellis Island.

I reach into my purse and pull out the postcards from earlier, checking each one to make sure that they are all properly stamped. Statue of Liberty stamp, seems appropriate enough. I pull the door open on the mailbox and stop. Looking at the postcards again, I pull the one featuring Ellis Island from the bunch, and I turn it over, reading what I wrote earlier.

Having a wonderful time here. I wish you could see how beautiful the city is at night. You would have loved Jersey Boys. Not Frank Sinatra but close enough. Found your name on Ellis Island today. I believe that you are now officially a star!

There's no mailing address on this postcard but that's OK. I drop the postcards into the mailbox and run across the lawn to catch up with my family.

Discussion Group Questions

1. How do you think Didi's friend Mari figured into Didi's mental well-being during her later years?
2. The narration in 1970 is told in first-person while the story in Germany is told in third-person. What does it do for the relationship between the reader and the characters?
3. How did the events from Didi's earlier years shape how she related to men later in her life?
4. While the relationship between the young narrator and her mother is never perceived as being close, how does the narrator fill that void?
5. Do you think Didi loved her children? How did she show it, or not show it?
6. Do you think Mickey's mother suspected Mickey's sexual identity? Why or why not?
7. How does Beth figure into the story? What role does she play in portraying how the Phillips family is perceived by the community?
8. How do you explain the father's relationship with his children and their mother? Did he do all he could do?
9. While the word *crazy* is considered insensitive and inappropriate today, the author decided to keep it in the dialogue of the characters in this book. Do you feel it was necessary? Why or why not?

Acknowledgments

The story I've told here is inspired from my childhood, most of which took place when I was very little. I have taken liberties with details and dialogue—inventing specific events and placing real-life experiences out of sequence. Upon the request of my editor, I also erased a sibling (sorry, Fred). I apologize to my brothers and sisters who will read this and say, "That's not at all how it happened."

This is for my children, who have asked about my mother and my childhood. Life with my mother has made me thankful for all I have today and, quite by accident, also taught me to cherish my children. This is a thank-you to my brothers and sisters who protected me from our mother when she couldn't help herself.

And to my wonderful husband, who, after meeting my mother, married me anyway.

Thank you to everyone at She Writes Press. I am honored to be a part of your community.

Join the conversation
Author Website: heidimccrary.net
Facebook: HeidiMcCraryAuthor
Twitter: @heidimccrary

About the Author

© Jon McCrary

Heidi is the youngest of five children and lives with her husband, Jon, in Kalamazoo, Michigan, just a short drive from Alamo where she grew up. She now owns the family woods that are depicted in the book, where her children have been known to use as a place to get away from their own mother and father. Her two sons, Tyler and Phillip, are doing great despite being raised by a mother with no formal training.

Embracing all that West Michigan has to offer, Heidi can often be found hanging with her family in Kalamazoo and the many unique towns along the Lake Michigan shoreline or on the local golf course, working on her goal of becoming a mediocre golfer. She remains connected to her siblings and is especially close to her sisters who also live in the area. Michael (Mickey) moved away soon after graduation and currently lives in Seattle, Washington.

Heidi has worked in the media world all her adult life—many years with the West Michigan CBS affiliate, and currently in the advertising/marketing industry. She is also a contributing writer for a regional women's magazine.

This is Heidi's first novel.

SELECTED TITLES FROM SHE WRITES PRESS

She Writes Press is an independent publishing company founded to serve women writers everywhere. Visit us at www.shewritespress.com.

The Sweetness by Sande Boritz Berger $16.95, 978-1-63152-907-8
A compelling and powerful story of two girls—cousins living on separate continents—whose strikingly different lives are forever changed when the Nazis invade Vilna, Lithuania.

The Belief in Angels by J. Dylan Yates $16.95, 978-1-938314-64-3
From the Majdonek death camp to a volatile hippie household on the East Coast, this narrative of tragedy, survival, and hope spans more than fifty years, from the 1920s to the 1970s.

An Address in Amsterdam by Mary Dingee Fillmore
$16.95, 978-1-63152-133-1
After facing relentless danger and escalating raids for 18 months, Rachel Klein—a well-behaved young Jewish woman who transformed herself into a courier for the underground when the Nazis invaded her country—persuades her parents to hide with her in a dank basement, where much is revealed.

Even in Darkness by Barbara Stark-Nemon $16.95, 978-1-63152-956-6
From privileged young German-Jewish woman to concentration camp refugee, Kläre Kohler navigates the horrors of war and—through unlikely sources—finds the strength, hope, and love she needs to survive.

Tasa's Song by Linda Kass $16.95, 978-1-63152-064-8
From a peaceful village in eastern Poland to a partitioned post-war Vienna, from a promising childhood to a year living underground, *Tasa's Song* celebrates the bonds of love, the power of memory, the solace of music, and the enduring strength of the human spirit.

Portrait of a Woman in White by Susan Winkler $16.95, 978-1-938314-83-4
When the Nazis steal a Matisse portrait from the eccentric, art-loving Rosenswigs, the Parisian family is thrust into the tumult of war and separation, their fates intertwined with that of their beloved portrait.